MEDICINE MAN

Also by Bill Burchardt

SHOTGUN BOTTOM
YANKEE LONGSTRAW
THE BIRTH OF LOGAN STATION
THE MEXICAN
BUCK

MEDICINE MAN

BILL BURCHARDT

DOUBLEDAY & COMPANY, INC.

GARDEN CITY, NEW YORK

1980

All of the characters in this book are fictitious,
and any resemblance to actual persons, living or
dead, is purely coincidental.

Library of Congress Cataloging in Publication Data

Burchardt, Bill.
   Medicine man.

   1. Kiowa Indians—Fiction. I. Title.
PZ4.B9387Md [PS3552.U65]   813'.5'4

Copyright © 1980 by Bill Burchardt
ISBN: 0-385-14903-4
Library of Congress Catalog Card Number 79-7192
First Edition
All Rights Reserved
Printed in the United States of America

MEDICINE MAN

The first hint came to Kor-Káy as he rode down into the stand of blackjack timber toward the spring. It was the peculiar keening snarl of a panther.

Kor-Káy kneed his hunting horse to a silent halt. The buckskin pony stood motionless, though Kor-Káy could feel the sudden acceleration of its heartbeat. Inside Pintí's rib cage, against Kor-Káy's knee, the buckskin war horse's heart was thudding with terror.

The sound had come from upwind, on the moist evening breeze sweeping up out of the draw. It came again. A rising, vicious panther snarl rising almost to a scream, half-muffled by the dense timber. Kor-Káy glanced at the sun line. The horizon still glowed white-hot beneath red-painted cloud haze.

Too early for a panther to be prowling. Kor-Káy puzzled at this as another squall keened up from the spring. Along his pony's withers, flesh tremors began to chase each other across the horse's skin. Too well trained to bolt, Pintí was barely mastering his own instinctive fear. Kor-Káy reached out along the gelded buckskin's neck to lay his fingers over Pintí's nostrils.

You, horse, are like me, he thought. *Alien to such alrededores, but wearing a sheen of training that makes you do the opposite of your natural bent.* Kor-Káy knew that the heritage of his first, short years as a boy in Chihuahua had been excised and altered. The years of Kiowa discipline had made him into a warrior he would never otherwise have been.

Now he rode naked in breechclout. His feet, in beaded

moccasins, were toed in against his frightened mount's barrel. His fingers filtered his horse's breath—a trick his Kiowa grandfather had taught him. The scent of Kor-Káy's fingers seemed to give the pony assurance, for to Pintí, man smell was better than panther smell. The flesh along Pintí's flanks stopped quivering. Kor-Káy slid to stand erect on the timber floor.

He moved silently up beside the buckskin's head, listening to the frolicking in the blackjack leaf mold down by the spring. His senses told him that a mother panther had brought her kittens down for an evening drink. But the rising snarl was not that of a mother simply playing with her kittens.

The antelope Kor-Káy had killed was tied behind his rawhide saddle. It was redolent of dried blood, for he had opened the antelope's belly and removed its viscera. But the wind current sweeping up away from the spring was strong. The panther would not smell the antelope's blood.

But it was a blood snarl she was uttering. Kor-Káy looped the buckskin's single rein about the trunk of a blackjack sapling and knotted it. Instinct might yet overcome Pintí's training, and he was too much horse to risk losing.

With his moccasined feet sorting the dry leaves as silently as serpents, Kor-Káy edged down the slope toward the spring. The sound of dripping water, almost a steady running stream of it, splashing into the spring-fed pool below the sandstone ledges, was broken with erratic rhythms of timber sound. The brush of the evening wind, increasing now in the leafy upper reaches of the thick timber, the raucous cry of a jay somewhere in the near south, both helped to cover Kor-Káy's approach.

He made small, almost no, sounds, and no smell, for the updraft from the cool canyon favored him completely. He used the panther's yowling outcry then to hide the noise he made covering the last distance, and prostrated himself on the bare sandstone ledge above the spring. What he saw down there raised a turmoil in him even greater than the fear his knees had sensed in Pintí's quivering flesh.

The panther had T'sal-túa!

The sixteen-year-old girl's deerskin work dress was shredded from shoulder to thigh. Her black braids were awry, torn and tangled, one of them still caught in the panther's claw. The panther was playing with the girl's limp body as a cat does a mouse, for the entertainment of her kittens. Tugging at T'sal-túa's thick braids, the panther pulled the girl along the edge of the spring pool until the entangled claw tore free, then backed away, creeping on high haunches.

The panther's forequarters clung to the ground, fangs bared. A keening snarl rended the air as the big cat tensed for another leap. Kor-Káy thought T'sal-túa was dead. The soft roundness of her body was slack and loose, a heap of melted flesh with no motion of life.

T'sal-túa certainly was dead. If not, the torture of fear alone would force her to move some muscle. The slow switching of the panther's tail paused, in suspension, as she reached with one paw, claws extended. With raking claws, she turned the girl over. This to the joy of the two panther kittens, who leaped joyfully, uttering imitations of their mother's snarls. Blood pulsed from an open wound in T'sal-túa's throat, and the sight of it swept Kor-Káy into motion.

Blood did not pulse from a dead body! Crouched and running, Kor-Káy returned to his buckskin pony in a flashing instant, his knife out and slashing the thong that bound the dressed antelope carcass to Pintí's back. From the rock ledge above the spring then, he hurled the antelope out across the pool.

It fell beyond the panther and her kittens. Distracted, the big cat pinioned Kor-Káy with slitted green eyes, then reached to cuff a bounding kitten into silence. Both kittens crept, stalking toward T'sal-túa's body. But the mother whirled and sprang upon the dead antelope. With a squall then that the kittens dared not disobey, she seized the meat in her teeth and leaped into the timber. The kittens followed.

His own jump, lengthened by his joy that the panther had preferred his antelope to T'sal-túa's human flesh, put Kor-Káy beyond the spring-fed pool and beside T'sal-túa. He knelt there, pausing to listen sharply to the flight of the departing cats. Their diminishing sound indicated that the mother was bound for the seclusion of some lair where they could feed in solitude.

In that moment, T'sal-túa sat up. Kor-Káy fixed his eyes on her in admiration of her bravery in lying so quietly before the torturing cat's onslaughts and of her incredible beauty. She was weak, her flesh pale, drained and sallow. Her face wrenched with a spasm of pain. Blood still spurted rhythmically from the pulsing wound in the hollow of her throat. The pool beside her was tinted red, either from her blood or from the reflection of the sandstone rocks above it. Traces of blood stained the sand beside the pool.

"Sister!" Kor-Káy exclaimed.

He made her lie down. It was easy. She was faint and weak. Her body trembled with shock and exhaustion, then went wholly limp again in unconsciousness. Forcing himself calm, Kor-Káy quickly stepped into the timber, his thoughts researching the medicine Asa-tebo had taught him. Carefully, he removed a thatch of viscous, mucilaginous webbing from the dry, forked twigs of a tree-caterpillar's nest. He returned to the spring to select a smooth oval stone of quartz crystal from the bottom of the pool of cool, red-tinged water.

Applying the cocoon of webs to the spurting wound, Kor-Káy forced the small stone down into the soft flesh behind her clavicle. The spurting stopped. Slowly, the blood coagulated, becoming mucoid in the thick interlacing of the webbing. Hurriedly, he retreated again to the timber edge where a patch of yellow spring buttercups grew in bright sunlight.

Murmuring his careful apologies to the plants, he selected

small healthy leaves untouched by insect blight and packed them in his mouth. Chewing this potion gently as he walked, he went to the head of the spring and removed larger leaves from a sapling ash tree, then stripped long tendrils of young bark from the tree's branches. Returning to kneel beside T'sal-túa, he applied the crushed leaves to the lips of her wound and selected another flat oval stone from the pool.

While supporting T'sal-túa's limp shoulders against his thigh, he tied into place a tight pressure binding using the two stones, the larger leaves and the bark tendrils. Knotting its final ties, he whistled sharply. T'sal-túa did not even stir but the thrashing disturbance in the timber behind him reminded Kor-Káy that he had left Pintí, not with dropped rein, but tied hard and fast to a blackjack sapling. His face flushed with frustration.

Reluctantly, Kor-Káy got up, leaving the unconscious girl, and went to retrieve Pintí. He led the pony back, then knelt to bathe the girl's face with cold spring water. It revived her slightly, barely enough to allow Kor-Káy to help her sit astride the buckskin pony. She wrapped her fingers in Pintí's long mane.

The necessary, but unsettling, display of T'sal-túa's long shapely legs fired anew the dull flush of shame on Kor-Káy's face. He hurriedly took his place beside Pintí's muzzle to lead the pony away, wondering at the power of this lovely girl to turn his emotions turbulent. A man should not be aroused by his own sister.

Proceeding with such haste that T'sal-túa could only precariously maintain her seat, Kor-Káy thought of that tortured night so long ago when he had first seen T'sal-túa. He had been a small boy then, she a toddler only four years old. He, a newly taken captive, filthy of body, with tangled, unkempt hair, overwhelmed with fear, exhaustion, and homesickness for his native Chihuahua; but tiny T'sal-túa had cooed at him, stroking his face gently with her fingers as she babbled soft words to him.

Her soft touch and voice were comforting, distracting him from weariness and emotional pain. In the immediately succeeding years, his occasional thought of escaping back to Chihuahua had often been driven away by the presence of T'sal-túa. Any contemplation of leaving her was even more agonizing than the thought of leaving his new parents, his foster mother Da-goomdl and father Toné-bone.

Yet the futility of remaining, as he had grown older and learned there was no hope of his marrying T'sal-túa, was for young Kor-Káy a cold shroud of despair. As they came near the village, the tepees of the Kiowa encampment stood silhouetted in the darkening light against the skyline above the cap rock. The tepees stood, facing east, in an arrangement approved by Asa-tebo, and agreeably so, as though set down there by the hand of a dexterous artist.

Pintí's hoofs rattled gratingly in the loose caliche, which impeded their slow ascent. To the south of the cap rock, the caliche became a cliff face that descended precipitously to the river. Kor-Káy's quick eyes perceived a human form in the thickening dark against the hillside and saw a purposeful Da-goomdl running angling down the mesa toward them.

Her passage was noisy, scattering the loose caliche as she came running on, but every movement of this graceful woman was identifiable as an expression of her concern. Da-goomdl, throughout their childhood, had been a loving and impartial mother to both Kor-Káy and T'sal-túa. She had been as fair and equal in her treatment of them as brother and sister as if she had borne them both. He dared not hurry toward her now. The semiconscious T'sal-túa sat too precariously on the buckskin pony.

Da-goomdl called out in anxiety as they drew together, "You have found her. I was worrying."

Kor-Káy, as a boy, had always thought of his foster mother

as beautiful and, seeing her here in the gathering dusk, knew that his durable conviction had not been wrong. She came up to the pony without lost motion, compact of body, still handsome, though past middle age. Da-goomdl reached up to steady her daughter's swaying figure. T'sal-túa's slumped posture astride the buckskin was convincing evidence that Da-goomdl had cause for worry.

"A panther was using T'sal-túa's body to instruct her young ones," Kor-Káy told his mother grimly.

"I had sent her to get cedar boughs and berries, to purify our tepee," Da-goomdl fretted.

Kor-Káy understood. Da-goomdl and T'sal-túa kept an immaculate tepee and camp, fragrant with cedar, and free of evil spirits.

"I knew as night came on that something bad had happened," Da-goomdl sighed. "I was afraid maybe the Utes . . ." she halted, unwilling even to express so terrible a thought. Solid forms like words too frequently tended to become reality.

Without pausing in their worried talk, Kor-Káy and Da-goomdl continued at a steady pace until they reached the tepee. Kor-Káy dropped Pintí's halter rein. The pony stood patiently while Da-goomdl worked at untangling T'sal-túa's fingers from the deathlike grip they had taken in the pony's mane. Pintí whinnied, as if in sympathy with the girl who slumped so weakly on his back.

The paralytic grip of her fingers was finally broken. Kor-Káy eased her down and she fell down into his arms. She had again lapsed into unconsciousness, which filled Kor-Káy with wonder—it was as if her suppliant body was an expression of her trust in him. He carried her inside the tepee and placed her tenderly on the bed of buffalo robes Da-goomdl had already prepared for her.

Kor-Káy stepped quickly aside then as Da-goomdl hurried in. She carried a beaver pouch filled with water, and began bathing T'sal-túa's face, shoulders, and breasts. Kor-Káy left the tepee, hurriedly and abruptly.

Firewood must be gathered against the coming chill of the early spring night. When he returned with an armload, Da-goomdl scrambled to her feet to face him in dismay.

"I cannot awaken her," she faltered.

Kor-Káy knelt. He felt for the pulse of blood in the soft hollow of T'sal-túa's throat beside the wound. It was feeble. T'sal-túa's face was pallid, ghostly in the near dark beside the glowing coals of the tepee's small fire. *She has lost too much blood,* Kor-Káy thought. He remembered the redness of the spring's pool, and the gouts of blood on the sand beside it.

Standing up, he declared, "I will go for Asa-tebo."

"It is of no use," Da-goomdl said in quiet agitation. "I saw him leave at dawn." She paused. "He was carrying that *tali-doy* bundle before him on his horse."

Kor-Káy kept his face impassive, despite the rise of inner turmoil. The presence of the *talidoy* bundle meant that Asa-tebo would be gone at least three days, and possibly seven. This, too, Da-goomdl knew, for she pleaded almost in despair, "Do you think that you could find him?"

Kor-Káy shook his head. "I do not yet know enough. But I will try."

Stooping out through the tepee entrance, he walked, slowly, in hard, thoughtful concentration, toward Asa-tebo's big tepee, pausing outside it, then turning into the smaller tepee alongside, where the *talidoy* god was kept. Only his certainty that he would one day fall heir to the *talidoy* bundle permitted him to enter.

As nugatory as he considered his present position, he felt that the buffalo medicine he had used this day, and perhaps the power he had already received from Asa-tebo, might in this dire emergency provide him with the strength to reach the medicine man.

Except for the glowing coals of a nearly burnt-out fire and

the white rack of bleached *palos* that usually held the *talidoy*, the small tepee was empty. Not only the *talidoy*, but all the sacred things used in caring for it, were gone. Kor-Káy knew this meant that in whatever mountain sanctuary Asa-tebo had chosen, he would unwrap each object inside the *talidoy*, pray over each of them and care for them, undergoing the long ritual of alternate fasting and eating of sacred foods necessary to carry out this ceremony.

It would take the full seven days. On the eighth day, Asa-tebo would return to camp. But before that, T'sal-túa would die. Kor-Káy did not know enough of the buffalo medicine to help her. He left the small tepee without a word. None was needed since the *talidoy* was not there. He walked directly into Asa-tebo's big tepee.

Old Darcie, Asa-tebo's wife, was sitting beside her small cooking fire. Recognizing him, she averted her eyes, accepting his presence, but keeping silent, as she should. Kor-Káy had long spent a part of each day in this lodge. He circled the fire now, approaching Asa-tebo's place, ornately blanketed, near the tepee's west wall.

Beside it hung the old medicine man's feathered war bonnet, his spear, short bow, long bow, two full quivers of arrows, and his war axe. Asa-tebo had taken no weapons on this journey, trusting himself fully to the protection of the *talidoy*. Behind him, Kor-Káy heard a hiss as old Darcie dropped a hot stone in the soup she was preparing.

Beside Asa-tebo's thronelike willow back rest, among colorful blankets and ceremonial garments, stood the eagle shield. It was slightly apart from all other objects, exalted on its own tripod. The firelight reflected on its medicine drawings, the symbolic owl, the looping rattlesnake coil, and in the upper center the dominant emblem of the shield, the golden eagle.

Kor-Káy reviewed with respect the shield's many scars and bullet-hole punctures. No bullet had ever penetrated completely through it. He voiced his request to the shield both in

Kiowa, *"D'ah-kih, tshegá'doc,"* and in Spanish, *"Con permiso, vuestra potestad."*

Behind him, as he lifted the shield from its stand, he heard Darcie's shocked gasp. Kor-Káy knew the risk that he took. The eagle shield had never left its place except in the hands of Asa-tebo.

Darcie's gasp became an outcry, shrill with horror, as Kor-Káy left the tepee carrying the shield. But she made no move to follow him. A woman's touch on that shield would be worse than anything that had yet transpired and she did not mean to involve herself in the imponderable consequences of such an act. Kor-Káy took the shield into the *talidoy* tepee and suspended it from the *talidoy* bundle's own resting place.

Then he pushed the charred ends of long, straight, dogwood fire poles into the smoldering coals of the fire before the shield, and sat down. A sufficient time of hard concentration here before the eagle shield might draw Asa-tebo's attention. If Kor-Káy could not reach him that way, he felt there was no way he could do so.

Ranging out beyond this Ouachita camp of the Elk band of the Kiowas were a thousand leagues of rugged and ancient granite mountains. Every draw and pass was choked with yellow-lichened granite boulders and long-thorned buckbrush. Its caliche-strewn earth was often barren, easily kept trackless. Over the years, Asa-tebo had taken Kor-Káy to many of his sanctuaries in these mountains; a multitude of places of power, but Kor-Káy knew there were others he had never seen, of varying distances far out from this camp, in many directions, toward the wide, encircling horizon.

The fire in the *talidoy* tepee took hold, popping and crackling sharply. It bit hungrily into the ends of the dry dogwood poles. That was a good sign. Asa-tebo was out there somewhere, perhaps very close, perhaps several leagues distant. Kor-Káy prayed that the eagle shield would speak to him, or that some beckoning would flow out from the intensity of his concentration. Surely Asa-tebo could feel the pain and need of his own granddaughter, T'sal-túa. Or the yearnings of her mother, Da-goomdl. Perhaps the spirit of T'sal-túa's father, Asa-tebo's son Toné-bone, who had so bravely staked himself out to die, would help. There was no other way.

Kor-Káy concentrated on the old priest, buffalo doctor, owl prophet, possessor of the eagle shield medicine. He visualized Asa-tebo in some hidden refuge of the darkness of the now fallen night, preparing himself for the sacrament of opening the *talidoy* at the first break of the sun's morning rays. Asa-tebo would then begin to unwrap, care for, and venerate a few objects each day.

For three days, Asa-tebo would eat nothing and take no water. From the fourth day on, as the sun rose each morning, he would partake of a single sacred food, gathered en route to his refuge. When the sun reached its zenith on the final days, he would sip a little water. Day and night he would pray, as long as he was strong enough to do so. Semiconscious or sleeping, he would dream, storing up visions and pondering them in deep meditation, praying over them until he fully comprehended the future meaning of each for the people to whom he ministered.

The thought that while Asa-tebo was so occupied with pious things, his own granddaughter T'sal-túa was dying here in camp, troubled Kor-Káy, but he forced such ironic, cynical implications out of his mind. To buttress his rejection of such thoughts, Kor-Káy prayed, closing off all thought except of T'sal-túa, Da-goomdl, and Asa-tebo. He sang their family song, concentrating on the fire's flickering reflections as they played over the painted surface of the eagle shield.

Kor-Káy remembered vividly the first time he had seen that shield. The broad *zócalo*, the plaza before the *ayuntamiento* and the cathedral in Chihuahua City, spread open before him in memory. He was a small boy then called Jorge, standing with his scolding aunt. She had been berating him in tense, covert tones while they stood waiting for his father, who was conversing with young Jorge's priest uncle.

Jorge remembered wishing that his mother had been there. Surely she would not have been like Aunt Beatrice, but he could not be sure. His mother had died when he was two. The priest, Father Ignacio, was his dead mother's brother. *Tía* Beatrice was his father's sister. Her voice was as sharp as her aquiline nose. *Tía* Beatrice, rarely silent, now harangued Jorge for his restless squirming during the long mass Father Ignacio had just celebrated in the cathedral.

It was a lovely, late Sunday morning and his aunt's acid monologue gradually faded in Jorge's inattentive ears to become a remote background for his survey of the sun-swept plaza. *Era bordado* with tall eucalyptus trees beneath which bootblacks polished to mirror brightness the boots of the *charro*-garbed *ganaderos* who relaxed now in easy luxuriant pleasure, as apparent as Jorge's, at being released from church.

Their handsome horses, ornately saddled and bridled, with silver-mounted rigging, stood tied in the shade around the plaza, along with carriage teams that had brought their wives and daughters and the townsfolk to church. A few scattered soldiers, on leave from the Chihuahua garrison, loafed about the plaza.

The sun bore down sharply on Jorge, making the sweat bead on his upper lip, turning his small body itchy beneath the expensive woolen suit that covered him. On his head perched a beribboned flat hat. Especially itchy were the dark blue woolen stockings that made his legs hot, and the high-topped leather shoes that imprisoned his feet.

Jorge stood waiting, patiently, hoping his father would reward him with a tall, cool glass of fruit juice from the *puesto de frutas* near their carriage at the edge of the plaza. His priestly but youthful uncle moved out of the cathedral doorway, reaching down to pat Jorge's shoulder affectionately and utter complimentary words about his nephew *pequeño, tan guapo y con paciencia fina de todo costumbre gentil* when suddenly the plaza was full of naked brown men astride hard charging horses, befeathered men gaudily painted and uttering shrill cries and yips and the *trémulo* as they swung *hachitas* and waved beaded and feather-decorated spears.

It was no *diversión*, no *espectáculo teátrico*, as Jorge first thought, for people were falling and running, screaming and bleeding. His priest uncle's sonorous compliment, *so handsome, with fine patience, and every custom of gentility*, still rang in Jorge's boyish ears, but he quickly forgot it as his father seized Tía Beatrice, pulling her toward the sanctuary of the cathedral. Jorge's uncle, Father Ignacio, shouting, was herding people toward the yawning maw of the cathedral's heavy, carved wooden doors. Jorge's sweaty hand slipped from his aunt's grasp as she pulled away. He turned to follow her when he saw her struck down, her head split open by one of the brown warrior's hatchets at almost the same instant the spear of another impaled his father, passing fully through his chest and thrusting out his back in a stain of crimson blood.

Jorge's frantic eyes sought his priest uncle but Father Ignacio had been swallowed up in the turbulent throng jamming the cathedral doors. Some were trying to keep the doors open, though others, inside, seemed to be trying as frantically to close them. Jorge avoided panic by following the crowd, his eyes still seeking Father Ignacio, when his passage was blocked by the squatting haunches of a spotted pony. The pony's hoofs clattered and slipped on the plaza's cobblestones as its Indian rider pulled it up, turning. The pony side-passed before Jorge's face, then, filling his view, appeared the shield. *Chihuahuense* sunshine glinted on the shiny, angry-eyed eagle and the other animals painted on its glistening surface.

Staring down over its edge was the owner of the shield, his smooth facial features grotesque with jagged lightning streaks of war paint. The shield bearer yelled something in incomprehensible gibberish at a younger Indian who rode a war horse that kicked, bit, and fought the fleeing victims near him. The young rider jerked his own horse up short then, to stare down intently at Jorge.

He shouted a reply to the older, shield-carrying Indian. Then the young warrior swung his horse toward Jorge. Responding to sharp heel kicks the horse circled Jorge, and its rider reached to snatch the boy up, throwing him across his horse's withers. There, across the coarse bristle-cut mane, wedged against the Indian's high rawhide-covered saddle horn, Jorge struggled for breath.

As Jorge gasped, trying to regain the wind that had been knocked out of him, his captor began edging outward through the jam-packed mob of people and horses. A pitifully few garrison soldiers were trying to make some kind of fight, with only pistols and knives, among fleeing people and flying hoofs. Jorge's captor rode toward the curbstone periphery of the plaza. His passage became easier as the clutter of frantic people thinned. Brown riders circling the plaza were cutting loose every tied saddle horse and slashing the harness of every carriage horse. Jorge's abductor paused in flight to whip his knife from his belt and add its sharp edge to the rein and harness cutting.

His comrades were already encircling the panic-stricken horses, rounding them up. As the horses bunched and crowded together, the horse stealers headed them into a narrow street bound outward toward the edge of the city. Then, down the narrow *calle* of iron-balconied building fronts, the herders drove them pell-mell.

Bringing up the rear was Jorge's kidnaper, slowed a little by the small boy he carried before his saddle. Not far behind, they were pursued by the rest of the Indian war party, fighting as a rear guard as they fled the city through streets that quickly became deserted. Back there, Jorge could hear a voice he at once recognized. It was the strong commanding voice of the shield-carrying man who had first blocked his way. The shield bearer was shouting, repeatedly, exultantly: *"Béy-hah! Ba-kó-bah!"*

The fire was so small it made little impact on the heavy darkness. Some childish first thought that the fire might be seen, that it might attract rescuers, had passed through Jorge's mind. But as he now saw how the towering canyon walls contained the fire's tiny light, he looked upward at the dark height of those walls and he gave up.

No flicker of light could escape the canyon, either around the bendings of its tortuous walls, or upward beyond the precipitous reaches of the narrow crevasse in which the war party had paused in its flight. No party would arrive during the night to save them.

The *indios*, obscure and shadowy forms in the surrounding darkness, were loosely gathered around the fire. One of the Indians came jerking a captured Chihuahua soldier up close to the fire. The soldier was led by a rough grass rope encircling his neck. His captor pulled cruelly at the rope from the opposite side of the fire, forcing the soldier so close that his boots were almost in the fire.

The Indian was holding a long, thin knife and it must have been very sharp. For the Indian began cutting and slashing at the Mexican soldier's uniform. He did not stop until the soldier stood naked before them, his slashed uniform a useless heap about his booted feet.

Jorge felt great embarrassment for the two Spanish girls who had been taken prisoner with him, and who sat beside him at the fire. In glancing at them he saw that their eyes were lowered, their faces blanched and frozen, whether stricken with horror at their predicament, with shame and embarrassment at the soldier's nakedness, or sickened by the great wound in his side, Jorge did not know.

The soldier had been stabbed in his lower right side by an

Indian lance. It was a raw and terrible wound that had bled profusely. In the dry, desert air, blood had coagulated and clotted in the wound so that it was not bleeding now. The soldier's right leg was covered with dried blood, but the man stood bravely, his face drained and pale with pain as the ugly Indian holding his neck rope harangued at him in vicious, incomprehensible, gutteral words.

Then the Indian thrust his knife into the soldier's wound, cutting and ripping at it until the blood gushed forth again. The soldier swayed reeling, and fainted, collapsing in an unconscious heap on his destroyed clothing.

Jorge's horrified gaze slid across to another Indian, the shield carrier who had blocked his flight across the Chihuahua plaza, and who had apparently ordered his capture. This older Indian stood across the fire from them. A grimness on his face seemed to convey disapproval of the torturing of the soldier. But he had done nothing to stop the brutalities. He still did nothing. The angry Indian threw the end of his grass rope down across his unconscious prisoner and stepped back from the firelight.

Then the older Indian sat down. He crossed his legs, placing the eagle shield between himself and the fire, and began talking. Jorge could not understand a word of this jargon, as he knew the two girls beside him could not, but at the first word directed toward them Jorge's heart leaped up in his throat to begin pumping with uncontrollable fear. An unknown fate awaited them, surely no different than the one that had brutally cut down the soldier, leaving him unconscious and bleeding here beside the fire.

The middle-aged Indian's voice, in talking to Jorge and the girls, was not harsh. It was soft, a mellow singsong that Jorge would have found soothing had not fear already seized its hold on him. With gentle chant and direct gaze, this more elderly one of their captors seemed to want Jorge and the girls to look at his shield, for he kept indicating it with his brown fingers. Jorge found his attention drawn to it and began examining it.

It was yellow in background, more than the length of Jorge's arm in diameter, and polished to a waxy glow. Around its periphery, the diamond-backed pattern of a rattlesnake was coiled. Inside the encircling snake were three animals, a trinity of turtle, owl, and buffalo. From one side, a lone coyote seemed to watch Jorge with sly amusement. Above, and dominating all, was the angry-eyed golden eagle. All these creatures were drawn, not artfully, as they were painted in the picture book Jorge had at home, but not crudely either.

They were drawn in a way Jorge found no words to describe in his limited understanding. Most of them he had seen personally, pointed out to him by his father during their rare walks into the sandy Chihuahua desert that surrounded their city. The buffalo he knew only from his picture book. But there was a singularly lifelike aspect to these drawings that so seized Jorge's attention that he began to forget that he was frightened.

The flickering fire seemed to lend its life to the animals, so that they began to take motion, the turtle moving slowly, the owl blinking its eyes lazily, the buffalo lowering its head to crop sparse bunch grass before its black hoofs. The Indian man's soothing voice droned on, further allaying Jorge's fears. Then the Indian did a strange thing.

He placed both hands near the base of the small fire and made a sign of lifting. The fire rose, floating peculiarly, lifting itself from the ground. It ascended, rising until it burned in mid-air, crackling briskly a hand's height above their heads.

The Indian eased forward until he sat, cross-legged, almost where the fire had previously burned. He was very close to Jorge and the two girls now. The fire burned busily not far above his head as he reached around the shield and scraped together a heap of sand, twirling his fingers in it. Suddenly he jerked his hand away and the heap of sand became a coiled rattlesnake. Its forked tongue darted, its tail rattles chattered their rhythmic warning.

Jorge, with sharp intake of breath, recoiled from the threatening snake's flat, triangular head, but the captured girl sitting beside him cried out with joy. She extended a caressing hand, cooing with pleasure as she reached to pet the rattlesnake.

Her hand had almost reached the rattlesnake's head when the Indian spoke an abrupt syllable. The snake uncoiled itself and slithered off into the brush. The middle-aged Indian seemed somehow to have become suddenly older. He moved back to his previous posture, and smoothed away the pyramid of dirt he had built as the fire returned to earth.

It was all confusing to Jorge, but he knew it would do no good to try to question this suddenly old and gentle man. Neither of them understood a word of the other's language. Anyway, the old Indian's hands were benevolently encouraging him to lie down now, and were covering him with some kind of soft-furred-animal skin.

Jorge went to sleep where he lay, beside the extinguished, earth-covered fire.

When he awakened it was still dark, but the sound of subdued talk, the noise of gathering horses, told him it was near
morning. They would soon be starting out again. Jorge sat up
where he had slept. He saw that the two girl captives were already sitting, glumly. The one beside him was crying.

Jorge asked her, "Why did you try to pet the snake last
night?"

Her crying suspended, she looked at him curiously.
"Snake?" she asked.

He pointed at the ground before them. "The one that was
there, between us and the Indian."

Her brows knitted. "There was no snake. There was a *per-
rito, muy chulo*, a cute little puppy lying there for a minute.
It jumped up and ran away when I reached out to pet it."

The other girl, stiff-backed and sulky, sat beyond them glaring off into the distance.

Jorge leaned to ask her, "Did you see the snake?"

She ignored him, frowning.

Jorge pressed, "Did you see the snake, or a puppy?"

Her glance flicked at Jorge angrily. "I saw nothing. A pile
of dirt!"

Jorge wanted to talk more, about the fire that had risen in
the air, the drowsiness that had overcome him, but there was
no time. The Indians were mounting up.

Jorge was taken aboard the horse of the man who had captured him, the younger Indian. Each of the girls was reclaimed by her captor, both of those warriors seeming to take a

proprietary interest in his captive. Jorge saw the captured soldier, still naked. He was very weak, still being led by the rope tied around his neck, barely able to stumble forward when the grass rope tightened, tugging at his red-chafed skin.

For a long time, Jorge thought of the rest of that journey as interminable. Much of it soon faded into a haze of exhaustion. He had become a maturing youth and was a member of the Herder's Society before he began to realize how much he had learned, how much had happened, during those days of incessant riding. He never slept beside the two girls again on that journey.

The girls, the one called Lupe, and the older one, Pilar, had been captured to be the wives of the men who had taken them. From that first day, each of the girls rode with and spent the night beside the man who had been her captor. Jorge could frequently hear the one who cried. It was Lupe. She seemed to cry all the time, though the man who kept her was clearly trying to comfort her and be kind to her. Jorge often heard Pilar, too, lashing out at her captor in the same harsh, strident voice with which she had so angrily spoken to him.

Lupe, when she quit crying, grew quiet, pensive, and at times seemed quite relaxed, her mood a mixture of sadness and defeat. Sometimes, strangely, she acted almost happy. Pilar remained resentful. It soon seemed as if the man who had taken her was the prisoner, instead of Pilar.

The captured soldier died on the first day. When he was too exhausted to go on he simply fell to his knees, then collapsed on the ground. When his Indian captor saw what had happened, he gave a war whoop, kicked his horse into running and rode off fast, dragging the man behind him. Jorge felt a trembling pity for the soldier, and cried for him. But the brave soldier was beyond pain now.

His naked and bloody body bounced along behind the horse that dragged him. The Indian dragged the body for a long time after the soldier was dead—more than two days. Then he finally got tired of dragging the skinless, stinking thing. The extra weight was tiring his horse too much. He got down to take the scalp. He cut the corpse in a few more places, carelessly, then untied his rope and rode off, leaving the body on the ground for the hovering buzzards and night-scavenging animals to devour.

It was more than a year before Jorge learned that during the raid in the Chihuahua plaza the brave Mexican soldier had, with his knife, killed his captor's only brother. That was why the Indian's heart had been so bad toward the soldier. He had caught him alive to torture him and kill him as slowly as he could.

During the long time of traveling, Jorge tried to talk with the two girls, although they were rarely permitted together for long. Even in those times they were so exhausted from long hours of riding that they were too tired to talk much. Pilar carried on with a burning, frantic energy of frustration, while Lupe smiled sadly, submitting in patient resignation to her apparent fate.

On some days, Jorge rode with the man who had captured him. Jorge learned that his name was Toné-bone. On other days he rode with the older Indian, whose name was Asa-tebo. Both of them tried to learn Jorge's name, which he willingly told them, but the closest they could come to saying it was Kor-Káy. So Jorge became Kor-Káy.

Asa-tebo and Toné-bone could not have been more diligent in trying to teach him. By the time they reached a wide river flowing with muddy red water which seemed to have some special significance for the Indians, Kor-Káy had been told the names of most of the plants and animals they had seen. He tried to respond by telling his captors the Spanish names of the plants and animals he recognized.

With no realization that he was doing so, Jorge—Kor-Káy—gradually shut the spectacle of the fight in the plaza and the bloody deaths out of his mind. His childish brain had begun the healing process of covering those grim memories with scar tissue. He wondered what had happened to his priest-uncle, Padre Ignacio, and if the spear wound had killed his father, but these things he had no way of knowing.

Since his father had been gone, on commercial trips buying herds of cattle for trade with the northern colonies, for so much of his childhood, Jorge did not really miss him. Thoughts of Padre Ignacio always aroused an image, somehow diffused and incongruently perfume-scented; they were vague recollections of his mother, who had died of the *mal*, fever, a long time ago.

His distant memories of his mother seemed as obscure as the angelic beings Padre Ignacio, her brother, often told him of in his frequent *cuentos de la Biblia*. As the days went by Jorge—Kor-Káy—found that he was learning a few Kiowa words, just by listening carefully to the sounds the Indians made when referring to a horse, the fire at night, a rope, saddle, blanket, the food they ate, the sky, the ground. Kor-Káy found it all interesting.

He was riding more with Asa-tebo than with Toné-bone now. Not because Toné-bone did not want Kor-Káy to ride with him, but because Asa-tebo was urging that it be this way, as if it were a kind of privilege to which he was entitled, and about which he had the right, and the responsibility, to be insistent.

One day when he was riding with Asa-tebo, the old Indian began sniffing the air and reining his horse to a halt. He thrust his arm skyward abruptly. They were riding through a country of rocky escarpments, low sandstone hills with tight entanglements of *encinos* lacing together the shallow valleys between them. The members of the war party were loosely grouped, each of the warriors apparently sunk in his own midafternoon preoccupations as riders dulled by a long journey are apt to be.

Asa-tebo was not dulled, and his upthrust arm brought the group to an immediate, silent, but alert halt. Kor-Káy could smell nothing, but Asa-tebo sat his horse as quiet as stone, his nose still lifted, carefully testing the air. His eyes were glazed, his ears vigilant, palpably sorting out each faint sound. He lowered his arm. It hung momentarily at his side as he seemed to consider all the evidence his senses had assembled, then he flung his arm in pointing toward the refuge he had chosen.

It was a rocky *brasada*, a tangled thicket of scrub oak perhaps a hundred *varas* distant. Every warrior put his heels to his horse and ran for it, lifting his blanket and waving it to herd the loose horses, the stolen ones, along with them. There was no shouting, no outcry. The flight was as quiet as it could be made with so many horses. Within moments they were all well concealed in the center of the thicket.

Each warrior dismounted. Some moved to insert a finger into the mouth of a nervous horse to prevent it from neighing. Such a signal of equine communication would have alerted the distant column that Kor-Káy could see now, coming along the shelved edge of a faraway talus slope.

The war horses were trained to hold their peace in such circumstances, but some of the stolen horses were skittish. Kor-Káy, from his vantage point, alone atop the back of Asa-tebo's horse, watched the coming riders gradually increase in size and distinctness. The broken talus over which they came made only occasional, distance-muffled, crunching sounds. Apparently it retained no print of the hoof that was lifted from it. The Indians, in fleeing across it, had left no trail.

As the approaching riders came on, Kor-Káy began to practice the counting his aunt had so impatiently tried to teach him. He got to *trienta y ocho*, and could not remember the next number, though there were still more riders to count. He was certain that there were more than thirty-eight men in the column, and there were not that many warriors hidden in the *brasada*.

The passing riders were not dressed alike, as soldiers would be, yet there were many things similar about them. Each man rode a fine horse. Each wore a broad-brimmed hat—not a hat such as the *rurales* wore, or as big as the hats of the *charros* of Chihuahua. The hats these men wore were brown, or dun, or buckskin color, and some were creased and some were not.

Their shirts had a rumpled, linsey, homespun look about them, and their legs terminated in high-heeled, fine leather boots. Each man wore a holstered pistol, a knife slung to his belt, and a rifle in scabbard beneath the stirrup fender of his saddle. Some wore vests, some shirts only, but pinned to the chest of each was a polished and shiny silver star.

Beside Kor-Káy one of the girls, Lupe—Lupita as Kor-Káy had come affectionately to know her—remained obediently silent; but Pilar caught her breath as if in preparation for sudden screaming. Her captor-husband seized her roughly, his hand covering her mouth, and the scream was choked into silence before it could rise in the hot afternoon air.

The column of men outside the thicket rode by to the accompaniment of rhythmic leather creaks and the gravel-muted clop of hoofs, accented when a hoof clipped glancing off a stone. There was the rare jingle of a spur rowel or some other piece of metal equipment, but no conversation among the passing men. The warriors hidden in the *brasada* waited in silence until long after they were gone.

Kor-Káy did not feel that the Indians were afraid, though he was certain there had been many more men in the column than warriors in the *brasada*. But the warriors had prisoners, the two girls and himself, and stolen horses. Perhaps they were satisfied.

The next day they entered the mountains. After that, the warriors seemed to get more cheerful. One or another would break out in a strange song, starting high, with coyote yelping cries, descending, and rising again. It was different from any singing that Kor-Káy had ever heard, yet pleasing and triumphant in sound.

During this time, Kor-Káy began to realize that Asa-tebo and Toné-bone were father and son. It was at first something in the way the younger man accepted the orders of the older and led the flight into the *brasada*. Increasingly now, although without real consciousness of why, Kor-Káy related the authority with which Asa-tebo spoke to Toné-bone with the tone his own father had always used in speaking to him. Asa-tebo's voice brought a sure and filial response from Toné-bone. Sometimes Toné-bone's responding or actions suggested a mild protestation but it was a slight and usually good-natured resentment that never bore any weight.

And they sang the same songs. Often together. Other warriors usually sang their own individual songs. Sometimes everyone in the war party sang a song together. When such a song was finished everyone would yip and yelp in appreciation of it. The war party made camp that night in a cheerful, relaxed mood, in which even Lupita seemed to join. Pilar stood aside, depressed and sullen, though she had quit fighting with her captor-husband all the time, and sometimes appeared to be almost content, or at least beginning to learn submission.

Occasionally some remark that she would make, *"¡Qué manera rara de vivir!"*—"What a strange way to live!"—would lead Kor-Káy to believe that Lupita had been reasoning with her, or that perhaps at last even she was beginning to find some surprising pleasure in the nomadic pattern of their increasingly leisurely passage northward.

The next morning they lingered long in camp, the warriors painting their faces and putting on their best clothes. Through hand gestures and the scattering of Kiowa words Kor-Káy had learned, he guessed that they were getting ready for some kind of *desfile*. There was an atmosphere of men getting dressed up for a parade, among friends and people who would appreciate and cheer for them.

By midmorning the procession was mounted and moving. There was a proud and colorful jubilation about it that was contagious. For some reason, Kor-Káy was to ride with Toné-bone today. Toné-bone, young and virile, was awesome in the paint of his warrior society. The lower half of his face was painted brilliant red, the upper half midnight black. Asa-tebo rode beside them wearing a cape of red strouding, a long, red sash, and a full war bonnet.

Three feathers jutted from Toné-bone's scalp lock; two V-notched and erect, the third notched and trailing. After much talking and hand gesturing by Asa-tebo, Kor-Káy got the idea —that one more victory and Toné-bone would be entitled to the full war bonnet.

As the procession started, it moved upstream parallel to a river somewhat more narrow, but clear, and deeper, and running between more precipitous banks than the wide, shallow, red stream they had crossed days ago.

Asa-tebo and Toné-bone led. Behind them came the captors of Lupita and Pilar. The girls rode astride, behind their new masters. Kor-Káy had learned now that their husbands were named Tsoy, and Intue-k'ece. The girls were pretty in spite of the worn, tattered condition of the dresses in which they had been captured. There had been no time to mend or replace garments during the long days of steady traveling.

Tsoy was painted black all over, symbolic of the complete-ness of his victory; a way of painting, Kor-Káy would learn, that had been given to him by a young warrior friend among the Southern Cheyenne. The rest of the party followed, herd-ing the captured horses. Their war cries imitated the excited yips of the prairie wolf that has brought down its prey and is celebrating victory.

Sporadic voices rose in victory songs. There were flurries of drum beating and, over all, the strident blats of a brass horn.

One of the Kiowas had stolen a soldier's bugle during the raid. The young warrior, Pein-hH, had snatched it from the aiguillette of the Mexican bugler after he had killed him. While in flight, Pein-hH had joyfully wielded the shining brass bugle and had, with tortured, red-faced, choking efforts, learned to strangle ear-splitting blasts from the horn.

Pein-hH's vociferous, unmusical blats were nothing like the piercingly lovely calls Kor-Káy remembered issuing from the walls of the small Chihuahua City garrison, but Pein-hH was proud of the merciless noise. His crude blasts drowned out the drumming, overrode the war songs, surmounted the victory cries of the warriors.

Their destination, in sight, became the first Indian village Kor-Káy had ever seen. Its tepees, some of them picturesquely painted, were luminous in the morning sunshine. The buffalo robes were brown and tan, the bleached skins snowy white; the painted ones ornamented with bright designs and figures he could not yet make out. They stood on the high bank of the river Toné-bone called Washita—a word Kor-Káy would learn the Kiowas had borrowed from the Choctaw-French *Ouachita*—big hunt.

No smoke arose from the tepees' open smoke flaps. The spidery patterns the upthrust poles made against the sky stood, sharply unobscured, in the clear air. No human moved in the open areas between the tepees, or among their adjoining meat-drying racks and brush arbors. Asa-tebo and Toné-bone led the procession down the gradual slope to the river crossing and plunged into the shallow edge of the ford.

The water became swimming deep a few *varas* out, and the herd of captured horses snorted and protested, bunching together as they swam the fast, deep current. They straggled out on the bank and stood drenched and dripping while the warriors held them in a tight herd. Everyone seemed to be staring up at the quiet, apparently deserted village.

It occurred to Kor-Káy to wonder, *how strange the people*

in that village must be. How could they be so incurious?

Every procession Kor-Káy remembered in Chihuahua City had brought the people out on their ironwork balconies to watch. The street dogs barked. All was excitement and confusion. But here there was no noise of celebration. All the warriors' songs and shouting had ceased. The Kiowas sat their horses warily, stonily alert, looking off in every direction, vigilantly watching the village.

A crescendo of chatter began to rise among them. A few warriors of the party broke from the group and rode with a thunder of hurrying hoofs up the rocky slope of the ford into the village. Kor-Káy could see them circle quickly and excitedly through it.

Asa-tebo did not seem to be perturbed. He motioned toward Toné-bone with a brief hand sign, and the two exchanged a short conversation in sign talk. The riders who had entered the village came thundering back, shouting bursts of Kiowa words that ricocheted from their throats like gunfire.

The rest of the war party broke and rode toward the village, driving the captured horse herd before them pell-mell in near stampede. Asa-tebo and Toné-bone followed along behind. The riders of the war party scattered through the deserted village, then regathered to mill in utter confusion.

The sign talk between Asa-tebo and Toné-bone went on. Kor-Káy, riding behind Toné-bone, clung to that warrior's narrow, muscular waist as Toné-bone's horse began to fidget and caracole nervously. Asa-tebo was pointing off across the *mal país*. His horse, too, was backing and filling, uneasy with contagion from the alarm that had activated the men and horses around them.

Kor-Káy looked where Asa-tebo was pointing. Off yonder across the sparse salt cedar, lay a tracery of draws and dry gullies. Asa-tebo rode toward the arroyos, shouting, shading his eyes with his free hand. Heads began to appear then as many pairs of eyes peeked out over the edges. Asa-tebo waved a beckoning arm.

People began, hesitantly, to climb out of the arroyos. They came then with greater alacrity until the two groups, mounted warriors and the appearing people, were making their way joyfully toward each other across the chaparral and shinnery that separated them.

It was months before Kor-Káy fully understood what had happened.

A small war party of predatory Utes had been skulking in the vicinity for days. They had been night prowling in the darkness outside camp, and appearing skylighted on the distant ridges during the day, too few in number to get up the courage to attack the entire village.

The Kiowa villagers, their best fighters gone on war journey, made nervous by the prowling Utes, had heard the approaching blats on Pein-hH's captured bugle. Stricken with fear that a troop of soldiers was also riding to attack them, they had fled to hide in the arroyos.

Asa-tebo had somehow understood this, which accounted for all his hand sign talk with Toné-bone. Riding among the reunited warriors and villagers, Asa-tebo told them, "Those Utes were as frightened by the bugle as you were. They have run away. We can chase them some other time. We are tired from a long journey and need to rest here for a while."

He sent an old man named KyHp-t'a—which means Old Man—to a high place to watch, and a boy, Tocp-k'—Jack Rabbit—with him as messenger. Then the war party dismounted, relaxing like soldiers come home, basking in the bounteous praise, exuberant in joyous reunions with family and friends.

Kor-Káy had not known that Toné-bone and his wife, Dagoomdl, had lost a boy child in death prior to the going out of this war party. He had been kidnaped to replace the dead

child. As soon as Asa-tebo had seen him there in the Chihuahua plaza he had urged Toné-bone to take him.

On that long ride of return, Kor-Káy's training as the foster
son of Toné-bone and Da-goomdl had begun. By the time of
their arrival at the village, his adoption had been well under-
way. When Toné-bone had swung Kor-Káy down off the back
of his horse into Da-goomdl's eager arms, his adoption had
been complete.

Da-goomdl had placed him on the ground to stand beside
the pretty little girl, four-year-old T'sal-túa, his new sister.
Kor-Káy was eight. Then Da-goomdl had knelt before them
to admire them together. Kor-Káy knew he was filthy from
the long travel, his hair tangled and matted. He felt overwhelmed with exhaustion and fear and a sudden flood of
homesickness for familiar Chihuahua.

But Da-goomdl had embraced him. Her family was once
more complete. The warmth of her emotion communicated
itself. Kor-Káy without understanding why, felt comforted.
He had stood there beside T'sal-túa and watched Asa-tebo
dismount from his horse with sudden inspiration in his eyes.
Asa-tebo approached the bugle blatter, Pein-hH, not to re-
buke him for frightening the villagers away, but to embrace
him and encourage him to blow the bugle every day until he
could learn to do it right.

At the victory dance of celebration held that night, the familiar, tattered clothing of Lupita and Pilar had been replaced with new, white deerskin dresses luxuriant with long
fringe. The camp women had heaped their arms with gifts of
bright trade blankets and beaded moccasins, with the culinary
and domestic articles necessary to set up their new house-
holds. Until even resentful Pilar's eyes were shining with astonishment. Lupita's content seemed to deepen even more.

In the years that followed, Kor-Káy quickly became a favorite son. He learned Kiowa and, at Asa-tebo's insistence,

taught his adopted parents Spanish. He learned that by custom Kiowa grandfathers do most of the raising of young boys. In that way there is no resentment between boys and their fathers, for grandfathers are more patient, less stern and demanding than fathers.

The whole tribe, in fact, pampered and petted Kor-Káy and all the young boys, who would soon grow up to be the warriors and defenders of the tribe. As Da-goomdl pointed out to her newly adopted son, "Those of you who may die in defending us deserve to be treated this way. If one of you is killed in fighting an enemy, we want to feel that we were kind to you and honored you when we had the chance."

His foster grandfather spent long evenings telling Kor-Káy the culture stories of the Kiowa people. Within the first few months, Asa-tebo put him on a horse and began teaching him to ride. The middle years of Kor-Káy's training came from Asa-tebo for a more tragic reason. Toné-bone staked himself out. When Kor-Káy asked his grandfather why, Asa-tebo explained that it was an act of courage to drive your spear down through the trailing end of your warrior society sash, and remain there, implanted before the enemy, until released by a fellow warrior. It was the supreme act of bravery.

Toné-bone had traveled north with a few warriors to bait the Utes. Anxious to win the one remaining honor that would earn for him the right to wear the full war bonnet, Toné-bone had staked himself out before a pursuing Ute.

'N'da—Smoke—the warrior who was fighting not far from Toné-bone, had shouted to the others that he would free Toné-bone, but in riding to do so he had somehow fallen from his horse. 'N'da, unable to reach Toné-bone in time to prevent his death, had caught up his own loose horse and managed to escape.

For a moment, Kor-Káy thought his own singing had awakened him. He was still sitting in the *talidoy* tepee, his eyes drowsily fixed on the hypnotic colors and medicine animals painted on the eagle shield. His hard concentrated effort to reach Asa-tebo through the shield, his intense prayers that Asa-tebo would come, had exhausted him and dulled his senses.

Kor-Káy wondered if he had dozed in this struggle of vigil, or if the glimmering recollection of things past had so distracted him from T'sal-túa's crisis that it gave him the illusion of drowsiness. He sang again their family song, strongly, adding to it the epic of Toné-bone's death.

Thoughts of the past still hung dreamily in Kor-Káy's fatigued mind as the first hint of morning breeze stirred through the open flaps of the *talidoy* tepee. He stared fixedly at the eagle shield, feeling himself begin to grow more awake and more distant from it. Perhaps it was only because morning was coming, but the sensation grew strong and urgent in him, and Kor-Káy got up and went out into the graying light.

Asa-tebo must have just ridden into camp. He was dismounting. Daylight was barely breaking. The old medicine man stood there, waiting, confronting Kor-Káy. The sacred *talidoy* was a shadow swinging from the tall horn of his saddle.

Asa-tebo said, "I am here," and looked off toward the tepee where T'sal-túa and Da-goomdl waited.

Asa-tebo lifted the *talidoy* bundle from his horse, carrying this sacred object with respect as he approached within hearing distance of Da-goomdl's tepee.

Here he paused quietly and began to sing. The song was soothing and elicited from Kor-Káy a deep feeling of gratitude that Asa-tebo was here. No sound came from the tepee. Kor-Káy felt a surging urge to hurry past Asa-tebo and enter. Surely there should be some sounds within the tepee. Unless T'sal-túa had not survived the witching hours between midnight and dawn. Kor-Káy held himself in check, tautly, resisting even the urge to speak to Asa-tebo, or call out to T'sal-túa or Da-goomdl.

Asa-tebo continued to sing softly. It was one of the buffalo medicine songs that Kor-Káy knew, so he began singing too, anxious to add the strength of his spirit. Asa-tebo motioned Kor-Káy to silence. It was good light now. The sun had not broken the horizon but its brightness suffused the eastern sky. Against it, Kor-Káy could clearly see every detail of Asa-tebo's appearance.

The medicine man was inclining his attitude slightly toward the tepee, not so much as if listening, but as if he sought to sense some other obscure information that might be emanating from within it. He wore his "going on a journey" clothes, buckskin leggings so battered and worn they hardly held together, their fringes ragged, uneven, or completely gone.

His shirt was dark from many years of wear, well ventilated from the many holes worn in through it, and fringeless. Asa-tebo's long black braids, as neatly and carefully prepared as always, were rich with otter fur and ermine and bright with red cloth. They looked freshly woven and added dignity to the face so lined with age and wisdom.

Kor-Káy realized that he had always thought of Asa-tebo as "old." Though he certainly had not been old that first morning Kor-Káy had seen him in the Chihuahua plaza, he had seemed old that evening by the campfire. Asa-tebo began another of the buffalo songs. The medicine man danced a few steps, placing each foot precisely and with care. He cradled the *talidoy* bundle in his arms. His soft singing was palliative, engendering hope.

Asa-tebo handed the *talidoy* to Kor-Káy. Kor-Káy accepted it and held it in awe. It was the first time he had ever been permitted to touch it. Continuing to sing, softly and gently, Asa-tebo entered the tepee. Kor-Káy leaned down to pass through the low entrance and follow. Asa-tebo sang his way inside and there repeated the same dancing he had executed before entering.

T'sal-túa was awake. Liquid eyes in a pale, feverish, and tired face that followed every move Kor-Káy and her grandfather made. Da-goomdl, her expression contorted with concern, sat beyond her daughter's head, with cool hands on either side of T'sal-túa's face. Asa-tebo ended his dance at T'sal-túa's feet where she could easily see him. He removed his wrinkled and frayed red neckerchief. Tying a loose knot in it, he suspended it over T'sal-túa's small toes.

"If the knot is able to untie itself," he suggested to his granddaughter, "you will get well."

He began singing again, quietly, patiently, and the neckerchief seemed to move slightly, although Kor-Káy detected not the slightest motion in Asa-tebo's suspending it there. Slowly then, like a lazily uncoiling serpent, the knot untied itself, and the neckerchief dropped and hung straight.

Asa-tebo replaced the red neckerchief about his throat and sat down beside T'sal-túa. He directed her to look up and out through the opened smoke flaps overhead. A white ball of cloud was suspended there, floating above the tepee. The tiny cloud, suspended high in the azure sky, was responding to currents of air that altered its shape, slowly, slightly, soothingly rhythmic in the steadiness of its change.

Asa-tebo spoke of sleep. When her attention wandered briefly from the cloud, he reminded her to fix her eyes on it.

"Do you feel tears forming in your eyes?" he asked. "Then do not resist them. They only say that your eyes are tired. Close them and go to sleep." He sang of sleep; and of water moving. Then of the wind that rises to touch the trees when the sun has risen and the day begins to warm. T'sal-túa's eyes drifted shut.

Asa-tebo continued his song. A muscle twitched in her eyelid as she relaxed, in sound, deep-breathing slumber. Asa-tebo gently removed the dressing Kor-Káy had put on her throat.

"You did well, my grandson," he told Kor-Káy, holding the

antiseptic leaves of the young sapling ash in his hand. "We
will need fresh ones."

Kor-Káy went out quickly, hurrying toward the Washita
where a grove of ash trees grew. The thought dominating him
as he walked rapidly toward it was the urgent desire to hurry
his own learning. Impatiently, Kor-Káy yearned for the time
when he could doctor and heal as Asa-tebo did.

Harvesting the needed leaves, he returned to watch Asa-
tebo replace the dressing on the sleeping T'sal-túa's throat.

The medicine man told Da-goomdl, "When she awakens,
have ready a weakened tea of peyote to keep her relaxed and
resting. She must be without motion; quiet. The wound must
heal enough not to open and start spurting blood again. Her
blood is thin now. If she loses more, she will die."

He arose to tell Kor-Káy, "I go to return the *talidoy* to its
place. Find for me 'N'da."

Kor-Káy wondered why but knew better than to ask. He
knew he would have no trouble finding T'sal-túa's most ar-
dent suitor since the death of Toné-bone. 'N'da was probably
within earshot.

Asa-tebo took the *talidoy* bundle and departed. Kor-Káy
found 'N'da, as he had been certain that he would, not many
yards from Da-goomdl's tepee, sitting with his blanket over
his head. 'N'da was a stout, big-nosed Kiowa, already too fat
though he was less than middle-aged. He had never been married and was so enamored of T'sal-túa that he was foolish.
Kor-Káy took him to Asa-tebo.

The old medicine man had returned the *talidoy* to its place
of honor and had restored his eagle shield to its pole rack in
his own tepee. When Kor-Káy and 'N'da entered, Asa-tebo
was seated in his place of honor, beside the colorfully displayed war bonnet and eagle shield on the opposite side of
the fire.

Asa-tebo was filling his pipe with a mixture of wild tobacco,
red sumac, and the white man's cured sweet tobacco. He mo-

tioned his guests to sit. Completing the ceremony with the pipe, he said, "The time for our long spring war journey is here. We must travel south and gather many horses for trading with the Comancheros. Our young men are restless to count coup and seek honors. I have sought the guidance of D'ah-kih. We go as soon as I have offered the pipe."

He promptly offered it to Kor-Káy.

Kor-Káy hesitated. He had already decided not to go. He must stay here and care for T'sal-túa. But Asa-tebo held the pipe insistently toward him, "Your preparations to receive power are almost finished. While we are on this journey I will give you all of the power that I am able."

"But I am needed here to take care of T'sal-túa," Kor-Káy protested.

" 'N'da will do that. He is a good man. That is why I asked you to bring him here. That is why I am not offering the pipe to him."

'N'da could hardly have been more willing. "I have been thinking I would offer my horses for T'sal-túa again," he said. He looked at Kor-Káy resentfully. "I have been wishing I had offered those horses to Toné-bone, before he staked himself out."

Kor-Káy suspected that he had, and that Toné-bone had refused them. He even wondered if that was not why 'N'da had accidentally fallen off his horse in the Ute battle and been unable to reach Toné-bone in time to free him. 'N'da, pretending remorse at having been unable to save the life of a brother member of his warrior society, wanted to replace Toné-bone by becoming the provider in Toné-bone's tepee.

Though young, Kor-Káy had determinedly assumed that man-of-the-family role himself. 'N'da had since offered five horses for T'sal-túa's hand. Kor-Káy had refused to accept them.

"She is too young to marry you," Kor-Káy declared hotly. 'N'da would probably offer six or eight horses this time. "I am still the head man of that tepee, and I will only refuse your horses again!"

"That will have to wait until we return from our journey," Asa-tebo ruled. "There is no time now. Besides, T'sal-túa is sick."

Kor-Káy sat silent. He realized his feeling toward 'N'da was rooted in his own dog-in-the-manger attitude, since by tribal custom he could never marry his own sister. He was doggedly determined that 'N'da would never have her, even if he was a good man and might be a dependable husband for T'sal-túa.

Asa-tebo, ignoring the bitter feelings between 'N'da and Kor-Káy, seemed to be thinking only of the journey ahead. "This will be a big war journey," he declared. "I have spent much time in planning it, and have talked with the owl about it." He fixed Kor-Káy with relentless eyes, "You will be the only helper I have. If you do not go it will leave all of the medicine I do not have time for to Gui-pah and Addo-mah."

Kor-Káy knew Asa-tebo's contempt for Gui-pah and Addo-mah, the medicine twins, for he knew their methods. If they were allowed to make much medicine, they would return from the journey with most of the loot.

He wondered if Asa-tebo feared Gui-pah and Addo-mah. They had once cast the spell over Toné-bone, simply stating that in all future war encounters Toné-bone would be afraid. Asa-tebo had negated that spell. But Toné-bone had still worried that others might think him afraid—that some might think Asa-tebo had failed to counteract the spell. It was part of the reason he had staked himself out in the fight with the Utes and fought there until the Utes killed him.

The twins would never stop trying to discredit Asa-tebo. With Asa-tebo out of the way they would become the head medicine men of the tribe, and Kor-Káy could only guess how they coveted the prestige—and the material profits—of that position. Should Asa-tebo become locked in mortal combat with that potent pair of sorcerers, Kor-Káy, as Asa-tebo's helper, would also be endangered.

Kor-Káy felt a twinge of unwelcome fear. Some Kiowas thought that Gui-pah and Addo-mah were the reincarnation of the original twins, whom all Kiowas mystically venerated. The one who in that ancient time had gone up into the sky to become the Milky Way, the other who had split himself into ten parts to become the ten sacred *talidoy* bundles. But Kor-Káy knew he did not dare let such dire speculation influence his judgment.

He knew, in fact, that he had no choice to make. If Asa-tebo insisted that he go, he must go. The tyranny of tribal custom simply would not countenance his refusing his own grandfather's request. Asa-tebo knew this as well, and was already giving 'N'da his orders.

"T'sal-túa has lost much blood. She needs some fresh blood right now. Go hunting and find a yearling buffalo calf. Bring it here alive with your rope. It will not be easy, but you can do it. Kill it and give T'sal-túa of its blood to drink and tell Da-goomdl that T'sal-túa must eat fresh red meat every day."

'N'da, arising to depart, said determinedly, "I will do it." His hooked nose was ugly and he was twice T'sal-túa's age. These thoughts tortured Kor-Káy. How could Asa-tebo believe that 'N'da would make a good husband for T'sal-túa?

How could he convince Asa-tebo otherwise?

Kor-Káy arose, "I go to purify myself, Grandfather," he said. A man does what he has to do.

Asa-tebo dismissed him with a wave of the pipe. "Make ready."

Kor-Káy went sadly to the river half a league from camp. Here it eddied back into a *rincón*, forming a deep, mirrorlike pool. His sweat lodge stood beside the pool, erected during the training he had been receiving from Asa-tebo.

He built a fire over the rocks in the low, round, sweat

lodge. The skins covering the lodge were hot from the morning sun. Working in the close dry heat of the tiny lodge started the sweat pouring down over his face and chest. He removed his clothing and lay waiting for the rocks to become hot enough to make steam. His skin had long ago lost its Spanish fairness. He was as dark as his Kiowa brothers. Asa-tebo's hard training had not permitted an *onza* of fat to form on his muscular body. When Kor-Káy went to the pool to fill his flint hide bottle, he saw reflected in the water the powerfully muscled youth he had become.

Asa-tebo's regimen was a hard physical discipline and Kor-Káy was as strong as a young bull. The bottle filled with water, he retired to the sweat lodge. Gingerly, with sticks, he turned the rocks, rolling them from the fire and flicking water on them. Steam hissed from the scalding stones, surrounding him, filling his nostrils and his lungs.

Sweatings, sprints, breathing exercises with stones piled on his belly, the necessary work of the acquiring of power had given his body a smooth and muscular agility. In serenity, he leaned quietly out over the stones to inhale the steam. With patience and hard work comes personal discipline, and even more patience.

Kor-Káy remembered the sun dance when he had realized beyond any doubt that he must seek power and become a medicine man. The decision had come during Asa-tebo's portion of the doctor dance. The sun dance had been held on upper Red River that year. Kor-Káy had been about ten years old, and it had been an unusually fine sun dance.

Asa-tebo, in charge of the *taime*—all the sacred things of the sun dance—had found just the right towering cedar for the center pole of the sun dance lodge. Lupita had cut it down that year, as a captured woman always must. She had now lived among them in harmony long enough to have many friends and to have earned such an honor. Lupita had carried out that important and dangerous task with dignity and joy.

The buffalo hunting party, amazingly, had that year found a sacred white buffalo. *Taime* man Asa-tebo had asked the sacred buffalo's permission to take its life, and astoundingly, it had been granted. All the tribe had eaten of the sacred meat, and as a celebration of thanks, Asa-tebo had offered up a special mystery ritual of his power from the eagle shield medicine.

On that special night, he had helpers drag in a large flat sandstone slab and set it up longwise, imbedded in the earth. A huge fire had been built in front of the sandstone slab. When the ceremonial dancing was at its height that night, Asa-tebo had appeared suddenly, in the darkened area behind the rock, seeming to have materialized himself out of the air. He shouted to the dancers.

They stopped dancing at once, standing still in an awe of shock at his startling appearance. Asa-tebo reached out into the air, and the eagle shield appeared mysteriously between his two hands. He held it there for a moment, tossed it into the air, and it disappeared.

He lowered his hands and reached out before him. In his hands appeared the horns of the sacred white buffalo. He raised them, each in turn, to his lips and issued a pre-emptory blast on them, as if summoning the spirits. Then the pair of horns simply disappeared, returning to the same mysterious source from whence they had come.

Asa-tebo faced the fire and began to pray. Flashes of firelight struck the wrinkled brown skin of his sternly dignified face. In the sincerity of its golden olive glow, Kor-Káy seemed to see a rapport with things eternal more convincing than any he had ever seen on the face of his priest uncle, Father Ignacio, during the early remembered years in Chihuahua.

Asa-tebo, in the dim reflections of the firelight behind the triangular-shaped flat rock, seemed attuned with the natural world of which he was a part and could, in many ways, apparently control.

He offered up a long prayer, his voice rising and falling in earnest Kiowa pleas and thanks to the great spirit, D'ah-kih. At times his prayer seemed more nearly a song than spoken words. Some of it was in Kiowa *antigua*, words so ancient their meanings had been forgotten by the tribe. Though Kor-Káy could not comprehend these parts, he knew they were the holiest of the holy.

Kor-Káy listened intently. Every word and phrase that Kor-Káy understood of Asa-tebo's prayer urgently asked for mercy and peace for all of the people. The medicine man was humbly eloquent, devoutly thanking D'ah-kih for all the good things that were part of their daily lives. As the prayer drew to an end, a short buffalo hunter's bow appeared suddenly in Asa-tebo's outreaching left hand.

At almost the same instant, an arrow appeared in his right hand. The arrow burst into flames. Asa-tebo set it smoothly and quickly to the bowstring and shot the burning arrow up toward the sky, out through the round opening in the roof of the brush arbor sun dance lodge.

He reached again into empty air and seized another arrow from nowhere. It burst into flame. This one he fitted into the bow and shot into the fire. From it a great shower of sparks arose as the flames leaped up in consuming the arrow.

He then grasped in the air above his head, where there was nothing but emptiness; the ample robe of the sacred white buffalo appeared in Asa-tebo's hands. The instant he touched it, it fell like a curtain, concealing him completely, then dropped on to the ground, and Asa-tebo himself was gone.

In the moment of the robe's passing through the air, Asa-tebo had simply vanished. The area behind the fire was empty.

Kor-Káy sat for a moment in stupefied wonder. Then he

leaped up and ran to look over the fire, banked and burning, against the triangular flat rock.

The robe of the sacred white buffalo was gone, too. The earth where it had fallen was bare. Nothing lay upon it. Kor-Káy returned to his place again and sat down. It was too much for his boggled, youthful mind. From where had the sacred objects come? From nowhere. They had suddenly appeared in Asa-tebo's hands for their moment of use, and then were gone.

All around him—the sun dance lodge was full of people— was a tumult of awe and admiring talk. The circle of drummers began a hesitant beat, slow, solemn, soft, on the big drum. Kor-Káy heard deep-throated expressions from the men, "Hough!" "Ah, ho!" A woman singer started a chant, high-pitched and eerie, a faraway wild coyote's crying, it descended strongly like an arriving winter wind. The drum beat strengthened, becoming regular, and the men singers joined her lonely singing until it became a powerful, thudding, rhythmic drive, a primal expression in song of elemental nature and of power.

Kor-Káy pondered Asa-tebo's power. He thought of the people he had seen Asa-tebo heal in the two short years since he had been captured as a small boy. How wonderful, Kor-Káy thought, to relieve sickness and misery, to make others well and whole.

During this sun dance, Asa-tebo had cured a middle-aged woman who had become so crippled with stiffening joints that she could hardly walk. Her relatives had brought her to him hobbling on sticks, leaning on their helping arms. Kor-Káy had seen her throw away her sticks and run, shouting joyfully, from that place.

Kor-Káy recalled every procession of this sun dance. Asa-tebo was always the man at its head. He was the most important man among all the people. They were almost always willing, eager, to do what Asa-tebo told them they ought to do. Constantly, men and women came to him for advice.

Asa-tebo sat as a judge to mediate their quarrels. He listened to their problems, then told them what would be the fair way to work things out. It came to Kor-Káy, with conviction, that this he must do. He must seek power and become a medicine man. He must become like Asa-tebo.

The dancing had fully resumed. Befeathered warriors performed their intricate steps in the center nearest the drum, mincing, artistic, sometimes aggressive and threatening. Women and children formed a solid procession moving in dignified meter around their perimeter. A few old men stood proudly around the edges, their blankets worn in careless neatness, suspended over forearms to drape below their waists. They pranced in place, rising on toes, descending on heels, to the stirring beat and song.

Kor-Káy made his way back around the edges of the crowd and went outside, hunting his grandfather. He remembered that Asa-tebo had once told him, "Power often comes to him who will use it, whether he seeks it or not."

Kor-Káy felt certain that he would use power if he had it. Perhaps he might as well see what would happen if he were to seek power right now. He walked to the edge of camp and stood facing the full moon, a ten-year-old boy letting its white light flow over him and surround him, wondering if he would feel any infusion of power from it.

He stood there until he knew that he could not. So he walked farther on down the slope to where the broad sheen of the stream made its circle around the camp. He had walked out into the water. Its coldness rose over his toes and ankles. Its sandy bottom gave way to hard pebbles as the stream bed deepened. The cold water rose almost to his knees.

He stood there in the running stream. Asa-tebo had often spoken to him of the power of water, and Kor-Káy knew his grandfather cherished this stream. Asa-tebo had pointed out the characteristics of the creatures that live in water and emphasized that the Kiowas did not eat them, for these creatures lived in a place of power. He said that he had heard some other Indians did eat them. He thought bad things must happen to such people, for it is dangerous to kill and eat creatures containing power, especially those that live in water and, on land, the bear. No one could tell what would happen from eating a power animal.

He had shown Kor-Káy the turtle, resting quietly in the sand on the bottom of a deep pool, and revealed that it was a sacred animal. Kor-Káy's playmates had secretly told him that his grandfather Asa-tebo had turtle power, and could sit underwater all day long without breathing, though Kor-Káy had never seen him do so.

Kor-Káy stood knee-deep in the water of the river with the full light of the moon beaming down upon him, certain that here he would feel an infusion of power rising up through him from the water or settling down upon the crown of his head from the mysterious moon. But he felt nothing. Except that in the chilly water, his feet were getting cold.

With increasing doubt, he waded out of the water and walked back up to the village. He went directly to Asa-tebo's tepee. Hesitating here, he scratched the tepee wall and was surprised to hear his grandfather's voice invite him inside. Kor-Káy crouched and entered, finding Asa-tebo in his accustomed place, leaning comfortably against his woven willow back rest.

Kor-Káy experienced surprise and a renewal of admiration. After the powerful happenings in the sun dance lodge, Kor-Káy felt that Asa-tebo should surely be tired, probably exhausted.

"Where did you go, Grandfather?" Kor-Káy asked. The question burst from him, for he simply could not contain it.

Asa-tebo did not answer. Reaching into the parfleche at his left he brought out his red stone calumet, and kept on rummaging. Presently his wrinkled brown hand produced his ornately beaded tobacco pouch.

"Sit down, Grandson," he invited.

Kor-Káy burst out, "Grandfather, I want to become like you! A doctor!"

Patiently, Asa-tebo filled his pipe.

Though Kor-Káy did not have power, he was certain he felt a strong surge of approval emanate from his grandfather, but Asa-tebo's present actions seemed to express hesitation, reluctance, even disapproval.

"It is hard to get power, my grandson," he said, "and even if you get power, it is harder to keep it."

Asa-tebo was packing the pipe. "I do not know if I can give you any of my power," he said.

Kor-Káy did not know what to say. He watched his grandfather reach barehanded into the fire, pick up a glowing coal, and lay it on the packed tobacco in the pipe. His face expressionless, he drew on the pipe until it fumed smokily.

As he began the pipe ceremony a gentle smile welled to Asa-tebo's lips from an affection unfathomed by Kor-Káy. The medicine man's eyes warmed with amused kindness. He passed the pipe to his grandson.

Kor-Káy choked and coughed tearfully on the pungent smoke; but he knew that his grandfather would try to give him power.

⊰ III ⊱

From that time, his training became intense. Asa-tebo spent more time with him than ever before, though it still seemed unpressured time, and none of it was spent idly.

"You must learn to see. Especially color," Asa-tebo told him. "You must learn to smell, to hear, to breathe."

Kor-Káy, on hearing these instructions, felt comfortable. He already knew how to do all those things. He soon learned that he did not know how to breathe while running for days and nights without stopping. But he began to learn. He found he did not know how to breathe with a big stone on his soft belly—a stone that was daily replaced with a heavier one.

He had always heard the birds sing. He knew many of their songs and could imitate them, as could most of his playmates. But he had never understood, or given thought to trying to understand, what they were saying. Now he began to learn.

What he thought had been seeing, had been casual, undisciplined looking. Now he began to see, and remember. Months after an occasion, Asa-tebo might ask, "Grandson, where was that feverwort plant we saw on the day the cardinal told us of his search for his lost mate?"

He learned to see color where, before, he would have insisted there had been no color. Asa-tebo could see and identify sickness by the color surrounding a patient, a technique Kor-Káy was slow in apprehending. Asa-tebo could infuse his whole surroundings with a healing color, which Kor-Káy could not even perceive, yet alone duplicate.

Slowly, Kor-Káy learned to infuse his own surroundings

with color but he was never sure which color he should seek, and it was always an uncertain and evanescent illusion for him. He sat in the sweat lodge pondering these uncertainties and all the great effort that went into them, and was suddenly aware that sweat was literally pouring off him now.

He knew there is such a thing as sitting in the sweat lodge too long, of leaving yourself too weak to travel, so he jumped out to run and plunge into the cool river. Swimming around there did not increase his eagerness to go on the war journey about which Asa-tebo was being so insistent.

Kor-Káy's spirit held the same reluctance it had when he had entered the sweat lodge. He wanted to remain behind in camp and take care of T'sal-túa. But his body felt refreshed and ready for action.

He dressed and hurried up the hill, still unwilling to leave T'sal-túa at the mercy of 'N'da. He had already been too long in the sweat lodge. The war party was mounting up as it made ready for departure. Asa-tebo had certainly not delayed in offering the pipe to those he wanted to accompany him. And they had not been hesitant in accepting, which was easy for Kor-Káy to understand.

War journeys led by Asa-tebo were usually more successful than those of any other leader. Those offered the pipe by Asa-tebo often returned having counted many coups, gaining much honor, and a great deal of material wealth in captured booty and horses.

Consequently those invited by Asa-tebo accepted with alacrity and prepared for the journey with eagerness. Horses were capering and prancing impatiently about the center of the village. Riders were swinging into their tall-horned saddles. Most were already mounted. Women were running about bringing last-minute needs that occurred to their warriors. Some of the women and old men were crying.

Kor-Káy had to make a final decision at once. He did so by

deciding that he would go now, but he resolved to return as soon as possible. Perhaps he could quickly sustain some minor wound that would render him useless to the war party, and he could return to T'sal-túa. He hurried to Da-goomdl's tepee to snatch up his short bow, arrows, rawhide, saddle, halter and bridle, blanket, rifle, the few cartridges he owned, and his sacred flute. He found his pouch of face paint, and wrapped the loose items in a piece of tanned elkhide. One must take as few things as possible on a war journey.

The warriors would live off the land and mend clothing and equipment from the raw hides of animals killed and eaten. Kor-Káy carried one blanket to use beneath his saddle, and one to wrap loosely about his waist. For this day only, he took a small parfleche and went outside to fill it with jerky at the meat rack.

Da-goomdl followed him out to urge sadly, "Please, my son, be careful. I cannot bear to think of both my children dead."

Kor-Káy paused, "I would not go, my mother, but Asatebo—"

She nodded understandingly. "We do what we must do," she murmured. Turning away, she went back into the lodge.

Kor-Káy ran out to the horse herd to whistle Pintí up from the midst of it. Two young boys were holding the horses, ready to drive the spare mounts south in the wake of the war party as soon as each of the warriors had roped out his favorite mount for this first day's riding. The boys were Koum-soc (Buckskin), about twelve years old, and a-A-dei (Magpie), surely no more than eleven; both too young to go as warriors, Kor-Káy realized from the superiority of his barely twenty years.

They were old enough to begin to learn how warriors comported themselves with dignity and bravery though, and this was valuable knowledge to acquire before you became old enough to learn how to fight. Pintí neighed excitedly as Kor-

Káy threw his rawhide saddle into place. He adroitly flipped his halter around the pony's black muzzle and Pintí snorted, moving into a fast trot as Kor-Káy bounded astride.

The village was deserted as Kor-Káy rode back through. There would be a period of lonesome quiet in the camp, he knew, then, gradually, normal activities would resume. But for the families of those warriors who had ridden away, the time of worry, of fear and suspense, would continue until their men had returned, or until sad news turned life hopelessly dark with the grief of death and loss.

The riders of the departing war party, now drawing away, brought to Kor-Káy's mind the panoply of victory, the procession that had first brought him to the Kiowas. But that remembering was short-lived. He rode fast to catch up, and only the spare horse herd was behind him now as the past was quickly overtaken by the present. As he approached, he could see that only a few of the riders were painted, and they with the insignia of departing, the symbols of their prayers for success on this war journey.

He heard the journey song being sung loudly by several of the warriors. As Kor-Káy ran his eyes over the group, he could see that Asa-tebo had wisely offered the pipe only to the strongest fighters, the most prudent men and young chiefs of the tribe. Even so, these Kiowas would be aggressively independent. Not one of them would take orders from Asa-tebo or anyone else. They would fight without restraint, *feroz y libre*, but to have anyone tell them what to do would outrage and affront their manhood.

Asa-tebo rode alone, far out in advance of them. Equally far away, over on the right flank, rode the medicine twins, Gui-pah and Addo-mah. Kor-Káy knew Asa-tebo had not offered the pipe to them, but he could not refuse them the privilege of accompanying the war party lest he lay himself open to accusation of being afraid of their medicine.

As Kor-Káy rode up alongside the riders he identified them

individually, for doing so told him something of interest about each one. Bringing up the rear were three warriors: Tsei (*zorro*—Fox), Kou-t (*duro*—Hard or Strong), and Sa-p'oudl (sometimes owl—but in this case, a Jest). The Kiowas considered the owl an omen of the devil, and Sa-p'oudl had a reputation of being a devilish fellow, a jokester.

The rest were loosely grouped together: Tsoy (Claw), K'a'dei (Being in a Bunch—for he was an outgoing extrovert, seldom seen alone), Intue-k'ece (Eggshell—he of the strangely light skin, with freckles, like a prairie quail's egg), Teigouc-kih (Pueblo man—he was not really a Kiowa but had come from a Tewa Pueblo far to the west to marry a Kiowa woman and live with the Kiowas), Pou-doc (Scarred, from smallpox).

Touha-syhn (Little Cliff), t'Hou-t'h (Dog), Koup-ei-tseidl (the Mountain Stands—a giant of a man with a hawklike nose), and Yih-gyh (Four Coups—many for such a young man). Kor-Káy felt sure that by the time this journey was over Yih-gyh would need a new name. Tā (Groin—because he was expert at striking his enemy in the groin with a knee thrust).

'H-'ei-p'eip (Hackberry Tree—because he was born under one), 'An-tsh' (Going on Foot—a fast runner), Ta'dei (Gall—because he liked to eat it), 'H-kou-e (Hawk), and P'-ou (Head Louse). Kor-Káy wondered how P'-ou's parents could have given so derogatory a name to so handsome a man. Perhaps it was evidence of the Kiowa sense of humor, for near him rode Tadl-doc (Hiccup—because his mother had the hiccups when he was born).

Pein-hH (Honey). Kor-Káy had often thought that it would have been an insult to call a man so in Chihuahua. Hanging from Pein-hH's saddle horn was the tarnished brass bugle captured years ago on the raid into Chihuahua. T'ou-teinei (Killdeer). Soun-goucdl (Illegitimate Child—his mother, an unmarried woman, would never reveal who Soun-

goucdl's father was, but the Kiowas did not castigate Soun-
goucdl; he was fully accepted and honored for his own
worth).

Kor-Káy had ridden past the war party and, approaching
Asa-tebo, thought of his name. The medicine man's name
was an ancient word from the prayer language of the sun
dance, Kiowa *antigua*, its translation lost, its meaning as obscure and mysterious as the man himself.

Kor-Káy was passing Medicine Creek, where he had turned
off to enter the mountains on his own vision quest less than a
year ago. Asa-tebo had summoned him one day to say, "We
have gone as far as we can down this road. It is time for you
to go away alone now, to see if something will take pity on
you and help you."

So Kor-Káy had set out for Medicine Creek and the high
bluffs above it. He had divided the daylight into eight parts,
during seven of which he traveled. Reaching the eighth part
of the day he found himself on a high ledge of the precipitous
cliffs the Kiowas called Medicine Bluff. Here he stripped to
his medicine bag and breechclout, then smoked a few puffs of
wild rustic tobacco. He had begun his vigil of fasting and
prayer beside a gnarled, ancient cedar, mostly dry and brittle,
though from its stunted growth a few fragrant evergreen
boughs still projected.

He spent a long night beside the old tree, wide-awake and
staring into the darkness. He remained there the next day,
using its few green limbs to protect him from the burning
sun, eating nothing, and taking no water. Another night and
a second day passed, and he began to doubt that any power
dream would come to him.

The hunger pangs from which he suffered died of their
own volition, but his thirst became a torment that permeated
his whole being, turning him dry and feverish. Toward evening of the third day he began to doze fitfully. He heard what
seemed like music, a singing in his ears and, in the distance,

the rumbling of a thunderstorm. As the storm came on to surround him it was overpowering.

Bolts of ozone-scented lightning unleashed themselves, splitting up among the rocks with thunderous crashes and blinding bursts of light. He seemed to hear a voice in the storm but could not understand what it said. A jagged thrust of lightning tore a dry branch from the gnarled cedar and hurled the branch to the earth beside him. The voice again spoke from the storm. This time he understood it clearly. "From this dry branch," it said, "you are to make a flute. The knots from which small branches once grew will show you where to make its holes; two in the lower body of the flute, one for the Spirit God, and one for the Mother Earth; four in the upper body will represent the north, south, east, and west. At the end of the flute you must carve a small bird. The singing of that bird will bless everyone who hears it."

An eagle swept over the horizon. It carried bolts of lightning in its beak, dropping them around Kor-Káy. Their bursts were deafening and dazzling. Black clouds rolling down upon him became a herd of stampeding black buffalo from which one giant *cíbola* emerged to charge Kor-Káy. A shower of flint sparks flew from its hoofs as it crossed the ledges, pawing the rocks and menacing him with its horns.

The buffalo's guttural throat sounds were like the throaty roars of a rutting bull in summer's heat. Lying there, Kor-Káy memorized the gutteral sounds in the hope that Asa-tebo might later be able to tell him what they meant. As the herd of buffalo stampeded past and over the ledge, the rutting bull followed. Rain came, inundating the mountain side.

The deluge drenched Kor-Káy, flowing over him so that he could not breathe. As he became completely submerged, he choked and strangled. Kor-Káy decided to inhale the water, thus filling his lungs and drowning himself. Then a turtle came swimming up to him. The green turtle said, "Remember the exercises Asa-tebo has given you in holding your breath. The water will subside. Lie quietly and conserve your breath." When the water fell away, Kor-Káy lay panting and gasping on the ledge. The storm was retreating.

With the last distant rumbles of its departure, Kor-Káy heard a ghostly hoot in the tree above him. Among the low branches of the cedar sat the softly defined form of an owl. Mist-shrouded, still hooting, the owl winged itself off the branch and settled, softly drifting down, to his bare chest. There was momentary pain as the owl's claws gripped his flesh, but it was a refreshing pain and brought clarity to Kor-Káy's muddled thoughts. He listened to all the owl told him, carefully fixing in his mind the rhythmic pattern of its hoots.

From sheer exhaustion of the ordeal then, Kor-Káy drifted off to sleep. When he awakened, the debris of the thunderstorm lay all around him. The dry branch from which he had been instructed to make the flute was held firmly in his right hand, while other broken branches lay all around him. The storm litter was laden with mud from the torrent of rain that had almost swept him off the ledge.

Tall bunch grass, growing down the mountain side to the ledge on which Kor-Káy lay, had been bent flat against the ground by the deluge. Kor-Káy assumed that the rain had washed out the hoof prints of the buffalo, but the claw prints of the owl were clearly cut into the flesh of his chest. From each of them ran a rivulet of dry, clotted blood. Kor-Káy shakily built a fire from dry branches of the gnarled cedar, dressed in his wet clothes; then cooked a small rabbit the lightning had killed.

As the tender young rabbit broiled over the coals, their heat and the sun dried his clothes. Kor-Káy thought over the visionary events of the past night. His spirits rose steadily. D'ah-kih had even used the lightning to provide him with breakfast, which he now ate. Kor-Káy arose jubilant, drank from a shallow rock basin filled with cool rain water, and returned to tell Asa-tebo.

Asa-tebo had been as jubilant as Kor-Káy. Listening carefully to Kor-Káy's account of the guttural roars the buffalo had uttered, Asa-tebo translated, "If you obey and do as D'ahkih tells you, you will become the greatest of blood wound healers, a buffalo doctor. The eagle with lightning in his beak clearly signifies that I will be able to give you the eagle shield medicine. The owl has touched you with the gift of prophecy. Even the turtle was willing to help you. You will be able to take sanctuary beneath the waters as I do."

Asa-tebo handled the branch of gnarled cedar with reverence. He helped Kor-Káy remove the knot holes as the spirit voice of the storm had told him. They carved a small bird near the tip of the flute. "This will be your strongest medicine," Asa-tebo said. "Its music will be happy and blessed. I have known of such sacred flutes that won the love of a beautiful girl and gave their owner a long life. Guard it as you would one of the *talidoy!*"

The war party was almost two hundred *varas* behind them as Kor-Káy caught up with Asa-tebo. Approaching unhurriedly, Kor-Káy rode alongside the medicine man for several minutes before Asa-tebo said in gratification, "You are here. *Gi-táhga.*" He made the hand sign for good, then, as if he had been following Kor-Káy's thoughts all the time, asked, "You have brought the sacred flute?"

"Yes, Grandfather," Kor-Káy replied.

Asa-tebo glanced back toward the right flank where the medicine twins rode together. "*Ah-hó,*" he nodded. "We will need the help of many sacred objects on this journey."

Kor-Káy looked behind, resting his hand on Pintí's sturdy rump. He saw the twins and, also riding together, Tsoy and Intue-k'ece, the husbands of the two Spanish girls. Intue-k'ece showed no reluctance at leaving Pilar. They were the scandal of the camp. Spats between Intue-k'ece and the shrewish Pilar could often be heard by everybody. But Tsoy rode sadly.

For Lupe, his wife, was great with child. Theirs was the sadness most felt, Kor-Káy knew, at leaving home behind on a war journey of unknown portent, distance, and duration.

Gui-pah and Addo-mah reclaimed his attention and Kor-Káy wondered tentatively how much Asa-tebo really feared them. Once more, the old medicine man seemed to read his thoughts.

Asa-tebo said, "Kiowa parents do not have twins often. But when that happens it is easy for the parents to make witches out of them. When Gui-pah and Addo-mah became doctors without coming to me for power, I knew what had happened. All their parents had to do was give them no mother's milk for three days, but feed them milk stolen from a bitch dog that has pups, and keep anyone from seeing them for three days. At the end of those days the mother drinks milk made from the sap of the baneberry bush to make her own milk start to flow freely. From then on she can nurse them. Nobody can change anything then."

Kor-Káy asked, "So while Gui-pah and Addo-mah call themselves doctors, they are really witches?"

"They know as many tricks as Tsain-day," Asa-tebo nodded, "and that is why everyone is afraid of them. That trickster Tsain-day's mischief is usually just for fun, but theirs is not. They can cure people but they always charge more than sick people can afford to pay. No one knows how many have suffered from a curse those twins put on them. And no one dares to accuse Gui-pah and Addo-mah of anything."

As the war party neared Red River, the twins separated themselves even farther from the rest of the group. They began disappearing and appearing, apparently diving under the ground, or flying off through the air. One of them, they were so alike Kor-Káy could never tell one from the other, appeared far out on the left flank.

The other one was nowhere in sight. Kor-Káy and the warriors would see one of them somewhere, first on one side of the war party, then on the other. Sometimes both of their horses would be in sight, but the twins would not be riding them. A few minutes later, you would see the twins walking but their horses were nowhere in sight.

As the afternoon wore on, they were no longer seen together at all, one here, one yonder, both gone, which seemed to strike Sa-p'oudl as funny. The brawny hawk-nosed warrior said nothing to anyone, but when you looked at him he might be riding beneath his horse, hanging onto its belly, or he was out of sight on the left side of his horse, or the right, with no part of him visible but the braided ring of his horse's mane and the stretched tight surcingle holding his leg, giving away where he was hiding on the other side of his horse.

Presently he was running along behind his horse hanging onto its tail; then chugging along in front of his horse, repeatedly being butted by the big *grullo's* head. Asa-tebo dropped back to tell them that this was a serious journey, with a serious purpose, but the warriors could not keep from laughing at Sa-p'oudl's antics, and by the time the party had crossed Red River any serious purpose of the journey had been, for the time being, forgotten.

Pou-doc rode his horse for almost half a league while standing on his head in the saddle. While everyone was watching Pou-doc, Touha-syhn slipped from his horse, approached Pou-doc's blind side, and loosened his saddle cinch. When Pou-doc's pony gathered strength in its haunches to ascend a small rise, the saddle slipped and the pock-marked warrior fell sprawling.

Pou-doc whooped and laughed louder than anyone, grabbing the rawhide kack that had slipped beneath his horse. Everyone straggled to a halt while Pou-doc tightened and re-cinched his saddle. Asa-tebo rode back. He lectured them again, telling them, "You are being foolish! If you do not settle down, your mischief and caperings could destroy the purpose of this whole journey. Anyone can hear us, from a long way off." But Asa-tebo had hardly resumed his place at the point when Koup-ei-tseidl noticed P'-ou.

The vain, narcissistic P'-ou was riding along watching his shadow. Like a conceited youth preening himself before his looking glass, P'-ou postured and posed as he rode along, intently viewing the effect of each movement of his shoulders. Koup-ei-tseidl nudged 'H-'ei-p'eip, pointing out this phenomenon to him. Then Koup-ei-tseidl, his bulging fat belly crowding against his saddle horn, began imitating P'-ou.

The whole war party began imitating P'-ou, riding along preening themselves. P'-ou's vanity so occupied him that he failed to notice. The long held silence around him at last penetrated his consciousness. Pricked by the utter quiet, he looked about to find all his comrades peering at their shadows, preening themselves as he certainly knew that he had been. Driving his heels into his pony's ribs, P'-ou rode off in hot anger.

Asa-tebo sighed, telling Kor-Káy, "There is not much that can be done until they decide to behave themselves and stop this rowdiness. Kiowas get this way. I have seen whole war journeys go on like this. Everyone just fooling around, making horseplay, until finally they turn around and ride back to camp, still full of mischief and having a good time, but empty-handed. The Comancheros will not trade blankets and guns for bad jokes when we get to Cibolero!"

The sun was setting, and Kor-Káy thought it was time to begin thinking about where they would camp tonight but Asa-tebo remarked seriously, "Until they decide to settle down, it will be a good time to continue with some of your training. I think I will give you part of the eagle shield medicine."

Discreetly, he looked back to see that the mischief making war party was far enough behind to be unable to perceive his activity. Then Asa-tebo removed his red neckerchief and tied a single loose knot in it. Just as he had for T'sal-túa. The neckerchief dropped down to twitch and agitate slightly, as dancing about slowly, like an uncoiling serpent, the knot in the neckerchief began untying itself.

But it was not as dark here as it had been in the tepee. The sun's last rays glimmering from the edge of the horizon were caught and reflected by a thin, transparent filament. Kor-Káy could see it; a filament of sinew looped about the third finger of Asa-tebo's hand, extending down through the knot and tied to the tip of the neckerchief.

Asa-tebo's hand, which had been so well concealed when the neckerchief had untied itself for T'sal-túa, was also visible here, clearly, because the medicine man intended it that way, and the third finger of his hand made the sinew agitate gently, steadily, almost a live thing as his finger dexterously manipulated it. First the finger then Asa-tebo's whole hand wound the sinew, unmistakably the result of tireless practice, and the far tip of the handkerchief came crawling up through the knot, snakelike, as though propelled by its own muscles.

The knot untied itself and the neckerchief hung limp as a live thing exhausted by its own efforts. Kor-Káy's fascinated eyes lifted from it to Asa-tebo's face. The first feeling to touch him was dismay. "You said if the spirits untied it T'sal-túa would get well. But the spirits did nothing. You did it. You do not know whether T'sal-túa is going to get well or not," he accused Asa-tebo. His dismay fast turned to shallow breathing anger. "The untying neckerchief is false—a trick of your hands. It does not tell anything!"

Asa-tebo was staring at his protégé in astonishment. Apparently he had been completely unprepared for such a reaction. He held up the neckerchief to show clearly how it was rigged, the sinew, almost invisible now in the failing light, running from the finger of his hand down to the tip of the stained, worn neckerchief. "T'sal-túa had to be given confidence," Asa-tebo declared. "She has to believe that she is going to get well."

"But you do not know," Kor-Káy pressed.

"I know that if those who are sick do not believe that they will get well, they may die," Asa-tebo insisted stubbornly. "T'sal-túa, like everyone, must be given confidence."

Kor-Káy, still angry, felt increasingly frustrated. His face was flushed and hot. "But that is a trick," he declared. "It is false." He searched his mind for a word, could not think of one in Kiowa, and said in Spanish, "Un engaño," a deceit.

Asa-tebo was offended. His aged features were set, unyielding, as he declared, "It is a part of my medicine, which was given to me. The eagle shield medicine is not easy to understand. It can be used in ways that are wrong. The twins have a medicine like it they use in wrong ways—"

Kor-Káy's mind was suddenly too full of the fear that T'sal-túa might die to hear any more explaining, or to have his attention turned away toward Addo-mah and Gui-pah. He turned Pintí and rode away. Perhaps he should leave here now and return to T'sal-túa. He would give himself until morning to decide.

Deep in the wild horse prairie south of Red River lies Mustang Springs, known to the Comanches, Kiowas, Kickapoos, all the tribes who frequented the north and south trails into Mexico. The war party, after dark, followed a draw that became one of the shallow canyons leading down to the springs.

They made camp congenially, with much laughter. The prankish mood provoked by Sa-p'oudl's antics early in the afternoon still hung on. But there was hardly time to get the fire burning before a shriek rent the air, followed by another from the other side of camp, and Gui-pah and Addo-mah leaped out into the light of the sputtery kindling fire.

They wore their medicine paint, Gui-pah's a spatter of red-edged black dots that almost resembled oozing sores. Addo-mah's slashes of vermilion were reminiscent of knife wounds. Gui-pah's headdress was a coyote's muzzle, its hide trailing down his back. Addo-mah's scalp lock was crowned with a spotted skunk's head edged with broad rattlesnake skins that hung down behind him to drag the earth.

The twins pranced threateningly through the primitive camp to confront Sa-p'oudl, then both stood before him and shrieked. Kor-Káy watched and listened, his neck hairs abristle.

Gui-pah howled, "You have ridiculed us!"

Addo-mah gave the tremolo and shrieked, "You have dishonored us."

Together, as if rehearsed, they shouted, "You are cursed. Before our journey ends, you will die. You will never see your family again."

With prancing and spraddle-legged hopping, making sure every warrior got the full effect of their grim medicine and terrorizing costumes, Gui-pah and Addo-mah circled the camp and ran off into the night. The mummery of these frightful apparitions had potent results. The warriors were aghast. Sa-p'oudl in particular was stunned and dismayed. His big-nosed face turned dull with shock and beaded with sweat. He looked away from the shadows the flickering tongues of the fire were sending out into the brush and moved to sit close to its warmth, pulling his blanket completely over his head. The others watched in awe, comprehending and understanding Sa-p'oudl's terror. Asa-tebo began singing and stripping branches from a cedar shrub that grew among the black-jacks surrounding camp. He interrupted his strong, aggressive singing long enough to apologize to the cedar, then carried his branches to the fire, spreading them thick over its flames.

As dense cedar smoke fogged up from the fire he bathed his hands in it. Singing steadily, he stepped into the drifting column of purifying smoke and bathed his whole body in it. He removed Sa-p'oudl's blanket, overcoming his slight resistance, and used his eagle-wing fan to waft the smoke thoroughly around Sa-p'oudl's huge frame.

Asa-tebo took out the curved horn of the sacred white buffalo. He tapped it and peered in it to be certain it was empty, then placed it against Sa-p'oudl's breast. The medicine man sucked hard on the buffalo horn, then removed it. A long mesquite thorn fell out of the horn and into his hands.

He repeated the treatment, sucking a second thorn from slightly lower and to the left on Sa-p'oudl's chest. Showing the thorns to the dispirited warrior, Asa-tebo told Sa-p'oudl, "Gui-pah and Addo-mah shot these into you. As soon as the thorns reached your heart, they would have killed you. But I have sucked them out. It is true that the twins are powerful witches, but Kor-Káy and I have become twins in spirit. You do not have anything to worry about. We will protect you from Gui-pah and Addo-mah's magic as long as we are alive."

Asa-tebo tossed the green thorns into the fire. Sa-p'oudl watched them turn brown as the sap boiled out of them. Their long, tapered shapes withered and twisted, then blazed up and were consumed by the fire. Sa-p'oudl gazed fixedly at the white-hot ashes into which they had disappeared. He sighed with relief and lay down, curling up in his blanket to go to sleep beside the fire.

Asa-tebo pointed out into the darkness. "I am going out there to sleep. If you are troubled, come and tell me, but do not come closer than twenty steps to where I sleep. Even if I do not answer, I will hear you and will do what I need to do. Whatever happens, do not come close to me and do not touch me when I am asleep."

Kor-Káy watched Asa-tebo depart. Sa-p'oudl's breathing was already deepening with slumber. Asa-tebo's mention of Kor-Káy in the medicine to combat the twin's magic made him think of the need for him here. His admiration of Asa-tebo had gone on too long to be entirely wiped out in a single revelation. Perhaps 'N'da should provide for T'sal-túa. If he returned now, it would be to the torture of being tempted by his own sister. It was best to wait until morning to decide finally. Kor-Káy found a sleeping place halfway between Asa-tebo and the rest of the war party and lay down for the night. In the naming of those who would stand the night's watches, his name had not been drawn.

The horseplay began again at daylight. K'a'dei, awakening at dawn, found a woods wasp, still chilled by the cool night, crawling along among the leaf mulch of the timber floor. Tā, as part of the medicine that gave him his name, wore his medicine bag beside his left testicle. While Tā slept soundly, K'a'dei lifted Tā's breechclout and placed the sleepy wasp in Tā's medicine bag.

In that warm place, the wasp threw off the night's chill and revived quickly. Finding itself entrapped it began to buzz loudly and freed itself from the medicine bag. It stung Tā's testicle and flew off in high dudgeon.

Tā's howl awoke the rest of the camp, everyone leaping up, grabbing weapons, standing half-ready, crouched, owl-eyed with puzzlement, as they tried to fathom the frantic capering of the wounded Tā. Kor-Káy, who had been lying awake, worrying, had seen it all.

Then, uncertainly fingering the sacred flute hanging on its suspending thong about his neck, Kor-Káy said, "Grandfather, I have concern about T'sal-túa. During this morning I must decide if I should return to her—"

Asa-tebo shook his head vigorously. K'a'dei, with loud shouts of laughter, was explaining his joke to the others. Asa-tebo drew Kor-Káy aside, out of the shouting and noise. "She is getting well," he assured Kor-Káy. "Before the morning star arose, a whippoorwill began calling from the timber there below Mustang Spring and told me."

Kor-Káy eyed him curiously.

Asa-tebo went on, "Then, in a vision, I saw them clearly."

"Who, Grandfather?"

"'N'da and T'sal-túa," said Asa-tebo. "She was sitting

against a back rest her mother Da-goomdl has woven for her in the tepee. She looked very pretty there. 'N'da is working hard to provide her with all the red meat she can eat. She is beginning to regain her strength. The wound in her throat is healing."

Kor-Káy listened. Doubt gnawed, but more of him wanted to believe.

"You are not needed there, Grandson. You are needed here. What you have to decide is whether you want power or not. You can get some power just by using it. But you cannot get real power unless you want it. I have told you this before."

"And I do not understand it," Kor-Káy said resignedly.

"Some men do not want power," Asa-tebo explained. "I know this. Power brings many responsibilities, even danger. Once you have power if you do not use it right it will turn on you and destroy you. You must decide. Let us go and get our horses."

Asa-tebo hurried to catch his hobbled pony. Kor-Káy beckoned to young Koum-soc to bring him a spare horse from the herd. Today he would rest Pintí. He was blanketing and saddling the spare horse when Asa-tebo returned.

"Why do you think I have made you work so hard?" Asa-tebo asked. "That is how you become the road to power. Your muscles must become as hard as a buffalo bull's! Look at me," Asa-tebo flexed his arms. "I have almost seventy winters. I do not even know how many—and do not want to know—but I am as strong as a young man."

Asa-tebo sprang up on the back of his pony as agilely as if his legs were steel springs. The others in the war party were mounted now and T'ou-teinei's horse bolted from the milling group, charging off toward the rising plains beyond the timber. A moment of silence passed, then Pein-hH shouted angrily and reined his horse around to follow in pursuit. T'ou-teinei had stolen the bugle from Pein-hH's saddle horn, and Pein-hH was chasing him to retrieve it.

It was Asa-tebo's turn to sigh in resignation. Shaking his head he declared, "This is going to be one of those journeys that comes to nothing. Someone is going to get too angry at a joke that is played on him. Somebody will lose their medicine. Or we are going to encounter a bad omen that is too powerful for us to defy."

⊱ IV ⊰

After six days of riding, during which they saw nothing, because high spirits and horseplay kept them from looking very hard, they came upon a strange trail. It happened during an impromptu horse race between Soun-goucdl and Tadl-doc.

Soun-goucdl won. When the stocky, aggressive warrior dismounted to congratulate his pony on outrunning Tadl-doc's war horse, Soun-goucdl found himself standing among horse tracks—too many tracks to have been made by the caracoling of his pony, as he pulled up at the end of the race.

Soun-goucdl examined the massed tracks and saw that they were strange hoof prints, not the prints of the ponies of the war party or their own spare-horse herd. Those tracks he was familiar with by now. Excitedly, he called the rest of the warriors. Within minutes there was general agreement that there were more than twenty-three horses in the strange remuda.

Pein-hH came riding in from the perimeter of the mass of tracks, exuberance in his shouting voice, to say that he had found the past night's camp of the wrangler. His bugle, long since recovered from T'ou-teinei, was bouncing loosely and crazily against his saddle. Everyone rode to see what Pein-hH had found.

Dismounting some distance away, approaching carefully on foot to avoid disturbing the camp site, the warriors examined boot prints around the dead fire. They were exultant. The wrangler was only a small boy—from the size of his boot prints surely not more than ten or eleven years of age.

"We will steal those horses from that little boy easy,"

crowed Pou-doc. His mouth, a wide, clownlike smile, cut across the pock-marked skin of his meaty face. "We will send him home crying to his mother."

"Or capture him and let him drive the herd of horses for us," 'An-tsh' suggested.

"I will count first coup," Yih-gyh predicted. His pride in his coups made it an out-and-out brag.

Asa-tebo interrupted. "Maybe there will be no honor in counting this coup." He was examining the footprints carefully.

"And less honor in killing a little boy." Kor-Káy knew that he spoke belligerently. He wanted to shame Pou-doc, and perhaps to warn the others, but Asa-tebo, with pointing lips, was urging him to examine the boot prints more closely.

Kor-Káy knelt to do so. There was something decidedly unusual about the boy's footprints, something peculiar, which kept trying to surface in Kor-Káy's thinking. But it was so vague, it kept slipping away, and he simply nodded in response to Asa-tebo's curious stare, then mounted his horse to take up the trail with the war party.

Following the horse herd was childishly easy. As evening approached bets were being wagered among the warriors as to exactly how many horses they were tracking. Soun-goucdl stuck to his original estimate of twenty-three. 'H-'ei-p'eip raised his guess and thought the herd was even larger.

It was he who first encountered the convergence of the second set of tracks. They came up from the southwest, flowing in like the confluence of two great rivers, to more than double the size of the herd. There were at least fifty horses in the second herd, and count estimates began to soar. 'H-'ei-p'eip raised his wager to bet they would capture more than a hundred horses.

Touha-syhn found, beside the trail, where the wrangler driving the second herd had stepped down to adjust his saddle rigging. A quick conference of the warriors at this spot confirmed that the second wrangler was a grown man. Probably the father of the young boy, 'An-tsh' suggested. Yes, that would be the way of it, several agreed—a father and his son, bringing a herd of mustangs together for a sale, or driving them to fresh graze beyond the blackjack cross timbers. There was no concern about that. One man and a boy would be no more difficult to handle than the boy alone.

When dark had fallen, they waited for moonrise, then followed the trail as easily as before.

'H-kou-e's hawklike gaze first spotted the wranglers' campfire when it was only a tiny spark glimmering and then disappearing in the night's far distance. The warriors held up briefly to collect their thoughts and gather a proper attitude of mind for attacking. Then they proceeded slowly, reconnoitering all aspects as they went.

They found that the wranglers had corralled the horses in a blind draw, closing it by tying their *riatas* to mesquite trees across its open end. Ta'dei was in favor of simply cutting the *riatas* and making off with the horses at once. Tsoy protested. He was engrossed with 'An-tsh's idea of capturing the wranglers and letting them do the work of herding the stolen horses.

Kor-Káy had always suspected that Tsoy was a little lazy. The tall, usually serious Tsoy had been enjoying the horseplay and sight-seeing in which the war party had been indulging along the way. He seemed reluctant to settle down to any purposeful work. The argument continued for a while. Asa-tebo was appealed to. He suggested that the warriors should proceed on for a closer look at the wranglers' camp.

Asa-tebo's manner in rendering this judgment hinted to Kor-Káy that there was yet some decision to make. In fact, the urgency of Asa-tebo's suggestion started Kor-Káy reviewing all that had occurred since Soun-goucdl had first encountered the tracks of the strange horses. Something was out of place in all of this. It piqued and tantalized him disturbingly, but he could not quite define it.

He dismounted with the others, leaving his mount in the care of Tā, Kou-t, and t'Hou-t'h, who would guard their horses. The rest of the party began a silent approach on the wranglers' camp. There seemed little unusual about the camp. As they came nearer, objects became clearer in the moonlight. Kor-Káy could see the wranglers' two night horses tied to the scrub brush.

One of the night horses wore a small saddle, with ridiculously short stirrups, perched on its back. One of the wranglers was nowhere in sight, but the other—the father, Kor-Káy assumed—stooped over the campfire. He was making coffee, warming something in a suspended pot, and frying meat. The other wrangler came walking into camp then from the brush, where he had apparently gone to relieve himself. He was not a small boy after all.

He was a dwarf. A squatty, awkward-moving little man with a big lump on his back, still buttoning the fly of his trousers. Kor-Káy could see Indian hands covering Indian mouths in astonishment. The hunchbacked dwarf took up a tin plate and poked at the meat with a fork, totally unaware of the eyes that scrutinized him from the cross-timbers darkness. He was as ugly as a half-man, half-animal gargoyle Kor-Káy dimly remembered, which perched on the cornice of the *ayuntamiento* in Chihuahua.

Addo-mah made hand signs to his brother, "Maybe he is a witch, as we are." Gui-pah replied, "It could be so." And Kor-Káy realized what had been disturbing and tantalizing his subconscious. The dwarf's boot prints, while boy-sized, were not the free and easy, prodigal footprints of a lively young boy. They were the stumping and inhibited boot prints of a stiff-gaited older man. They portrayed the economical body movements of the middle-aged.

Kor-Káy knew that Asa-tebo, seeing them, had known or

suspected this truth. He had predicted that there would be no coup counting here. The freakish, the feeble-minded, the insane, aroused great caution among the Kiowas. These were special people, endowed by D'ah-kih, the great spirit, with special gifts. It was incredibly dangerous to kill, capture, or in any way plague such special people. D'ah-kih's retribution on those who did so was sure and usually disastrous.

Without exception, and without discussion, the war party recoiled from stealing horses from, or attacking, the dwarf. The warriors backed away from this project which had at first seemed so choice a morsel. Easing back to where their own horses were being held, they were confronted by Tā. He testily raised the question of why this hurried retreat. Then Kou-t angrily demanded to know why were they leaving behind a herd that could be so easily stolen. Asa-tebo himself replied, softly, a single word, "Kōc'-dei (evil)."

They mounted up and rode silently off into the night.

The loss of the horse herd further discouraged Asa-tebo, convincing him that the signs for this war party were not presently right. Rather than return to the people with empty hands, he was willing now to wait, to proceed along from day to day, letting the warriors amuse themselves, sportive and sight-seeing, living off the land. Asa-tebo persevered, watching the signs, waiting for good omens and a change to better luck.

The journey lengthened down across the country of the *tejanos*; through leagues of low hills and round-topped ridges, rocky ground with short but lush grass for grazing. Emerging from this terrain they found what at first they thought was a small cave. They camped in it for the night, near a clear, cold river.

Next morning, a curious Touha-syhn ventured back into the cavern. Then his shouting, echoing voice summoned his comrades. With resin torches cut from the evergreen trees near the entrance they explored deep into the cavern. It was a wonderland of crystal springs, bewildering passages, and towering rooms. The labyrinth became so confusing that a growing fear of becoming lost prompted them to begin following the smoky odor of the trail of their own torches back out the serpentine way toward the entrance.

Wrong turns, and as the scent grew faint, the necessity of retracing their way out of blind passages, was time consuming. For Kor-Káy, the fear of being forever lost in this dark, underground maze of damp rock tunnels gradually became near claustrophobic, a pulse-pounding terror as their attempts to find their way out lengthened. The fear sharpened his sense of smell to the most acute pitch it had ever reached.

He felt that even Asa-tebo would be proud of the wolflike way with which he at last selected the proper threads of odor of old pine smoke and sweaty bodies and led the warriors back to the bright daylight of the entrance. Asa-tebo had not accompanied them. He had complained that the damp of the cavern's interior passages might make his aging bones ache.

They had left him sitting by the fire, resting and watching their horses and equipment, though their own reconnaissance had told them there was no other human creature in half-a-day's ride of them. But when the excited warriors came out of the cavern, Asa-tebo was gone, nowhere in sight, anywhere. Kor-Káy, scrutinizing the surroundings, had a hunch where they might look for him.

A large spring-fed lake of unusually clear water drained from just below the caverns into the wide river. They climbed up a rock *rincón* to reach a high place above the cave entrance. Looking down from there into the clear water, they could see Asa-tebo, sitting on the lake bottom. Not a ripple disturbed the lake surface. He had evidently been there for a long while, for not a bubble arose from the place where Asa-tebo sat.

He has probably been there ever since we entered the cave, Kor-Káy decided. They stood there for an incredibly long

time, watching the old medicine man sitting utterly motionless on the lake bottom. Pou-doc became sharply alarmed,
"Maybe he is dead! Somehow he has fallen in, drowned, and
sunk down in that strange way. See, he does not even
breathe!"

Kor-Káy moved out on the boulder. If somebody had to
dive down to Asa-tebo it would probably be his responsibility.
But then something happened. A green turtle came swimming up to Asa-tebo. It was astonishingly like the one Kor-
Káy had seen in his power dream. The more he watched it,
the more certain Kor-Káy was that it was the same turtle. The
water turtle's snapping jaws opened, emitting bubbles. Asa-
tebo turned toward the turtle, nodded his head, and sat in an
attitude of listening intently. Then he moved all at once, rising gracefully to the surface.

"The turtle told me you had returned," Asa-tebo smiled
with water dripping from his smoothly combed hair and long
black braids. He was not even breathing hard. "The turtle
also told me there is a big village to the south. The *tejanos*
call it San Antonio. We must circle around it. It would be
bad medicine for us to go there."

As a result of the turtle's telling, the war party turned west
from the place of the cave. They struck a big trail and, thinking the hunting for horses might be good along it, followed it
for six days. They saw only one man. He was riding a mule,
and Yih-gyh wanted to count coup on him and take the mule
but Asa-tebo warned Yih-gyh; "That man is carrying two pistols and a rifle. He looks like a fighter. He might kill you, or
he might wound you and you would get angry and kill him.
That would stir up the whole country. We must wait until
our fighting will count for something. We need many horses,
for trading with the Comancheros. Not just one mule."

So they rode far to the south, around Fort Stockton, where
they encountered another trail. "I know of this road," Asa-

tebo told them. "It is called the Salt Road, and I have raided on it before. The *tejanos* use it for carrying salt to their settlements, to trade for other goods."

They moved off into the fringe of rimrock bluffs alongside the trail, made camp, and set the watch. As evening came on, Asa-tebo, as before, moved away from the others. He asked Kor-Káy to come with him. "Perhaps the owl will have something to tell us," he suggested mysteriously.

When full darkness had fallen, Asa-tebo showed Kor-Káy how to make an arrangement of rocks and sticks, covering them with his blanket in such a way that it would appear that he lay there sleeping.

"Tonight we will see how well you have learned your running lessons," said Asa-tebo.

They were in an arid region where the uplift gradually falls away to the coastal plains of the Mexican gulf. A country of *llanos* dotted by mottes of encinos, widely interspersed with creeks already beginning to dry up as spring became summer.

Asa-tebo had chosen for his bed ground a slight rise where his own clever likeness of a sleeping man would be plainly visible to the warriors scattered along the flat below.

Then Asa-tebo announced, "I will run up the trail toward the fort, you south toward the mountains. Go as far as you can until the Great Bear"—he pointed upward toward the bright constellation—"is halfway descended, then return. I will meet you in the little thicket of mesquite where this ledge breaks apart. Then we will see what the owl says."

Kor-Káy turned to go. Asa-tebo grasped his arm, "Remember all you see. And if anyone detects your going or returning, I will know I have taught you nothing."

Asa-tebo, departing, faded away into the night so silently Kor-Káy might have suspected him of being an owl.

Kor-Káy ran, hoping his feet would find no rut in the unseen trail. He jogged downhill through cool, stagnant night air, crossing a wide canyon where two dry creek beds converged. Climbing again then, he emerged from the hollow into the pale light of a rising quarter moon which gave little light.

Kor-Káy's eyes searched the night, with no purpose other than to report anything he encountered, which seemed to him unusual. He smelled the vague scent of a burnt-out fire. That led him to the camp. These campers, like the Kiowas, had secreted themselves among the rock ledges, not far from the trail. Kor-Káy guessed that he had run at least two leagues since leaving Asa-tebo.

Veering downwind, he approached the unknown camp at a squatting run; then on his hands and knees; then on his belly. As noiseless in the rock-littered sand as the serpent he imitated, he skirted the camp's guard, a rangy, big-hatted man sitting on a round rock with a rifle cocked skyward against his thigh.

The man was singing a lugubrious song, softly. He sang in the white man's language, of which Kor-Káy knew only a few words, learned from Pou-doc. The pock-marked warrior had been cured of the disease that left his face scarred at the white soldiers' fort hospital. At Asa-tebo's urging, Pou-doc had kept on visiting the soldiers at the fort to learn the way they spoke.

The guard's song had a funereal sound, not unlike the mourning wail of the Kiowas for the dead. Its noise gave Kor-Káy comfort, for he felt that it might help cover any small sound he accidentally made. He counted fifteen sleeping shapes. By what he could see of the clothing beside their bedrolls, by the smell of the camp, and by the odors of the food they had cooked at the now-defunct fire, he felt certain they were all white men.

Kor-Káy slithered back to stare up from a prone position at the singing guard. Through the branches of the scrubby greasewood that concealed him, Kor-Káy could see the glint of pale moonlight on bone buttons. As he crept back away from the guard he caught a glimpse of the yellow light reflecting from a metal ornament the man wore on his jacket.

A glance at the Great Bear told Kor-Káy that it was not quite time to start back, so he eased down from the ledges and continued on downhill toward the trail, retracing the tracks of the white men. They had been coming up from the south and were surely bound in for the fort, he decided. Another glance at the lowering constellation. Kor-Káy jogged to a halt and stood, deliberating. He turned then and headed back to meet Asa-tebo.

From deep within the mesquite grove below where the Kiowas slept, the hooting imitation of a horned owl beckoned Kor-Káy as he approached. Breathing deeply and easily, he circled in to meet Asa-tebo, and described the camp of the white men. His aging mentor recalled for Kor-Káy the incident on the trail up from Chihuahua where he had first been kidnaped, reminding Kor-Káy how they had all hidden in the *brasada* while the troop of mounted white men had gone by, all wearing metallic ornaments attached to their breasts.

Asa-tebo was pleased that Kor-Káy remembered. It was a good sign. "*Tejanos*," Asa-tebo declared. "Texas Rangers, a war party like ours, but they do not propose only to count coup and steal horses. They will kill us if they can. Come."

In the blackest dark before the dawn, Kor-Káy followed Asa-tebo back to dismantle the blanket-shrouded forms they had left to simulate their bodies. Asa-tebo then seated himself on the edge of the camp and resumed his hooting imitations of the courting female owl. This time loudly enough to awaken the sleeping Kiowa warriors.

He was as persistent as he was skillful, and by the time he had a male owl cautiously approaching in reply to his calling, the warriors were awakening. The curious, shadowy horned owl drifted closer. The warriors were awake now, listening to the dialogue between Asa-tebo and the owl. When the medicine man was certain he had the full attention of the members of the war party, he intensified his conversation, terminating it by beckoning the war party up to join him on the knoll.

"Brothers," Asa-tebo reported, "the owl tells me that a force of Texas Rangers is camped down the trail from us. They will be starting up soon, and it will be only a little while before they are upon us. Go and paint yourselves. We will make ready an ambush to receive them."

Kor-Káy went, but as he worked at applying his paint, the doubt that had plagued him before had begun to gnaw anew. Asa-tebo's bold chicanery created a growing confusion in him. He thought of the thorns sucked from Sa-p'oudl's flesh after the twins' witching, and found himself involuntarily wondering how Asa-tebo had done it.

Covering his lower face with blue paint so dark it was almost black, Kor-Káy thought of the night he had summoned Asa-tebo through the eagle shield. Asa-tebo had sensed that calling. He had returned to doctor T'sal-túa. Kor-Káy thought once more of other healings he had seen from Asa-tebo's hands, yet still something urged him that it was wrong to make people believe things that were not true. He found his own mind seeming to ask what was real and what was unreal.

Asa-tebo had no discernible reluctance to use any device of trickery or deception. The old medicine man worked skillfully, without guilt. If he was being dishonest, it caused no self-doubt. He did not manifest even a pretense of remorse.

Kor-Káy himself had not the slightest doubt of Asa-tebo's capabilities at healing with plants, roots, and herbs. But he had also seen the rallying of the sick at Asa-tebo's incantations. He had seen Asa-tebo sit in clear water on the bottom of a lake . . . without breathing.

Kor-Káy paused in his face painting to remember his own power dream. He had himself been spoken to by a medicine turtle, likely the same one that had addressed Asa-tebo. But with white-eyes fighters bent on their destruction riding toward them, there was no time for these mental wanderings. Kor-Káy seized his paint pot and hurriedly finished staining his jaws.

Above the stormy midnight blue of his lower face he painted his forehead and around his eyes a bright sunshine yellow. Asa-tebo had divined these colors for him in interpreting his power dream. Kor-Káy made sure his medicine bag was securely in place. Then he ran to launch himself in a leaping mount of Pintí, and rode down the ledges with the others.

Following Asa-tebo, they circled down a grassy wash onto the flood plain of one of the two dry creeks that converged farther down the trail where the *tejanos* were camped. They concealed themselves behind the mound of a gently rounded hill from which giant cottonwoods grew. From here, they could see the trail clearly and also the grassy meadow beyond it. Listening to the wind as it fluttered the leaves of the towering cottonwoods, they waited. From this natural concealment they could let the Rangers pass, then ride out to attack them from the rear.

Touha-syhn mused, "They will not be expecting a fight this close to Fort Stockton."

Koup-ei-tseidl hissed, "They are coming."

Kor-Káy listened to the spur jingle and saddle creak so reminiscent of the remembered *brasada* of his boyhood. He sat quietly and watched the first linsey shirts ride into vision.

Yih-gyh boasted hoarsely, "I will count coup on more than any of you. I will do it the first time we ride through them."

Touha-syhn hissed, "*Tou-hei!*" Silence! It was too late. Yih-gyh's hoarse brag had carried. Most of the Rangers were in sight now. Their leader spoke in a low conversational tone, but their horses became a swirling mass of motion as they turned defensively. Yih-gyh's war cry rang out bravely and the warriors were riding.

They burst among the Rangers in a melee of coup counting and colliding horses. Kor-Káy smartly hit one of the enemy with the coup stick in his right hand and another with his open left hand as they rode through the group and went bursting out onto the grassy meadow beyond. Arguments as to who had counted coup, on how many, began at once.

The Rangers quickly regrouped. Kor-Káy thought their hurried counting must have revealed to them that they were outnumbered by the Kiowas. Asa-tebo was shouting, "hH-dl H! Hurry now!" and turning to lead a second charge but the Rangers were already in flight. The Kiowas were too occupied with arguments over the coup counting to pursue immediately.

Kor-Káy watched the almost leisurely retreat of the small covey of Rangers. There were only eleven of them, instead of fifteen as he had thought the night before. There were twenty-six Kiowas. Perhaps he had counted some of the dark lumps made by saddles and packs as sleeping men. The Rangers were here clearly illumined by the morning sun, eleven fleeing backs of linsey-woolsey and crossed galluses, above brown ducking britches.

Flapping chaps, hung across the withers of some of the Rangers' horses, popped in the breeze which was made stronger by their running. A hornet zinged by Kor-Káy's ear. He saw the puff of smoke from a Ranger's gun then and knew that it was no hornet. All of the Rangers were turning and firing back at the Kiowas now, quartering, slowing their horses as they turned to take quick but careful aim.

"They want us to chase them closer to Fort Stockton," Asa-tebo confirmed, "where we will run into patrols of soldiers." Kor-Káy could hear anger in Asa-tebo's voice. He scolded the warriors in restrained fury, "We were more than twice as many as they are!"

Resignedly then, Asa-tebo headed the Kiowas off toward a motte of live oak brush that flanked the trail down toward the creek bed beyond the cottonwoods. They were riding through the same trees from which they had ridden in ambush. Ranger bullets sheered peevishly through the cottonwood leaves, splitting and splintering twigs, thunking into the earth of the rocky knoll, wheeing and whistling in ricochet from the hard trunks of the oaks as they rode toward them, and K'a'dei, Tsei, and Koup-ei-tseidl were hit, falling from their horses.

Asa-tebo pulled up to ride in a tight and angry circle on the exposed ground behind them. The Kiowas milled at the timber's edge, their coup counting arguments ended as they stared back at the wounded scattered along their trail of retreat.

Asa-tebo shouted at them in rage, "They're running away now—the *tejanos* you could have killed. They have escaped. You will only have to fight them some other time, and then maybe they will kill you." He rode charging toward them in full fury, "What is worse, three of us are on the ground bleeding. Tā! Pou-doc! Yih-gyh! Pick them up! We are going to have to find a place to hide so I can doctor them."

For three days they ran. It was hard on the wounded warriors, especially Tsei, who had been shot through the body, but the medicine man was insistent.

"Those Rangers might follow us," he said. "It is not enough for them to win. They never let go. They are like ticks and never get enough blood. Once they have found you, you can never be free of them until you are dead, or until you have killed them."

He hoped to cross the Rio Bravo into Mexico. For some reason, Asa-tebo told them, no one was likely to follow them into Mexico. Also, he said, "That is a good place for medicine. There are things there that will clean these wounds, and others that will cure them. There are things that will be good for all of us. That whole country around the Rio Bravo is the best medicine place I have ever seen."

He let them stop only at hidden springs, scraping together such food as they had to provide sustenance for the wounded men. Everyone else went hungry, for Asa-tebo urged them on at such a pace they could not stop long enough to hunt and make a fire to cook anything.

They crossed a much-used Comanche trail north of Lajitas, then turned, running for the fastness of the rugged country just north of the river, in the big bend of the Bravo, for Tsei was near the end of his strength. A Ranger bullet had entered near his navel, ranging upward, and had not come out. He had much pain. Asa-tebo sucked the horn of the sacred white buffalo near Tsei's spine until a lump appeared there. He took his knife, cut open the lump, and removed the bullet.

Koup-ei-tseidl remained unconscious. He had been struck in the temple and the lead slug had plowed a bloody furrow through his hair that exposed white skull when the lips of the furrow were spread apart. Asa-tebo shook his head and did nothing for him. He told the warriors to take turns riding behind Koup-ei-tseidl to hold him on his horse.

K'a'dei's wound was painful, but it was a clear shot through the meaty part of his upper leg. Gui-pah and Addo-mah came to him and subversively offered to heal him by witchery if he would give them his share of the booty captured on this journey and certain other of his possessions when they returned to the tribal camp, but Asa-tebo found out about it and scourged them, "Everyone knows you do not ask pay for healing those wounded on a war journey." The twins, already in disfavor for their attempt to place a curse on the well-liked Sa-p'oudl, slunk off and disappeared. Nobody cared whether they had gone under the ground, gone home, or what had happened to them. As the days went by, nobody saw them. No one even asked about them.

So it was that, three nights after the ineffectual clash with the *tejanos*, with limping horses and weary men, so hungry they felt like they were starving, the impotent, aborted war party rode in darkness into the Chisos Mountains. Asa-tebo seemed to know exactly where he was going. He led them single file into a black fastness that grew increasingly constricted by looming, towering precipices. It was so dark Kor-Káy could not see where the hoofs of the spare horse he was riding fell on the narrow trail.

Asa-tebo had been clever in keeping the spare-horse herd well to the rear in every incipient encounter thus far. The boy wranglers Koum-soc and a-A-dei, could occasionally be heard grumbling that they would learn nothing about fighting this way, but Asa-tebo had countered that they wouldn't lose any horses either.

An occasional glow of ghost light bloomed around the forefeet of the mustang Kor-Káy rode, or the hind hoofs of the horse ahead of him—some strange reaction between the horny crusts of the horses' hoofs and the rocky volcanic rubble through which they rode. Kor-Káy sensed by the shape of the encircling ramparts above that they were moving toward the center of a vast amphitheatre. That Asa-tebo had been here before was evident.

When at last they stopped, black, hulking walls and high ramparts hovered over them. "I have seen no sign at all of those *tejanos* following us," Asa-tebo mused. "Maybe, because we took nothing from them and did not hurt any of them, they are going to let us go this time. Maybe we can build a fire here."

He told the warriors, "You will find prickly pear blooming here. Its white leaves are tasty and will assuage your hunger. Just do not eat too many or they will purge you like the black drink."

While they foraged, nibbling the yucca leaves, Asa-tebo told Kor-Káy, "This is a place of much power. The Apache people call these mountains Chisos, which means 'ghosts.' Maybe we will stay here for a while if the *tejanos* do not attack us."

Kor-Káy stared up at the darkly towering spires. "These walls seem to have claws," he said, "as if they were ready to jump down out of the dark and pounce on us."

Asa-tebo chuckled, "The old people say that in ancient times this was a place of great quaking and shaking. One time a whole band of Apache people were wiped out here in an earth upheaval. Their chief, Alsate, was preserved in stone not far from here. Early in the morning I will show you his face. You had better not eat any more of those yucca leaves now, or you will be spending the most of the night in the bushes."

In the slanting rays of earliest light, Asa-tebo showed Kor-Káy Alsate's face. They climbed to the top of the huge, recumbent, natural sculpture, so resembling a man's face, to check the horizon for distant dust, or smoke, any evidence of pursuit. Asa-tebo pointed out the abundance of medicinal plants growing, "There is the candelilla, which yields wax good for many things. The seeds from this sunflower, mixed with candelilla sap, are good for those who fall sick from too much sun. It makes a paste. Spread it on wild tobacco leaves and put them on the forehead. When the leaf turns red, replace it. Sometimes it takes several to draw out all the heat. Then you can bathe the skin with a cool solution in which sunflower leaves have been boiled."

Asa-tebo pointed out the abundance of peyote cactus buttons, listing ailments they were helpful in curing. Cenizo, lechuguilla, desert willow, maguey, Apache plume, persimmons, piñón. "Some of the plants are good to eat," he added. "The piñón nut, of course, and sotol hearts—pitahaya. There is much wild honey here, and it is not hard to find. We will eat well and build up our strength. Let us go and doctor our sick."

K'a'dei's wound was a running sore. Asa-tebo soaked an eagle feather in a stewing solution of roots from the creosote bush. He ran the feather through the wound, cleansing it thoroughly. He washed the feather, drew it into the wound, and left it there.

Koup-ei-tseidl, who during the flight had been carried on his horse like a dead man, now lay like one. Asa-tebo made a rubbery dressing from the raw sap of the guayule. He covered the open furrow in Koup-ei-tseidl's scalp with it, giving instructions that the big, unconscious warrior must be kept in the shade of a huge boulder and moved regularly as the sun made its daily tour.

After a few days the medicine man had him moved beneath a big mesquite where flecks of the sun filtered through to strike him. During those days, Asa-tebo boiled and blended, using liquids taken from the lechuguilla, from a pit gouged in the center of the tall maguey, and peyote tea. He made Tsei drink copious amounts of all of these. Over Tsei's thinning, weakening body, the medicine man made incantations, and prayed. Tsei's wounds would not stop draining. It became difficult for the thin, mildly complaisant warrior to retain the potions Asa-tebo forced upon him.

On the fifth morning of their camping, when Asa-tebo pulled the creosoted feather from K'a'dei's wound, it brought with it a poisonous flow of pus. K'a'dei's leg scabbed over then. Within a few days he was not even limping, and was mounting his horse with ease. On the eighth day Asa-tebo took Kor-Káy climbing to the high south rim of the basin.

"I have seen more power animals here," he said, sweeping his arm out over the thousands of hectares that lay exposed to their survey, "than in any other place I have ever been. You have to be careful of every creature you encounter, for most of them are witches of some kind or another."

Kor-Káy could not share Asa-tebo's enthusiasm for the wild and rugged landscape. Taking up the sacred flute, he played a brief song to distant vistas, feeling homesick for the gentle, rolling hills along the Washita, for the cool water of that sandy stream where he and T'sal-túa once swam and waded. But he kept quiet, not wanting to seem unmanly to his stern mentor.

Asa-tebo stood there on the precipice for a long time, looking at Kor-Káy steadily. He moved aside then, far enough to reveal the presence of a huge gila lizard, clinging motionless to the rough bark of a fallen tree behind him. He greeted the lizard as if it were an old friend, and thanked it for coming to see him. In soft monologue, with words like flowing water, Asa-tebo's arm eased out toward the monstrous lizard until his hand stroked its palpitating throat.

He lifted the chest of the heavy creature. It came crawling up his arm until the colorfully beaded skin of its jaws rested almost on his shoulder. Its reptilian eyes locked with Asa-tebo's.

"This one's eyes are windows to another place," said Asa-tebo. "Through them I see T'sal-túa and 'N'da. They are swimming. I think it is in the Washita—"

Kor-Káy felt again the stir of amazement at Asa-tebo's ability to pick out parts of his most private thoughts and give them back to him.

"—no, it is a deep pool in Cache Creek," Asa-tebo divined, "not far from where the panther and her cubs were playing with T'sal-túa. T'sal-túa is climbing up on the ledge now to catch a vine and swing down into the water. How she has matured! Her breasts are high and firm. The wound in her throat is all healed now. I can see only a small pink scar. Now 'N'da and T'sal-túa are holding hands. They seem mutually agreeable—not quarreling and fighting as Pilar and Intue-k'ece always are—"

Involuntarily, Kor-Káy tried to move so that he could see into the gila's eyes, but the giant lizard's stare seemed to turn malevolent. It raced down Asa-tebo's arm in reverse, leaped to a pitted lava stone nearby, and disappeared behind it. Kor-Káy heard an explosive flurry in the dry, deciduous leaves beyond the stone as the lizard slithered toward security.

"I hope you have not offended her," Asa-tebo said worriedly. "If you did, you will surely encounter difficulty, for that lizard is enchanted."

Half angry that Asa-tebo would be friendly, and conversant, with a creature that could do him harm, Kor-Káy struck out to descend from the ridge. Purposely, he sought a shorter, more precipitous route down the slope. He knew that he did not have the patience to retrace the gradual climb of more than four hours that had brought them to this height. He often heard Asa-tebo struggling with the steep and sheer faces of rock down which they climbed, but the medicine man had no inclination to protest or admit that the way Kor-Káy had chosen was taxing. Instead, as they worked their way down among the sparse vegetation of the rocky cliff face, he continued his teaching. "This plant," he said, touching its small dry leaves and stems, "is called the bloodroot. If someone has blisters or sores in their mouth, have them rub the juice from its roots on their sores."

A road runner paused in its clownish trot down the abrupt slope to peer at them with cocked head. "Now that chaparral bird," Asa-tebo said softly, "is good medicine. For someone who is weak you should kill that bird without losing any of its blood. Cover it with clay, put it in a hole under the center of the fire, and let the coals bake it. The sick person must take off the clay and feathers then, and eat the whole bird. One of these birds might help Tsei—" he stopped, staring far down the slope as if he had seen something besides the chaparral.

Kor-Káy had seen it, too. There was movement in the basin below them. Not a single movement, but a long, curving line of movement, and Kor-Káy caught the blue color of uniforms.

"Soldiers from Fort Stockton," said Asa-tebo. "That is why the Rangers did not follow us. They went to the fort and told the soldiers."

He watched the line of blue-uniformed men, tiny figures in the distant basin below them, silently stalking the Indians through the timber. "It took them a long time to get here," Asa-tebo mused. "The *tejanos* move faster. The soldiers are usually slower, but they can be just as determined. And they have finally found us."

The skirmish line of soldiers had succeeded in surrounding the Kiowa camp. They crept toward it in ever-tightening circle, keeping their concealment in the surrounding timber.

Kor-Káy looked for the army horses, and found them grouped together, being held by foot soldiers, beside a knob to the south, against the far heights.

It was all happening too far away to shout any intelligible warning to the war party. Kor-Káy thought his loudest yelling might reach the Kiowas, but the words would be indistinguishable from this distance. Shouting would only hasten the attack—and inform the soldiers that two Indians had escaped their tightening net.

The ambushing cavalrymen were almost upon the camp. Kor-Káy wondered frantically where the camp's watch was. Could the warriors have become so complacent that they had set out no guards? Were they dozing in the pleasant morning sunshine? He and Asa-tebo could do nothing but wait helplessly, and watch. It all looked so far away, unreal, from this distance.

They looked like tiny costumed dolls, made of sticks and cloth, such as those T'sal-túa and her girlhood friends had played with years ago. Kor-Káy saw one of the soldiers stand, lift his arm, and wave his rifle, ready to signal the charge. After what seemed an interminable time, the vague sound of his faraway voice shouting its command reached Kor-Káy, but the soldiers were already erect and running then, their guns at ready, surging forward to attack the unsuspecting warriors.

The grappling and hand-to-hand fighting was only a moment away when, from the eminence above the tethered and hand-held horses, a bugle call sounded, piercingly sharp and commanding. The charge in the basin stopped as abruptly as if a natural disaster had frozen the soldiers into instant ice. A moment of fixed tableau, and the bugler in the heights sounded a second, urgent and clarion call.

The soldiers turned and fled. Running toward the command post from which the bugle had sounded, they gained their horses, mounted, re-formed with military precision under the faintly heard commands of their sergeants, and re-treated from the basin. Not a shot had been fired.

Asa-tebo and Kor-Káy hastened their descent. By the time they reached camp, the Kiowas were mounted and ready. Tsei and Koup-ei-tseidl, the two wounded men still unable to help themselves, had been loaded in horse-drawn litters. Pein-hH came in, jubilant, carrying his bugle.

Asa-tebo went to grasp his shoulders and congratulate him, "You did well, my son!" He reached to touch the bugle. Days before, Kor-Káy had observed Pein-hH polishing it brassy bright in the glass sand of a Chisos Mountain stream.

"Thank you," said Pein-hH, telling to the others, "Asa-tebo told me long ago to learn to use it right. I spent many days in those hills around the soldier houses at Medicine Bluff, the place the soldiers call Fort Sill. I listened to those who blow this kind of horn, and saw what the soldiers did when they heard it."

Pein-hH said that when it had been his turn to go to the high place on watch this morning, he had taken his bugle as always. Then when he saw the Fort Stockton cavalry coming, he had known to wait until the critical minute before surprising the soldiers with the bugle.

"I crept up close to the place where they had left their horses," Pein-hH related jubilantly, "then I waited. The first song I played is a little one, Officers' Call. It always makes them stop whatever they are doing and wait for someone to tell them what to do next. Then I played the one the soldiers call Retreat. It made them run like rabbits!"

Asa-tebo impatiently brought an end to Pein-hH's talking. "All of you have done right in getting ready to go. Those soldiers will not be fooled long. They have probably already discovered that they have been tricked. We must leave as quickly as possible. Perhaps we can get across the river, into Mexico, before they catch up with us again. I have never seen the blue-coated soldiers cross that river!"

The passage to the river was over rough country, but they did not delay in making it. "It will be painful for Tsei," Asa-tebo commented to Kor-Káy, "but less painful than if the soldiers had caught him. Koup-ei-tseidl is beginning to look like he is going to wake up from his long sleep. I think a little ride will do him good."

At the edge of the river, the medicine man drew rein. Kor-Káy, following Asa-tebo's upward-looking eyes, saw why. Gui-pah and Addo-mah were sitting on their horses high on the bluff above them. No one had seen them since Asa-tebo had shamed them for trying to get K'a'dei to pay them if they would cure him by witchery. Everyone stopped to stare up at them. The medicine twins were looking down at the war party and making sign language.

Soldiers chasing you, Gui-pah signed, his closed fists jammed together, then opening to make the zigzag sign for chasing.

Many soldiers, Addo-mah added, heaping them up with his hands.

You die! All! Gui-pah's pointing finger swept beneath his right hand, cutting off their lives, then made the great sweeping circle that included all of them!

Asa-tebo, clearly upset by the twins' interruption and their threats, shouted, "Go on across the river. Now! Hurry!"

Kor-Káy watched Tā, Pou-doc, and Yih-gyh, who were carrying the wounded, start across the broad sheen of water, then he looked back up at the bluff. Gui-pah and Addo-mah were gone.

Defiantly, however, Asa-tebo himself had paused there, on the north side of the river, watching a chaparral cock playing boldly among the small sand dunes along the Rio Bravo banks. The clownish bird was busily hunting sidewinder rattlesnakes, a prey it loved to kill and eat. Signaling for Kor-Káy to wait, Asa-tebo dismounted and stripped salt cedar bark to set up a small snare. Procuring Kor-Káy's help, they rode to round up the bold bird. Together they herded it, running thoughtlessly ahead of them into Asa-tebo's snare. The road runner had barely been captured when the advance guard of the Fort Stockton soldiers came riding out of the cedar brakes.

The rest of the Kiowas, who had already crossed, were disappearing out of sight in the Mexican chamizal. Asa-tebo, clutching the squawking bird, motioned Kor-Káy into the river. Asa-tebo followed, their horses splashing across in knee-deep water to the far side.

"We caught the chaparral without losing any of its blood," Asa-tebo exulted, deeply pleased. "Now we can use it to heal Tsei."

As they turned their ponies into the thickening chamizal, the Fort Stockton soldiers arrived in strength on the Rio Bravo bank behind them. They halted, precisely aligned in groups. No soldier even raised a rifle.

Asa-tebo glanced back at them, and shook his head. "I do not understand it," he said. "Perhaps they think it is not worth crossing the river now, just to catch two Indians."

They rode on deeper into the chamizal, setting a course to intercept the rest of the Kiowas.

Planning aloud, Asa-tebo rode in thoughtful concentration. "When we cook this medicine bird for Tsei," Asa-tebo said, "I am going to make a strong doctor dance for both him and Koup-ei-tseidl. There is a cave down the river where I have made that medicine before on war journeys."

Intercepting the rest of the war party, Asa-tebo led them to a camping place where the badlands north of the Rio Bravo lapped across to continue their upheaval on the Mexico side of the river. A considerable stream flowed from the south into the big river here. On the west side of its entry canyon, near the mouth, was the cave Asa-tebo sought.

Facing eastward, it cut deeply back into the rock. Within

it, water seeped from dark walls to make a black pool. The entrance was partly shielded from exterior view by a rugged pillar of volcanic plug.

Completing his plans in camp late that afternoon, Asa-tebo added, "We will make our doctor dance tomorrow evening just as the grandfather sun is going to bed. That way D'ah-kih will hear our prayers and have all night to think about them. He will give us our answer the following morning."

Asa-tebo told Kor-Káy, "When I am ready tomorrow evening I will tell you to cross the river and watch out for soldiers. There is a bald hill over there that makes a good guard post. Start off that way," he gestured in the direction he wanted Kor-Káy to go, "then when you get out of sight, cut around through the chamizal and come back here. You will find a crevice in the cave back there—a big crack where the bats fly up out of the ground. Come down through it and you will be inside the cave to help me."

Asa-tebo spent the next day ceremoniously preparing and cooking the chaparral bird. Smoke often poured from the cave in black billows far in excess of any needed for cooking. Sa-p'oudl, Touha-syhn, and Kou-t went hunting and returned with a *venado*, a small deer. The rest of the war party rested in camp, surreptitiously watching Asa-tebo's preparations for the doctor dance with interest tinged with awe. Toward sundown, a steaming hot ball of clay launched itself from the mouth of the cave.

Asa-tebo's voice, echoing hollowly and mysteriously from the interior of the cave, followed it, instructing those outside to break open the ball for Tsei. "The feathers will come off with the clay," informed the medicine man. "Be sure that Tsei eats the whole bird, every part of it."

Asa-tebo's previous performance of the doctor dance here had left a fire-scorched flat stone in place in front of the cave's entrance. It was, to Kor-Káy, reminiscent of the triangular flat stone that had confronted the spectators when Kor-Káy had first seen Asa-tebo perform this sacred rite, at the sun dance that had convinced him that he must himself become a medicine man.

As the sun fell into the chamizal behind the cave it reflected its rays into the eyes of the warriors who sat before the cave entrance and turned its interior into impenetrable darkness. Asa-tebo's voice issued from that darkness to tell Kor-Káy to cross the river, find a high point, and keep watch for the soldiers. Kor-Káy crossed the river well within sight of the others, then obeyed Asa-tebo's orders.

Having disappeared into the chamizal on the north side of the river, he cut upstream beyond the first bend and swam back across. To be certain that he remained unseen, he swam across the narrows here beneath the surface of waist-deep, fast-running water. The breathing exercises Asa-tebo had so long forced him to practice made it easy. He surfaced for air only once during the entire crossing, near the south bank, and that executed sportively, just to practice doing it, on his back. Only his nose broke water.

Emerging from the river, he quickly regained the concealment of the brush, and found the bats' rear entrance to the cave, just where Asa-tebo had said he would. As he slipped inside, Asa-tebo was waiting for him. "Blacken your body with the candelilla ashes," he directed. "Stay behind the pillar. Keep your back turned so no one will see the firelight reflecting in your eyes."

It had been Asa-tebo's burning of the mass of candelilla that had kept the black smoke issuing from the front of the cave during the day, Kor-Káy thought, as he stripped and made himself black all over. He observed that Asa-tebo had thoroughly blackened his own back, but the front of his body and arms were coated with white limestone clay. Dusk had become darkness now and Asa-tebo shouted out orders to light the fire before the flat rock at the cave entrance.

The bright fire flickered up, its crackling flames sending a little light back into the cavern, but most of the light was reflected back into the eyes of the warriors who sat watching before the entrance. Asa-tebo had been standing with his black back to the entrance. He turned abruptly and the clay-whitened front of his body caught and reflected the dim firelight. Kor-Káy knew that he had "appeared" to the warriors who sat watching.

At the foot of the volcanic pillar behind which Kor-Káy worked, he saw the bow and arrows Asa-tebo would use in the ceremony. On a small ledge near the top of the pillar a heap of glowing coals smoldered. The medicine man sang a striking song to D'ah-kih, then began his long prayer. It was eloquent with thanks for deliverance from their enemies, with long eulogies to the bravery of each of the warriors, including Kor-Káy *"who is now across the river, his eyes alert to warn us should danger appear."*

Asa-tebo prayed for the recovery of Tsei and Koup-ei-tseidl and for the success of their journey in the gathering of many horses to trade. As the prayer ran long, Kor-Káy, remembering this spectacle, recalled almost instinctively what to do. He picked up the clay-whitened short bow at his feet behind the volcanic tuff which hid him from view. The bow was made of driftwood, a brittle, toylike thing, useless except to weakly shoot the medicine arrows a few *varas* out into the night.

Kor-Káy held the bow hidden behind the edge of the pillar, knowing that his black-painted hands and arms would be as invisible to the warriors outside as the white-painted front of Asa-tebo's body was visible. Sure enough, Asa-tebo's white fingers reached to pluck the bow from Kor-Káy's black ones, and as the bow appeared so miraculously to those watching, Kor-Káy made ready the first arrow.

Asa-tebo picked it neatly from Kor-Káy's black hand and as the medicine man lifted it to hold it high he touched the tip of the tinder-dry greasewood arrow to the smoldering coals on the ledge. The arrow burst into flame. Asa-tebo quickly fit it against the clay-whitened bowstring and sent it arcing out into the night.

As sparks flew smokily from the flying arrow, Asa-tebo picked the second arrow from Kor-Káy's fingers, contrived its burst into flame, and shot it into the fire before the stone in front of the cave. The greasewood arrow became a shower of sparks flying up into the night darkness.

This time Asa-tebo made his exit with a smooth step backward and again the sharp turn, so that his black-painted back made him seem to disappear to those outside the cave entrance. He side-stepped to join Kor-Káy behind the pillar. "Wash yourself quickly in the pool of water at the back of the cave," Asa-tebo whispered. "Return then to your watch post and wait for your relief. He will come giving the cry of the mourning dove."

The spring water was icy cold and sharply refreshing. Reasonably sure he must have removed most of the evidence of the black candelilla ashes, Kor-Káy stepped from the spring as Asa-tebo entered it to wash himself.

"I will not return until I have prayed the dawn into being," he told Kor-Káy. "Be sure you leave the *crevasse* as silently as the bats that use it, and that no one sees you, or all our medicine will be useless."

A nettle of resistance pricked Kor-Káy. "What if the soldiers had come while I was helping you in the cave?" he asked.

"I knew they would not," Asa-tebo said shortly.

Kor-Káy persisted, "How did you know?"

"The owl told me." Evidently sensing that this might no longer forestall Kor-Káy, Asa-tebo turned to confront his protégé. Kor-Káy could see him only dimly in the faltering light. He could feel Asa-tebo's breath on his face. The keeper of the fire outside had apparently ceased to throw on brush now that the doctor dance was over and its flickering fell rapidly.

Asa-tebo's voice was hard. "It is not too late to turn back," he said obdurately. "But once you get power, if you don't use it right, it will turn on you. Decide," he admonished Kor-Káy, and dismissed him with finality. "Go."

Kor-Káy departed, sliding out through the crevice. Across the river he climbed almost to the top of the bald knob and sat by a rocky protuberance that helped to conceal him by its mere presence. *If I do not move,* he thought, *I will become as much a part of the hill as the rock beside me.* He wanted to become an indistinguishable part of the night-shrouded landscape, and think. The moon waxed and waned as he sat immobile, keeping only the horizon in focus.

He thought of the neckerchief; of the "owl telling" Asa-tebo of the coming of the Rangers along the Fort Stockton road; and he thought of the wonder and awe with which he had first seen the short bow and flaming arrows appear in Asa-tebo's hands during that memorable long-ago sun dance.

The wonder and awe were gone now. Asa-tebo's attitude toward the loss of that wonder and awe seemed inexplicable. Kor-Káy felt an emotion he had never been taught by his foster Kiowa grandfather—guilt. It had been so long since he had felt that emotion he had almost forgotten it. And he did not know why he felt it now. Asa-tebo clearly did not feel guilt.

Kor-Káy thought again of the coming of Asa-tebo when he had summoned him through the eagle shield. He thought, *If T'sal-túa is not getting well it may be because of my doubts, my refusal to believe, my own lack of faith.*

Kor-Káy thought carefully, reconstructing all the medicine things he had seen Asa-tebo accomplish, his sucking the thorns out of Sa-p'oudl. His removing of the twins' curse. The mound of Chihuahua earth that had become a live rattlesnake with darting, forked tongue beneath Asa-tebo's hands—it had hissed, coiled threateningly, and slithered away at Asa-tebo's dismissal.

Kor-Káy thought of Asa-tebo sitting underwater, at the bottom of the clear lake, where neither his mouth nor nostrils made even a single bubble. And the turtle that had come to talk with him, the turtle Kor-Káy had seen in his own power dream. He knew that Asa-tebo was often aware of, and could envision, things that were happening a long way off. He *could* heal wounds and cure diseases. Kor-Káy had too many times *seen* him do so. He recalled a time in his own childhood when he had been hot and restless with fever, vomiting, unable to eat. Asa-tebo had come with his singing, with his cool hands, and with an incantation in Kiowa *antigua* that Kor-Káy did not understand. His medicine man grandfather had shown Da-goomdl how to dose him with the medicine he had left. Kor-Káy remembered that he had gone to sleep. When he had awakened, his fever was gone. He felt fine, and was hungry for the soup Da-goomdl had spooned into his mouth.

Kor-Káy had seen sick people made to feel better by Asa-tebo's just talking to them. He knew that his grandfather's knowledge of healing roots, leaves, bark, herbs, was so vast that Kor-Káy often found himself despairing of remembering even a little of it.

Searching to the bottom of his concern, Kor-Káy knew that something was trying to shake his conviction that he must learn all Asa-tebo could teach him. And the root of that conviction, while loosened, was not dislodged. Kor-Káy knew that he still had to learn the road to power, and in learning the road, had, as Asa-tebo had told him, to accept the risks of that road.

He had to learn the eagle shield medicine; become a buffalo doctor; an owl prophet. He had to accept the responsibility of power and learn to live with the dangers of using power. He had to pray that he would be shown how to use

power right. He had to push aside these doubts that troubled
him, for they did not trouble Asa-tebo.

The sinew that untied the neckerchief was as much a part
of Asa-tebo's medicine as the boiled poultice of sunflower
seeds that drew out fever, or any of the other pharmacopoeia
of herbs and remedies for ills that beset the people. Kor-Káy
knew that Asa-tebo would insist the same about the flimsy
driftwood bow and the greasewood arrows that burst into
flame.

All were parts of the medicine that had been given to him
by elders before him, by D'ah-kih himself, and to Asa-tebo all
parts of the medicine were equal, all worthy, and all useful.
Perhaps losing the wonder and awe was just a step on the
road to power, a part of maturing as a doctor, part of becoming a medicine man.

Beyond the mysteries of the medicine, it was plain to Kor-
Káy that his grandfather had another wisdom, a knowledge
that made him perceive the possible uses of things far into
the future, like telling Pein-hH so long ago to keep trying to
learn how to use the soldier's bugle, like encouraging others
to learn Kor-Káy's childish Spanish while he was learning to
understand Kiowa. Pou-doc, on this war journey, knew some
of the white-eyes' language because Asa-tebo had suggested
that he learn as much as he could while he was kept at the
soldier house.

A mourning dove's plaintive cry came from the chamizal
below. Kor-Káy waited, listening for a second cry, and analyz-
ing it. It was the voice of Touha-syhn.

≫ VI ≪

It was barely daylight when Touha-syhn relieved Kor-Káy. He returned to camp, and by the time he had crossed the river everyone was up except Tsei and Koup-ei-tseidl. Tsei, however, was, for the first time, sitting up, and appeared to be taking an interest in what was going on there. Could it be that eating the chaparral bird—or the doctor dance—had helped him?

Koup-ei-tseidl had recovered consciousness. Presumably. Tā reported to Kor-Káy that he had opened his eyes late in the night, long after the doctor dance was over, and had called out for water. But he had recognized no one, and now seemed almost as unaware of everything as when he had been in complete coma.

The long rays of the dawning sun were reaching across the camp, and Koup-ei-tseidl lay beneath a river willow, his eyes dull, but open, and seeming to focus on the interplay of the early morning sunlight through the long, slender, summer-dry willow leaves. As the sun became a sheen on the river, turning its water into a winding metallic mirror of eye-blinding light, Asa-tebo came stumping into camp from the direction of the water, his stiff gait warped by the arthritic bending of his hips. The stiffness was plaguing him more and more these mornings, Kor-Káy thought, until the activities of the day freed his joints.

Beckoning Sa-p'oudl and Intue-k'ece, the medicine man had them lift Koup-ei-tseidl and carry him toward the cave. The slighter built Intue-k'ece could hardly bear his half of the burden of the brawny, heavyweight Koup-ei-tseidl, who took little note of being carried. The mountainous warrior's eyes hung open, rolling viscously in their sockets like obsidian rocks in thick syrup.

They carried Koup-ei-tseidl directly to the cold spring, and at Asa-tebo's signal, threw him bodily into the icy water. For a man who had so long been in a coma he reacted galvanically. As the bitter cold water enveloped his whole body he went rigid, then began to thresh about like a buffalo bull in a wallow. On his feet in an instant, he came floundering up out of the water. Moaning and shivering, he stood briefly with the water running off him, then with a shout of rage he rushed out of the dark cave into the chilly half warmth of the sunshine. There he stood capering heavily, trying to warm up.

After so many days of being unconscious, his energy was brief. He soon sat down on the ground in the growing warmth of the sun, his hands massaging warmth into his quivering flesh. His rubbing encountered the rubbery mass of guayule Asa-tebo had used to protect and heal his head wound. Koup-ei-tseidl pulled it off and threw it away.

Tā and 'An-tsh' came bringing Tsei into the cave. He came reluctantly. Hanging back, protesting weakly, at the edge of the cold spring he recoiled completely. Asa-tebo said, "No, no. Do not throw him in." He spoke soothingly to Tsei, dipping his hands into the spring to bathe Tsei's face and shoulders. At last he threw double handfuls of the water, still streaked with the greasy black candelilla stains Asa-tebo and Kor-Káy had washed off into it last night, over Tsei's body.

Asa-tebo accompanied Tsei outside and dried his skin with bunches of dry grass. Rubbing him briskly in the now fully warm sunshine, the medicine man said, "I think they can ride their own horses now, if we stop and rest once in a while." He nodded briskly, thus pronouncing the benediction of success on his doctor dance of the previous night.

So they ate, saddled up, recalled Touha-syhn from across

the river, and departed, traveling southward, farther into
Mexico.

"This is the way to do," Asa-tebo told Kor-Káy, "when
there is a reason for it. When you have sick men who need to
get well before they can fight, then you need to see new country. New country is always a place to learn new things. Until
Tsei and Koup-ei-tseidl are as strong as they used to be we
will see what we can learn."

The wounded men did seem to improve a little every day,
regaining strength, becoming more nimble as their muscles
became more supple, and Kor-Káy reflected with something
like a glow of personal satisfaction that perhaps the doctor
dance *had* helped them. Certainly Asa-tebo's willingness to
risk his own life in halting to catch a chaparral bird while the
pursuing soldiers caught up with him had had a salubrious
effect on Tsei. Since eating the road runner Tsei's wound had
stopped draining and began healing. The skin-and-bones gunshot victim began to gain flesh. His appetite increased. Asa-
tebo seemed entirely content with these results, and he rode
on eagerly, day after day, leading them farther southeast.

The country through which they rode changed constantly;
at first desert, then becoming a rain forest, steamily humid, at
the foot of mountains. The scarce trails were tangled, matted,
impenetrable; game trails only; narrow, *estrecha*. They encountered one small primitive village of people native to the
region, obviously Indians, like themselves, but Asa-tebo made
no contact with them. Except for examining their garbage
heaps minutely, he guided his war party silently around them.

He explained to Kor-Káy, "There are trees and plants here
that I have never seen. By examining the seeds and peelings
in trash people have thrown out, we can know what is safe for
us to eat and use. They seem friendly and gentle. Maybe we
ought to try to get acquainted with them. But you can never
know when strangers are going to be stingy with their food, or

jealous of their women, so to avoid any chance of trouble right now when we don't really need anything anyway, we will just go on."

Which they did, for a few more days—then one day they came upon a village even Asa-tebo could not resist. The first indication of its presence was the sight of it. They had simply come up over the crest of a foothill and there it was, lying out between them and the higher mountains. There had been no warning sound, no distant dog barking, no smell of any human nor any outlying human habitation. T'ou-teinei, who had been riding advance guard, had reached the crest of the hill first.

The others, following along behind, had seen him pull up suddenly, his horse febrile, then instantly backing away from the crest. T'ou-teinei dismounted to prostrate himself, then crept forward. So they, too, dismounted and went forward with great caution, leading their horses. What they saw stunned them. There it lay in the valley below.

For the most part it consisted of great symmetrical hillocks of earth. But at various places shapes of rocks thrust out from the hillocks. Not heterogeneous piles of rocks heaped up by nature, but shaped rocks, like those made by men in the pueblos where the Comancheros lived. There was a kinship to the humble rock structures the white men made in their little towns, but somehow it was more nearly similar to a great Mexican city.

Having first seen the strange city in the late morning, they lay hidden on the crest of the rise, observing it, until midafternoon. By then they were certain the village was deserted, or occupied by an unusual people who had no odor and who never exposed themselves to the light of day. It appeared to have been deserted for a long time, for in many places the building stones thrusting out from the hillocks were crumbling and tumbling down.

At last, as the afternoon grew late, Yih-gyh, adventurous

and eager, suggested, "Let us go down there. We may find
something we need." So after a final period of patient obser-
vation, Asa-tebo agreed.

Timidly, like curious children, they began the descent toward the big village. As they approached and entered it, Tā
said in amazement, "Look. There has not been anyone here
for so long there are not even any tracks!"

It was true. The tall grass grew almost to their loin cloths.
Other than the presence of the structures, there was no evidence at all that anyone had ever lived here. There was no
castoff trash, no evidence of human occupation. Only the
brush-covered hillocks, the weathered stones. Built in something like a great square were the giant stone tepees. One of
them had many niches carved in its sides, and many steps
leading up to its platforms, each of which was smaller than
the one below it.

They became so engrossed in exploring the wonders of it
that time was forgotten. They seemed unable to find an end
to the city. There were always more mounds of earth, more
exposed cornices, caving walls, and carved rocks. The jungle
had almost devoured it. On the crumbling stone platforms
and walls, some of the rocks were deeply etched with devices
a little like those they painted on their own hide tepees,
parfleches, and other belongings.

Asa-tebo said that some of the carvings were more like
those he had seen among the Tewa people of the pueblos,
and the Hopi, far to the north and west. The work was beautifully done. All of the Kiowas on this war journey were awe-
struck at the skill of these people in decorating their ceremonial stones with fine carvings of men, serpents, eagles, fanged
animals, and intricate feather designs. They became so preoc-
cupied with these wonderful sights that they did not see the
coming of the clouds, and the gradual overshadowing of the
sun, until a reverberating crash of thunder burst among them.

As the thunder shattered the hot and humid air of the rain

forest, forks of lightning began to dart down, seeming to sting the remnants of buildings, with accompanying crashes that blotted out the earth in darkness after each vivid crash. Sprinkles, then raindrops, then torrential tropical rain came pouring down. They stood, drenched and petrified, in the din of the storm, trying to huddle against their horses and the fallen walls.

Asa-tebo started shouting. His voice reached through to claim their attention and they began as best they could to follow him. In growing terror, trying only to keep in sight of one another in the pouring sheets of rain, the war journey turned into an open rout. They fled without thought, stumbling, falling in the rain and mud, clinging to their horses' reins and being dragged up again by their horses to run farther.

As the storm abated they were able to increase speed, and by the time the rain began to slacken they could no longer see anything of the strange, deserted village from which they had fled. So they stopped here, and squatted, exhausted. The chests of both horses and men were heaving.

"It is clear," Asa-tebo puffed, "that D'ah-kih did not want us in that bad medicine place. No wonder no one lives in it. In our own country I have a friendly arrangement with storms. Usually they will come and go as I bid them, and I have an agreement with them that they will never damage my tepee. But a storm like this one—it is too wild and crazy to reason with."

They continued south somewhat numbly. The thunderous storm had been an overwhelming *abrumado*. But as the shock of it faded, their curiosity about this fantastic country, so strange and different to them, began to freshen. Only Asa-tebo did not respond. Instead of being inquisitive and enthusiastic, he seemed restive and depressed, even avoiding Kor-Káy.

Kor-Káy, after days of wondering if he had done something to displease his grandfather, came then to realize that it was because Asa-tebo felt inadequate in this increasingly tropical country. The plants they encountered in these hot, humid jungles were unfamiliar to him. He did not know their curative powers, and so had nothing to teach Kor-Káy. He seemed to have lost his own power. There was no great horned owl here to advise him.

There were no buffalo, none of the familiar animals and plants he used for confidants and advisers. But this did not trouble the rest of the warriors. Enjoying the journey to the fullest, they traveled east until they could see the limitless blue of the great water—*el Golfo de México*. They ate the banana, which Kor-Káy approved, remembering it as the *plátano*, also the *mango*, and *papaya*. They speculated as to how far these great blue waters along the edge of which they traveled might extend. Asa-tebo from time to time made speeches in which he urged them to realize that they had gone far enough, too far, now they should turn back.

He became insistent, even admitting that he felt ill at ease and insecure here. But the others would not agree and refused to turn back. They even began to discuss the merits of returning to their homelands only long enough to gather up their families, friends, and personal possessions, then move here permanently. That way they could escape for all time the white eyes, the soldiers, the *tejanos*, the drovers and raisers of herds of *wohaws* who were crowding in on them, the farmers, whom the soldiers sometimes promised to stop, but never did.

Here they would live in a land where they could easily pick their food from the trees, then, at night, sleep under those same trees, in warm air that never grew cool enough to need even a single blanket. The prospect was pleasing, but Asa-tebo warned them that there were already people living in these jungles. Large groups of them, especially along the shores of the great blue water. They were careful to avoid these people and their villages, and could now move stealthily, Asa-tebo told them. As an unencumbered and freely mobile war party they could move rapidly enough to avoid attack, but if all the Kiowas were to move here to live, Asa-tebo assured them that all these strange people would band together to defend their land and drive the intruding Kiowas away.

He reminded them of the troubles they had once had with the Comanches, of the fights they still had with the Utes, who continually tried to encroach on their hunting lands. Peace with the Comanches had not come until Asa-tebo was a young man, and they still had to defend themselves from the Ute raids. To try to capture these lands, where so many other people already lived, was foolishness. "We should turn back now, before going any further," Asa-tebo urged repeatedly.

"We would have to go back to the place of the hurricane," K'a'dei protested. His wound still gave him pain, especially when stormy weather came. That prospect was not inviting, even to Asa-tebo. He let them wander southeast for two more days, curving around the shore of the great blue waters where the palm trees grew tall and slender, where the banana groves were luxuriant. They began to grow accustomed to almost daily afternoon rains and tropical thunderstorms.

The storms were never long—a brief hour or so and the rain stopped, the water drained off, absorbed by the sandy shores, and the sun again shined warmly. Soon feathered *pájaros*, myriads of multicolored birds, were singing and calling and clacking their bills again.

Early one morning, as they awakened in the leisurely, unhurried fashion that had become their habit in this land of never hurry, first one then another of the warriors began to spot movement high in the towering, shady palms and *papaya* trees beneath which they had slept.

Kor-Káy had been watching what, at first, appeared to be darkened streaks moving among the tops of the tall trees. But as the light grew brighter, the streaks took on more and more human shape. Soon Teigouc-kih was gesturing skyward. Others, t'Hou-t'h and 'An-tsh', joined him in pointing. Asa-tebo had not arisen from the sandy place he had chosen for his bed ground. He lay staring upward in fixation with, to Kor-Káy's mind, the nearest to an expression of real fear on his deep-lined, bright brown face that Kor-Káy had ever seen.

A thrown fruit struck the ground among them.

Huge, hawk-nosed Koup-ei-tseidl, leaped to his feet holding it. "They are going to attack us!" he cried. He cocked his arm and hurled the *papaya* upward. Even his great strength was insufficient to throw it high enough to reach the leafy tops of the trees, but it elicited an angry chattering from one of the attackers, and another *papaya*, this one mushy and overripe.

Sa-p'oudl shouted, "The trees are full of hairy little men!"

The hairy little men appeared to be even smaller than the dwarf whose horses they had been afraid to steal. The little men were surely more agile than the dwarf. These little men leaped and swung from branch to branch, and they had long tails to help them. All the Kiowas were standing now, staring up at them.

Sa-p'oudl shouted invitingly, "Let us not be enemies, little men. We will not hurt you. Come down and talk with us."

But they did not come down, and they would not talk. They only chattered wildly, and Kor-Káy commented, "They do not sound as if they were afraid of us. They sound as if they are taunting us."

Kou-t and P'-ou had drawn together and were talking secretively, with fearful animation. Kor-Káy thought they looked as if they might be ready to flee.

Pou-doc said in awe, "Hear them all jabbering at once! Those little men are very angry with us. They may be even more powerful witches than the little man with the horses."

Tsoy agreed. "We have invaded their lands, and we are bigger than they are. But there are many of them." He turned to Asa-tebo, "What are they saying, Grandfather?"

Asa-tebo's face was working angrily. He looked as if he might start hopping about, like the hairy little men. He exploded, "Saying? I do not know what they are saying. I do not speak that language. Apparently they do not speak ours. I think they are medicine animals of some kind, for they sound crazy. Like this crazy country that grows more crazy the farther we wander into it."

Asa-tebo ranted on, "This was supposed to be a war journey. We started out that way. But you have acted crazy from the first. Now I am going to go crazy with you. We are approaching the full moon, and will soon see the third new moon since we left our homes. If we do not end this craziness, and turn around, and begin to do what we came to do, those Comancheros at Cibolero will have traded off all the things we need before we even get there. We will return home hanging our heads like foolish women, as empty-handed as when we started out.

"Ask the little men in the trees if what you are doing makes any sense?" Asa-tebo demanded. "I am going home from this crazy place before it is too late and I lose all my power here!"

He ran to uproot the picket pin of his horse.

≽ VII ≼

"You will guide us past the place of the hurricane so that we do not have to go through it?" Asa-tebo voiced this request as if it were an order.

"If I can, Grandfather," Kor-Káy replied.

"If you can?"

Kor-Káy shrugged. "It is somewhere north of us. I do not know where."

"But this is your country," Asa-tebo protested. "You were born in it."

"Grandfather!" Kor-Káy exclaimed. "I was only a little boy when you captured me."

They had turned their peregrination back northward days ago. The shocking encounter with the little men in the trees who would not talk to them and Asa-tebo's fury had sobered everyone. Especially sobering was Asa-tebo's · fear that he might lose all his power. They seemed suddenly to feel the weight of the great distance they had traveled, and how far this journey had taken them from the familiar things of home into strange, often fearful surroundings. To be in such a place without strong medicine was an intolerable thought. Everyone was suddenly eager to at least regain surroundings in which Asa-tebo felt that his medicine was secure. So while they traveled in a subdued spirit, they traveled fast. Kor-Káy had never seen the warriors more amenable to orders. They were moving northwestward cohesively, co-operatively, as fast as Koum-soc and a-A-dei could keep the spare horses following along behind.

"This is the first time I have ever been this far south," Kor-Káy said. "The Rio Bravo must yet be two hundred leagues to the north."

"We have a long ways to go," Asa-tebo agreed thoughtfully. Kor-Káy understood his desire to avoid a revisit to the deserted city of pyramided stone buildings. He had no desire to return there himself. The utter alienness of that place, its emptiness, its silence, he was sure had magnified and colored the memory of the storm they had encountered there.

Anticipating Asa-tebo's desire to avoid that place of bad medicine, Kor-Káy had been guiding the war party northwestward, away from the great water. Setting each day's course to the left of where the moon had set the night before, they had left behind them the pleasant country where the nights never grew chill and the abundant fruits of the trees so easily provided all their food.

Now they were moving into a higher country, where they had to hunt for food. Strange gray quail were plentiful, though much different from the bobwhite singers along the Washita. Rabbits and squirrels, wearing coats differing in color from those of their homelands, were easy to find, and small deer came in numbers to drink at the banks of the cold streams they crossed.

The increasing depth of the streams led Kor-Káy to suspect that the *sequía* was over in the high country they were approaching, that they were moving into the rainy season, the time that at home they would have known as "thunder moon." They were likely to encounter some rain wherever they went for a while.

As the country climbed up out of the tropics it became rocky and undulant. Not a terrain of towering mountains, but rising heights of barren, gray-green-appearing stone, dominating fortresslike *prados*. But as they traveled over the first ridges of these rocky heights they found them not barren, as they had appeared from the distance, but interspersed with nutritious high plains grasses that Asa-tebo immediately said would be good for adding bone and muscle to their horses.

Expansive hectares of the gray-green to yellow stone spread out before them, gradually rising, and interrupted by areas of soft turf, luxuriant with the short, tough grass. They went on, less hurriedly now, letting the war ponies take advantage of this superior grazing.

As they moved on northwest, they began encountering dry cow chips littering the high *prado* pastures. The cow chip litter told them theirs were not the only animals grazing these pastures, and following the general directions of the wandering cattle trails Kor-Káy was convinced they would eventually find an hacienda. Increasingly, also, Kor-Káy was reminded of the rare cattle-buying trips on which he had accompanied his father during his early childhood in Chihuahua. Recollections of those bygone days began to flood in upon him.

They made landfall on the hacienda during midafternoon of a bright, sunny day and, had a great fiesta not been in progress, it is likely they would have been discovered before they found it. From the first sight of it, vague memories began to intensify in Kor-Káy and they sought out a tight grove of *ocotle* trees, where they were not sky-lined, and could carefully observe the activities of the celebration in progress.

The hacienda itself made up one side of a walled courtyard enveloping a large, square plaza. It seemed deserted. A long, low adobe stable made the second side of the hacienda. The third side consisted of a towering *iglesia*, a magnificent church, now only a burnt-out hull, probably a relic of some countryside bandit uprising. A thick wall at least twelve *varas* high enclosed the fourth side, its center portals now swung open. When closed, the hacienda would become a fortress.

The reason for the hacienda's desertion was clearly apparent to Kor-Káy. Perhaps half a league away, to the right of the *ocotle* grove in which the Kiowas waited, was a circular arena with adjoining corrals. Here all the people were gathered.

From the uphill rise of their concealment, the Kiowas could view the activity down there. As his recollections took tangible form, Kor-Káy identified the events taking place there, and quickly became the narrator.

"It is the *tientas*," he told Asa-tebo and the members of the war party. "This is surely a *ganadería* where they raise the brave bulls, the *toros* that fight in the plazas of Mexico on Sunday afternoons. These people, the *patrón*, his guests, and the *toreros*, and possibly an *impresario* here to purchase bulls for his plaza, have gathered to try the cows. They want to see which ones are brave enough to become the mothers of brave bulls. And they come to test the *becerros*, the young yearling calves, to see if they will run at the cape. Those that do not charge the cape, and the cows that flee from the *picador* and his iron lance are put aside to be butchered for meat."

The Kiowas watched with hard-to-contain excitement as each aggressive cow released charged the *picador* mounted on a horse well protected by quilted matting. They watched him halt each charge by implanting his iron lance in the cow's shoulder muscles. "If she retreats and charges him again," Kor-Káy told them, "she will be confined among the cows that will be bred to produce brave sons. If she only retreats, she will be rejected." And, truly some cows ran away, while others stood and took the punishment of the lance bravely. The afternoon wore on as the warriors began to wager which cows would fight, and which would not. They watched the chosen ones herded into a corral on one side of the arena, the rejected ones shunted off into a corral on the opposite side, near the butcher's rack.

Later, the *toreros* came singly into the arena, each to taunt successive calves with *veronicas* of his swirling cape. "It will not do to let each calf make more than a few charges," Kor-Káy commented. "They learn quickly. My father once told me that a calf that has been permitted to charge the cape too often learns it is the man he should attack, and not the whirling cape. This makes them too dangerous to be used later in a real bullfight."

As the calves were tried, separated, and corralled, the afternoon waned. Kor-Káy observed the fine horses the *caballeros* rode about outside the arena, and the circulating of wineskins among the *caballeros*, the *toreros*, and their ladies, even among the *vaqueros* and *peones* who handled the livestock. He saw the bottles and *jarros* of *aguardiente* and *cerveza*, then, presently, they watched the *cocineros* raking back the thick bed of glowing coals from the great barbecue pit. The smoky scent of the succulent cooked meats floated through the air all the way to the *ocotle* thicket where the Kiowas hid, sharpening their hungers, activating their digestive juices to a point that would have been almost unbearable had it not been for humor of listening to and giggling at their own growling stomachs.

"Quiet!" Asa-tebo poked Koup-ei-tseidl's great brown belly. "They will hear you clear over there!"

As the feasting grew long the shadows grew longer, and with the *puesta del sol* came the lighting of lanterns, which sparkled like fireflies. In the *oscurecimiento* of the cooling evening, ladies were donning their *rebozos*, and Kor-Káy saw many a *vaquero* flip his *serape* across his shoulders. The chill may even have increased the drinking of stimulants, for the fiesta celebrants became quite noisy.

It seemed an interminable time before the sparkling lights of the lanterns began to flicker their way across the *prado* from the *tientas* arena to the hacienda. The Kiowas waited with Indian patience. Approaching midnight, the lights dwindled, becoming fewer and fewer until only one remained, bobbing about in the vicinity of the arena. When all the lights had returned to the main hacienda except for the single lantern of the lone watchman who had been left to close the corrals and sleep in a lean-to with the livestock through the night, Kor-Káy asked Asa-tebo for permission to go. It was granted.

"When I swing the lantern in a wide arc, beckoning you," he told the warriors, "come quickly."

Kor-Káy went first to the corrals. He followed the bouncing light of the watchman until the advantage was his, and then attacked. The *pelado* left to oversee the *tientas* arena was aged and feeble, for who would suspect the presence of Indians here so far south in Mexico, in open country where only the workers of the hacienda lived and rode. Kor-Káy overcame him easily, locking the old man's arms behind him, muffling his shouts with an iron-fingered hand. He dragged his victim to the roofed area where the *tientas'* spectators had sat to observe the afternoon's events. There, using the *pelado's* own ragged shirt, Kor-Káy gagged him and tied him to a stanchion.

He then went among the corrals of cows and calves, arranging their pole gates for easy opening, and found a surprise. In a strong corral set apart were six black fighting bulls, yoked to oxen for easier driving. These six bulls, not yet used to their ox partners, were grunting in throaty, angry voices, a sound not unlike the grumbling and roaring of jungle *tigres* in the hot tropical forests farther south, where Kor-Káy and the warriors had so recently been.

Kor-Káy eyed these bulls in contemplation, then set out running, as silent as a ghost, for the hacienda itself. He circled around the burnt-out shell of the church, bringing up at the far corner of the living quarters of the hacienda. Here the length of the adobe back wall of the hacienda's rooms stretched out in the night before him. The wall was inset with iron-barred windows. He hunkered down to proceed along the wall beneath the level of the darkened windows.

Odors emanating from the first black window opening he passed told him this was the *cocina*. It smelled of old cooking, stoneware crockery filled with tortilla *masa*, the *le-*

gumbres in the *dispensa*. Next, the *comedor*, dining room, then the *sala*. As he raised to peek into the darkened room he could see the bulky shapes of its heavy Spanish furniture and a few dimly luminescent sparklets from its cut-glass chandelier. Only one window, the next to the last one at the far end of the long back wall, showed light. From it, soft lamplight shown out across the *prado*. It was still a long distance ahead of him.

The next room smelled of paper, ink, and leather, and as he looked in through the window he could dimly visualize long rows of leather-bound ledgers and a wide roll-top desk. It was the hacienda office, smelling exactly as his father's office had smelled in the big townhouse in Chihuahua City where he had lived as a boy. As he stood at the window savoring these smells and his poignant memories, the sounds coming from the next window offered diversion. He could hear hard breathing and the passionate sounds of drunken love-making, which suggested that the rest of the rooms along the wall would be bedrooms. Kor-Káy thought of all the wineskins, the *aguardiente, cerveza,* and *mescal* he had seen consumed during the afternoon.

He must have arrived alongside the first bedroom in the final moments of the orgy of passion *adentro,* for while he waited there the stertorous breathing in the room abated. The following sighs of contentment and fulfillment, which emanated from the bed, were brief. The lovers were going to sleep. Kor-Káy passed slowly along beneath the remaining windows, listening intently to sounds of the deep, regular breathing of sound sleep, and of *los borrachos'* varieties of alcohol-drugged snoring.

When he reached the next to the last window, he stopped short. Voices were talking in there.

"—se encuentra emocionante la bravura sembrada en mis toros bravos por la sangre Miura—" it must be the *patrón*

himself, Kor-Káy decided, bragging about the bravery the Miura strain had implanted in his brave bulls.

The reply was worried and querulous, "*Ojalá que sea así, señor. No que ando yo conmovido. Los últimos toros que tuve fueron un desastre, y los mismos toreros un escándalo: ¡Qué barbaridad!*"

Kor-Káy was certain this would be the *impresario* from some *plaza mayor*, here to purchase the six bulls he had seen yoked to tame oxen for ease of handling on the trail. While the *impresario* complained about the inadequacy of past bulls and the clumsiness of *toreros*, Kor-Káy heard the *patrón's* chair creak as he moved from it. There was a clink of glasses as they toasted each other in "*un último traguito*" to top off the infinity of drinks quaffed during this festive day.

"*Buenas noches, don Teófilo.*"

"*Buenas noches te de Dios.*"

After the final good night, the door opened and closed as the *impresario* retired to his own bedroom. Kor-Káy could hear the *patrón* throwing off clothes, then the creak of his bed, as with weary sighs he turned in. The room went dark.

Kor-Káy squatted beneath the window and practiced his Indian patience while he listened to the coming of sleep. When, by the *patrón's* sleep mumbling and an occasional snorting snore from the adjoining room, he felt it was safe to proceed, Kor-Káy followed on around the hacienda, behind the stable wing. Small windows, high in the adobe stable wall, were sufficient to reassure him here. He could smell horses, the dung and straw of the stable, and heard the crunch of jaws masticating grain. An occasional impatient hoof stamped the stable floor, for these were high-bred horses, Arabs and Barbs, the proud steeds he had seen ridden by the haughty *caballeros* and *vaqueros*—during the afternoon *tientas*.

He hurried a little, on around the wall, bringing up before the wide double gates of the hacienda. Now a rapid sniffing of dogs alerted him and he knelt before the portals.

There were two of them, their inquisitive black muzzles thrusting beneath the heavy gate portals. Kor-Káy gave quick thanks to D'ah-kih that their curiosity had momentarily overcome any instinct to bark an alarm. But the half-wolf strain an hacienda *patrón* released within his compound at night were more likely to be stalking assassin dogs—dogs that come silently upon any unknown human entering the compound, not to bark and threaten but to attack, pull down, and kill.

Speaking the words of respect that Asa-tebo had taught him, Kor-Káy addressed the animals. He placed his hand beneath the gate to let the dogs sniff his fingers. They would smell no fear on his hands, and they heard only calm assurance in his voice as he reached in farther to scratch behind their ears and inform them that he was about to enter.

Hanging down beside the gate was a bell rope for the convenience of visitors wishing to alert the hacienda's inhabitants. His intention being the opposite, Kor-Káy pulled out his knife. He reached, silently, to cut the bell rope where it passed through the gate portal. Knotting the rope end, he cast the knot upward, where it fell to lodge between the gate and portal near the top of the wall.

Testing his weight against the rope, he used it to climb to the top of the gate, where he perched for an instant, scanning the courtyard, then dropped down inside. The squirming, tail-wagging dogs, emitting restrained whines of pleasure, greeted him like an old friend, wrapping themselves around his legs and flailing him with their tails as Kor-Káy spoke.

"I would like to request your help with a chore," he explained pleasantly.

Kor-Káy slid back the heavy oak beam that locked the hacienda gate, and opened the portals wide. He and the dogs then trotted together, eagerly, to the stable. Clearly they were accustomed to the work of herding, for as soon as Kor-Káy's intentions became apparent to them they ran about, nipping horse heels and hurrying up laggards to send the horses streaming out of the stable.

Kor-Káy leaped on the bare back of one running near him. They exited the courtyard with a considerable clamor, which he hoped would not awaken any of the sleepers from their alcoholic stupor. He ran the horses across the half league that separated the hacienda from the *tientas* arena, and dismounted to open the arena gate. Hazing the horses inside, he left them there in the circular bull ring and went to fetch the old man's lantern.

From atop a hillock of manure that had been cleaned out of the corrals, he swung wide arcs of lantern light to beckon his friends. His answer came in a moment, in the prompt, charging arrival of Asa-tebo and the warriors. As if they had rehearsed it, which in a sense they had on many earlier such expeditions, they emptied the corrals, circling up the livestock, the calves and the cows, both the brave and the cowardly ones.

Kor-Káy noticed t'Hou-t'h preparing to slash the ties that yoked the fighting bulls to tame oxen. "No, no! Leave them together," he said.

"But we can travel more rapidly," t'Hou-t'h reasoned craftily.

"Having them tied together will slow us down," protested Asa-tebo. "It was I who told t'Hou-t'h to separate them."

"These fighting bulls are more valuable for selling than even the best horses," said Kor-Káy. "If we release them they will fight each other or run off like deer into the first thicket. They know only to fight and run. The ox is trained to restrain the bull."

The Kiowas were keeping the rest of the herd bunched impatiently. Asa-tebo shrugged as Kor-Káy gave the signal to move.

They proceeded as fast as the yoked bulls could plod. Toward dawn they found and filed out of the hacienda's entrance gate, having at Kor-Káy's urging, gone a league out of their way to do so, for that was faster and easier than tearing down a section of the thick rock wall that surrounded the hacienda.

As they passed through the entrance gate Kor-Káy looked back at it over his shoulder; *Hacienda Piedras Negras;* the letters were burned into the slab crossbar above the gate, along with the mark of the hacienda's branding iron. *Marca de Toros Bravos* said the *escudo,* and beside it fluttered the red and green *divisa* ribbons of the *ganadería.* Kor-Káy suspected the *patrón* had those fresh and new *divisa* ribbons replaced daily, with the same pride as they were darted into the shoulder of each of his bulls as it entered the fighting arena.

Noon approached, and Kor-Káy began checking their back trail from the top of each rise they crested. He suspected that they had escaped with every riding horse on the place. He also felt that by evening the *patrón* would have obtained help from some place. Then there would be pursuit.

Without stopping, they invoiced their take. Twenty-eight yearling calves, all healthy and able to travel. Thirty-two heifers, all prime and ready to breed. The six bulls of the *corrida,* each with its ox. Thirty-six horses, all Arabs or Barbs, most of them gelded, each a mount of which any man would be proud. Kor-Káy eased Pintí into the drags of the now steadily moving trail herd, casting an occasional glance at their back trail, and watching with hopefulness as the clouds mounted through the sky during the afternoon.

The warriors were in high spirits. The feeling of having taken a worth-while prize of booty had been a tonic to these pirates of the plains. Their mood was effervescent. Kor-Káy hoped their high spirits would not lead to resumption of horseplay. He kept watching the building clouds, becoming darker and more ominous. In late afternoon, a shower of the rainy season began to fall.

Kor-Káy relaxed a little. The rain would dampen the spirits

of the playful, and Asa-tebo became exultant, enjoying even
the thunder and the lightning, for this seasonal downpour
would wipe out every sign of their trail. "Eh ha!" he cried.
"Now they can never find us!"

Kor-Káy was somewhat more restrained. "We have carved
a thick layer from the fat of that *patrón's* fortune," he said
doubtfully. "He is not likely to give up chasing us. Some
place, he will catch us. What will we do then?"

"Fight!" Asa-tebo declared. "That is what we came to do.
When you are on a war journey it is good to fight. And to die,
if you need to."

It rained all night and they did not camp for there was no
place to camp anyway. The next morning the rain let up.
They made a wet camp, ate a little, and slept less, for the rain
started again. This time a real *chubasco*, falling in torrents.
They plunged ahead blindly.

As the weather cleared, the rain stopped completely. Then
they had cloudless days in which to proceed as fast as the
herd could move. Throwing the spare horses driven by Koum-
soc and a-A-dei in with the stolen stock helped them to make
even better progress, for the spare horses were trailwise
and experienced. They traveled by habit now, with little lost
motion. On the fourth day, the two dogs from Piedras Negras
caught up with them, which worried Kor-Káy momentarily,
but Asa-tebo said, "They have just come to be with their new
friends. They will help us."

Kor-Káy then decided that they liked him better than the
patrón they had deserted, for they sought his attention constantly, and zestfully followed his instructions in helping the
Kiowas drive the stolen animals.

An increased frequency of Indian huts, a few standing
alone at first, then growing in numbers, told them that they
must be approaching a pueblo of people, so they turned the
herd a little east of north, and ran headlong into another
deserted city. Approaching and entering it in the dusk of late

evening they found themselves in it, and by that time it was too late to do anything but keep on going. Most of it seemed to be covered with dirt anyway.

Intue-k'ece was the first to notice anything, almost falling into a walled pit as he rode forward leading the herd. He signaled the turn to the left and they circled an area enclosed with great, square, black stones. Almost impossible to see now in the gathering darkness, still they could make out other huge stones carved in the shapes of the heads of serpents, with bared fangs.

Continuing ahead they found themselves on stone paving. Asa-tebo kneeled to feel of it. "I can hardly believe it," he murmured. The herd marched across it on noisy hoofs, especially the shod ones among the horses, clattering and clonking on the big square stones.

"Those people have smoothed these stones in some way," Asa-tebo marveled, "and covered the whole ground with them. Look, my moccasin does not sink in at all, and it makes no track."

A sudden and totally unexpected barrage of thunder and lightning transfixed him then and he cowered. The blue flash of the lightning had starkly revealed a pair of monstrous pyramided mountains of stone. They stood at either end of the deserted avenue down which their animals were proceeding. Kor-Káy comprehended Asa-tebo's terror, and himself shared it. There was something in the empty unreality of these places that stunned the heart and mind. Surely they had been built by men, but, as surely, they had not been built for men. They had been built for unearthly creatures, for the purpose of overawing men, and terrorizing them.

It seemed to Kor-Káy that he knew this; these structures stood as monuments to ancient, unknown, and terrible gods. With faltering heart, he watched flickering lightning cross the sky, trailed by rolling thunder, and sure enough, it began to rain.

The rain intensified and fell relentlessly. Asa-tebo bent beneath its drenching weight. "The people who lived here must have had a powerful rain spirit. It is still working." He crouched, looking toward first one end of the long paved avenue, then the other. Between the lightning flashes it was pitch dark.

"We must be away from this magic place," the medicine man declared. "This power here is old and evil. The strongest my bones have ever felt. It comes up out of the ground and is all around. It is a death power."

Forced by the rain to keep traveling, they camped the next morning soaked and exhausted. Even Kor-Káy had forgotten pursuit. On too many of the days and nights since leaving the hacienda, the rain had washed out every hoof print almost as fast as it was made.

As they descended from the *meseta central*, the country became Coahuilan desert. The rains tapered to nothing. An occasional *tormenta*, a desert shower of the season, fell to soak them, but the dry sunshine here was refreshing. And the wind blew, sweeping the desert sand into new designs around the towering saguaro, ocotillo, cholla, all the kinds of cactus that kept the desert itself from departing Coahuila and crossing over into Tamaulipas or Nuevo León.

The herd traveled well. The drenching rain had helped subdue the spirits of fractious animals; the oxen yoked to the fighting bulls provided a steady core of restraint against stampedes. K'a'dei, who had the strongest herding instinct of any of the warriors, suggested to Kor-Káy and Asa-tebo that he believed the bulls might be sufficiently trail-broken to be freed from the yokes, which would enable them to make better time.

They tried unyoking one. It worked out; perhaps K'a'dei was right. Before evening of the next day all six had been freed. The steady, unremittent travel had sapped their aggressive instincts. Remarkably, each of the fighting bulls continued to travel alongside the ox to which he had been yoked. They distributed themselves along the length of the herd according to some bovine concept of protocol, ignoring each other, and were so doing the day P'-ou, who had been riding advance guard, came riding back toward the herd.

Kor-Káy saw him coming, his pony at a hard run. While he was still a long way off, P'-ou began making the hand signs for "many horses," both hands scooping the air and ending with the fist and fingers of his right hand astraddle of his left hand.

Kor-Káy rode to meet him, but P'-ou reached Asa-tebo first and had completed his report by the time Kor-Káy got there. Asa-tebo was saying to P'-ou, "Go with Touha-syhn. Swing the herd away around to the left—" he paused. P'-ou's handsome face was resentful and rebellious.

"But I found them!" he protested angrily.

Asa-tebo, discernibly frustrated, but knowing better than to try to force his will on the vain P'-ou, turned to Kor-Káy. "Go with P'-ou," he said briefly.

P'-ou heeled his horse and was off. "I will show you what to do," he yelled back.

Kor-Káy, watching Asa-tebo and Touha-syhn ride to take point and begin swinging the herd to the left, hurried to catch up with P'-ou. "What have you found?" he asked. "What are we going to do?"

It was hard to talk, riding at such speed. The wind was blowing their words away. P'-ou replied mysteriously, "You will see."

P'-ou reined his horse in abruptly, its haunches digging down into the sand atop a dune, and Kor-Káy, in reflex, pulled Pintí up just beyond him. Yonder, in the undulating heat waves rising from the desert, stood a country *cantina*. Lined up before the *cantina*, a long row of handsome dun and buckskin horses waited, tied to the hitch rail. There was no town; no other buildings. Only the *cantina* and the long line of well-groomed horses.

Kor-Káy would have thought that it might be a mirage, except that, from inside the *cantina*, floating down to them on the stiff wind, came the sound of music, violins, guitars, one strident overriding trumpet, and a masculine-sounding voice singing a *corrida*, one of the folk songs of the north of Mexico.

"He has a fine voice," P'-ou smiled.

"He is a she," Kor-Káy corrected him.

"No!"

"Yes," Kor-Káy nodded. He remembered the beautiful, but always deep-voiced contraltos of his native Chihuahua and their *ranchera* singing too well. Undoubtedly there was a troop of *rurales* in there, enjoying a break in their endless patrol of the Mexican countryside.

P'-ou suggested, "I will bet you the best horse among those tied there that the singer is a he."

"The horses, if we can get them, belong to everyone. Besides, I cannot prove that she is a girl—"

"I will go look!" P'-ou was off again, his pony scooting across the deep, shifting sand.

Kor-Káy made a move toward pursuit, intending to fetch him back, then decided he had better pause and give thought to what he might do to save this situation, which could become a rapidly deteriorating one. P'-ou rode his pony up behind the tied horses, slipped from its back, and ran crouched and swift to a dirty window. He raised up to peek through, and came running back to his horse.

Mounted, he ran his pony back to Kor-Káy to say frankly, "You are right. Look, I will swing back the way that we came to gain speed. You go cut their reins. Then I will come running to start them quickly." He was gone.

Kor-Káy knew the vain and impulsive P'-ou would give him barely time to act, so he had better act quickly. Grasping the hair ring woven into Pintí's mane, he slid down to conceal himself on the off side, and rode to the foot of the row of tethered horses. He left Pintí ground-tied, dismounted, and on hands and knees began to work his way along the hitch rail, crouching beneath it, his sharp knife cutting the reins as fast as he could wield it. He was knifing toward the last pair of reins when he saw P'-ou circle and start his run. The horses along the rail were growing increasingly nervous. They had been sternly taught to stand ground tied so well that they would not run away without strong reason, but the strange Indian smell of the sweaty Kor-Káy working beneath their noses with his flashing knife blade had them on edge.

As Kor-Káy cut the final horse free P'-ou came charging hard. There was no time to return to the other end of the line for Pintí. Kor-Káy swung up into the uncomfortable, ill-fitting Mexican stock saddle of the horse he had just cut loose. P'-ou was whooping and shouting, and waving his short, grass catch rope. Fortunately, the horse beneath Kor-Káy did not choose to try to buck free of the strong rider on his back. Instead, it chose to run.

Kor-Káy whistled shrilly for Pintí to come along. The *rurales* were swarming out of the *cantina*, as aroused as hornets. P'-ou flanked to the rear, Kor-Káy held the lead, and they swept the *rurales'* horses away like a high wind. The *rurales* were shooting, a little high, and Kor-Káy applauded them with silent inner enthusiasm for being so careful to avoid hitting their own horses.

P'-ou came thundering up beside him, driving all the horses in full flight. The handsome Kiowa glanced back over his shoulder at the *rurales* and shouted to Kor-Káy, "What fine figures of men they make!"

Bullets still buzzed overhead. Kor-Káy turned in the uncomfortable Mexican saddle, resting his hand on the rump of the dun horse, as he watched the troop of *rurales* attempting to deal with their own frustration as they found themselves unable to pursue. Their tan uniforms *were* very handsome. The broad-brimmed Chihuahua hats crowning their heads were ornately embroidered, and held in place by long, leather thongs knotted at their chins. They wore tailored shirts, tight-laced breeches, and high-heeled boots; *muy macho.*

Several had come running afoot after the Indian horse thieves. When the foolishness of such a gesture occurred to them, they had stopped, some thirty *varas* ahead of their fellows where they now stood firing most of the remaining shots. It was the gunfire of frustration rather than sense—for P'-ou, Kor-Káy, and the horses were out of pistol range. Kor-Káy whistled shrilly at Pintí. Without slowing the dun horse, he transferred to his own pony and his own comfortable blanketed rawhide saddle while their flight continued at a dead run.

Glancing back occasionally at the milling, angry *rurales,* Kor-Káy was struck with their similarity to the Rangers of Texas, and the *rurales* at that moment surely would have sub-scribed to the *tejanos* sentiment that, "A man without a horse ain't no man at all!"

≫ VIII ≪

Kor-Káy and P'-ou added their string of thirty-two *rurale* horses to the Kiowas' already acquired livestock when the two groups converged some *siete leguas* on up the trail through Coahuila. Encountering then a high-wheeled *carreta*, driven by an *arriero* and drawn by six-span of oxen, a little further up the trail, they appropriated this equipment. T'ou-teinei wanted to kill the *arriero*, claiming that privilege as it was he, riding in advance, who had first seen the freighter.

Asa-tebo remonstrated. "Look here at us," he reasoned. "We now have almost a hundred *wohaws* of many kinds, and sixty-eight fine horses to trade with the Comancheros. A killing will only tell people where we are, and make them crazy mad. We need to go on to Cibolero, not stop here to fight. We will fight if we have to but if we do we will maybe lose the animals we have. T'ou-teinei, since you first saw the *carreta* driver, you can kill him at Cibolero if you want to, but do not do it here. We need to keep going as fast as we can."

They loaded into the *carreta* all the saddles and bridles from the *rurales'* horses—the riding gear of a *compañía* of thirty, with their *capitán* and *segundo*. Tying the submissive *arriero's* arms and legs securely with rawhide thongs they placed him atop the load.

Delegating T'ou-teinei to control the *carreta*, they continued north and soon found that they were in trouble. The oxen pulling the cart would not respond to T'ou-teinei's commands. So they untied the *arriero* and once more placed him in charge of his vehicle. Asa-tebo added 'An-tsh' to the *carreta* detail since he did not object to traveling on foot, could help watch the *carreta* drover, and keep him from making mischief. Asa-tebo told T'ou-teinei and 'An-tsh' to try to learn the *arriero*'s commands for driving the oxen. Throwing 'An-tsh's war pony in with the horse herd, with 'An-tsh' walking beside the *arriero* and T'ou-teinei riding his pony alongside, they started again.

"This is like the herds of *wohaws* that are driven up across our country," Asa-tebo said. "They always have a wagon going along with them. I have seen them. T'ou-teinei can kill some game as we go along and throw it in the wagon and we will have meat to eat when we stop to camp."

They continued across Coahuila, with temperate haste, in the intemperate desert heat. It was hard to keep the ox-drawn *carreta* up with the moving herd. The moon that at home they called the "heat moon" had waxed and waned while they were still much farther south, returning from the tropics. But as they crossed this desert country the reigning "thunder moon" seemed to grow hotter than the familiar "heat moon" back on the Washita.

They struggled through hot, dry days, swept by hot winds, trying to conserve their energy and that of the stock they drove. There was no scarcity of water, for Asa-tebo used his gifts, observing the distant flight patterns of birds, the traces of movement left by desert wildlife, and the patterns of the desert vegetation. Some might have thought it magic, others might call it instinct, but Kor-Káy knew, and felt a small glow of pride in his own computations, each time Asa-tebo led them to water at a place Kor-Káy had calculated it would be found.

Guarding their *arriero* prisoner, riding *ojeos* on the captured livestock, keeping their waterskins filled, they slowly trailed across Coahuila, searching out eatable desert plants and killing enough animals to sustain them. Being Kiowas, they were not adverse to eating meat raw while staying in the saddle, in times when haste seemed wise. Steady going kept everyone busy and the nights were short. They were so tired there was little talk. For traveling is always work, and fast traveling is *only* work, with no energy left for complaining. It became so hot approaching Texas that they changed, and began driving the herd at night, trying to rest a little in the shade around a water hole during the day.

The days and nights began to run together, making it seem they had been on this journey forever. One morning, when Kor-Káy felt they must surely be drawing near the Rio Bravo, Asa-tebo led them to a place of water, *una noria* of sudden and unexpected beauty. It was a well dug by the *anasazi*, an ancient and primitive people, and left there, rock-walled and overflowing, for later centuries of travelers and wild creatures.

"We will stay here all day, and for a full night of rest," Asa-tebo announced wearily. It was an idyllic spot. Centuries of seepage from the well had created a shallow pond and seeds sown by passing and roosting birds had surrounded it with trees and vegetation not native to this desert country.

In relief, anticipating the rest, they bedded the herd down north of the well, roasted themselves some meat, and napped. Some set about repairing garments and tack that needed mending. As evening approached the usual wind sprang up, this time cooled a little by the leafy deciduous trees and the water. Kor-Káy thought, *It will even blow the mosquitos away from the pool tonight* and he, with the others, began to look forward to the most pleasant sleep they had had since the nights beneath the trees beside the great blue water.

Some of the warriors scarcely waited for darkness to take to their blankets. Arranging low shelters for protection against the stiff night wind, most of them had already gone to sleep. Kor-Káy sat drowsily across the fire from Asa-tebo. He slumped, half-dozing, enjoying the pleasant languor of just sitting here by the fire resting, doing nothing, deterred from finding his own place to sleep only by the knowledge that he had to ride a turn of guard duty before he could give up completely to somnolence and lie down for sound sleep.

Having tired of listening to P'-ou retell the tale of how he had captured the *rurale* horses, though his story varied and improved with each telling, even the last small group of warriors had wandered off to bed down, leaving Asa-tebo and Kor-Káy alone and facing each other across the fire.

Sleepily, Kor-Káy began to play softly on his sacred flute. Asa-tebo slowly raised his arm toward the fire, pointing cataleptically, directly into its flames. "There," he said, "you see there is a new tepee among those of the Washita band."

Kor-Káy lowered the flute and looked. He saw a thick bed of greasewood coals from which sporadic flames sputtered up lazily. Yet, hazy, in shadows, through a thick curtain of smoke, Kor-Káy saw something like the tan shape of a newly sewn tepee. Its circle of tepee poles seemed clearer then, thrusting up above the smoke flaps, a wavering but identifiable shape among the flames.

"It is the new tepee of 'N'da and T'sal-túa," Asa-tebo said, mesmerized. "I can see inside it. Da-goomdl your mother and the women of camp have been very generous in helping T'sal-túa to set up her new household. Da-goomdl has tanned and with her own hands cut hides from the buffalo 'N'da has killed. Together the women have sewn T'sal-túa a fine tepee. Even the women of 'N'da's family helped, for they felt sad that there was no man from T'sal-túa's family there to whom 'N'da could give a gift of horses. These things I see," Asa-tebo concluded, "and I foresee that T'sal-túa will soon be with child."

The tepee Kor-Káy saw in the flames became translucent. Inside it, Kor-Káy could see two figures. One of them, the girl, though her image was tiny in the flames, moved with T'sal-túa's distinctive body movements. Her hand and arm gestures were intimately familiar to Kor-Káy. The male stood aside, his out-thrust pouter pigeon chest certainly that of

'N'da, posturing and posing to impress his woman. T'sal-túa moved to him.

Kor-Káy sat as though stunned. The vision Asa-tebo had pointed out to him in the firelight seemed irrevocably real while everything in his wounded spirit rejected it. Doubt touched his conviction, creeping up through it as though in utter desperation. He stared angrily at Asa-tebo.

"It is not true," Kor-Káy said through clenched teeth, seeking to keep his voice low so as not to awaken the others and to enable him to keep this intensely personal grief personal. His disappointment and shame was a private matter. Struggling to retain his composure, Kor-Káy declared, "It is a trick! Like the knot that unties itself, and the magic of white arrows that appear out of darkness and catch fire. It is all of your making. If you had not tricked me, and forced me to come on this journey, I would have been there to have prevented that marriage."

"That would have been a mistake," Asa-tebo's voice was soft and sad.

"I love her, and would have taken care of her."

The medicine man reached to touch Kor-Káy. "You forget, my grandson. T'sal-túa is your sister."

Kor-Káy looked away. "I could have guarded her from harm."

"Such would have been an unnatural thing," Asa-tebo insisted. He withdrew his hand and shook his head sadly. "I know," he said, "of a brother and sister who went from a guarding relationship to that of a man and wife. One of their children was weak and died, and two were crippled and remained infants in everything they did, even though they grew as tall as any of us."

Asa-tebo paused, then added quietly, "I feel the heat of your anger, my grandson. Do not give in to it and do something crazy. As time goes away, so will your anger toward me. Do not do anything that will cause you sorrow when your anger is past. When enough time is gone, you will understand that T'sal-túa is not the person you should take to be your wife."

Kor-Káy turned away. He strode off to the horse herd, carelessly roped out a mustang pony, mounted it bareback, and rode to relieve 'H-'ei-p'eip. For two hours he circled the captured livestock and their own spare-horse herd, silently meeting young a-A-dei twice each turn, then Tadl-doc and Koum-soc came to relieve them both.

Throwing the horse he had been riding back in among the spare horses, Kor-Káy returned to camp. Still so disturbed by the vision Asa-tebo had induced that he could not sleep, Kor-Káy sat long, staring into the troubling fire, before finally giving up to restless drowsing in taut exhaustion.

When he awakened it was barely daylight. Asa-tebo was standing at the edge of the oasis shading his eyes with his hands, and staring out over their back trail. He greeted Kor-Káy with brisk good humor. "You see," he said, sweeping his hand out over the desert, "the strong night wind has brushed the sand thoroughly. It has removed every sign of our tracks to this place." From the look on Asa-tebo's face it was evident that he felt very smug and safe.

It seemed more difficult to arouse the warriors and to get the livestock lined out on the trail after the night of heavy rest than it had on other mornings. Even the fighting bulls were lethargic and utterly weary. They followed their custom of stringing themselves out, up and down the length of the herd in the order of seniority they had themselves determined, then moving along with no apparent interest in fighting, with each other, or with any other creature.

By the full heat of midday they had reached the Rio Bravo, arriving at the same Boquillas Canyon crossing they had used almost three months ago on their way south. They drew up beside the river to consider its depth and the swiftness of the current. Asa-tebo turned, cantering his pony back to Sa-p'oudl

to ask him to ride across and check for quicksand near the far
bank.

Sa-p'oudl rode toward the river, then suddenly turned his
own horse back, wheeling about excitedly and pointing across
the river. Everyone looked where he was pointing. Riding
out of the chamizal came two Indians, and a moment more
sufficed to identify them. Kor-Káy saw no joy in anyone's face
as they stared across the running water at the approaching
twins.

Asa-tebo's eyes lost their focus and he said, "I think we had
better not cross here after all. When we came down that way
we had only our wounded to worry about, but now we have
all these *wohaws* and horses. We had better go north along
the river and find a place where the country is flat, not all
wrinkled up with mountains like that on the other side."

Kor-Káy knew it was not the roughness of the terrain here
that altered his grandfather's plan. It was the presence of that
pair across the river. Even after twice defeating them, he still
wanted no more of their witchery. But it made no difference
anyway, for by the time they had turned the herd and started
it moving northward, Gui-pah and Addo-mah came splashing
out into the stream, riding across to greet them.

As their horses came up wet and dripping out of the water,
Gui-pah shouted, "We had made some medicine over there
to destroy all of you. But our hearts are good today and we
have decided to give you another chance." The twins seemed
frankly glad to come riding once more into this group of old
acquaintances. Kor-Káy saw no evidence that their sentiment
was reciprocated, until Tsei, in his way of trying to get along
with everyone, went riding to meet them with a fawning
smile and almost doglike demeanor.

The afternoon was hot, contrary to socializing, and the
twins essayed no magic in an attempt to impress anyone. In
contrast, Asa-tebo, probably to impress the twins with his dis-
dain of the soldiers, said, "If we cross the river in the morning

about where it turns east again, Fort Stockton will be only two days' ride from us, and directly on our way to Cibolero. Although we have enough stolen animals now, we ought to ride over that way and see if the soldiers have left any of their horses running loose."

So, after crossing the Rio Bravo where Asa-tebo suggested, they drove the herd across the hot *tejano* prairie for two days during which the medicine man was busy planning with members of the group, especially Pein-hH, as to how they should proceed, and how they might make use of bugle calls, in case they did run onto any horses that could be stolen.

Fort Stockton, Asa-tebo reminded them, was an old fort, having been there for as long as he had been making war journeys southward. The Comanches had once told him it had been built there by the white-eyes because there was a fine spring there. The building of the fort had stopped them from using the spring on their own forays down the Comanche Trail. The buildings of the fort were all down in close to the spring, but there were hills around it.

Some of the warriors urged that they pass south of the fort itself, since that was the shorter way to Cibolero, and should they be caught by surprise they could easily scatter back into the mountains of the Rio Bravo's big bend and flee once more into Mexico.

Kor-Káy used the two days of leisurely traveling toward Fort Stockton to get better acquainted with the *arriero* whom they had captured when they had stolen his *carreta*. Though he had spoken to him briefly before, there had been no time for long talks during the bad weather and forced marches that had plagued their flight out of Mexico.

The name of the *arriero* was Juan Diego. He was a good fellow, thankful to be alive. It was pleasant for Kor-Káy to be able to converse freely with someone in the flowing Spanish of his childhood. Diego was cheerful and good-humored.

"Half of us Mexican Indians lost our Indian names and

were named 'Juan Diego' by the Spanish friars who baptized us," he told Kor-Káy. "It is confusing sometimes. You learn very young to pay no attention when someone calls 'Juan Diego,' for they are always calling some other Juan Diego and not you."

The *arriero* was the first man Kor-Káy had encountered since childhood who could comprehend and pronounce Kor-Káy's real name. After so many years it sounded strange, even to Kor-Káy, when he spoke it:

"Jorge de la Vega Valdez y Valdez . . ."

"*Es un nombre distinguido,*" said Diego, "it is a distinguished name. I have heard it spoken with respect during my freighting trips into Chihuahua City."

Diego was a small man, wiry of build; a willing worker, and expressed his willingness to take over his share of camp duties, including all the cooking, if the warriors wished, whereupon he became a captive in name only, and in reality a full participant in the war journey. He had heard of the Comancheros and had once been offered a contract to drive a *carreta* loaded with trade goods north along the *Jornado de Muerto.*

He had been afraid, but, "Now that I am going there with friends," Diego grinned at the Kiowas riding out in the van herding the stolen stock, "perhaps I can arrange some business. It would be better than hauling a *carreta* of woolen garments from Saltillo to Monterey, then returning empty."

Kor-Káy had suggested that the Comanche Indians carried mostly hides and peltries to Cibolero—buffalo hides, deer and bear skins, the pelts of beaver, otter, muskrat. Perhaps Juan Diego could arrange to haul these raw hides and untanned skins back to Chihuahua, returning with trade goods, firearms, lead for bullets, Saltillo blankets, other textiles and gewgaws beloved by both the Comanches and the Kiowas.

"It has possibilities," Juan Diego agreed. He suggested that Kor-Káy join him and become *patrón* of the venture. The conversation was left there, for they were nearing Fort Stockton

and Kor-Káy wanted to join the long sweep out in searching
for any band of stray horses that might be running loose near
the fort.

They were already so close to the fort that some of the
Kiowas were beginning to grumble and urge that they turn
straight west. "It would be foolish for us to risk getting too
close and have so many soldiers attack us that they take everything we already have," Tsoy had complained at last night's
council.

For this reason, Pein-hH was asked to keep his bugle handy
and be ready to use it to make the soldiers run. As many as
could be spared from moving the herd scattered over the low
foothills as scouts. Gui-pah and Addo-mah had adopted their
old practice of disappearing to be seen only occasionally. Kor-
Káy was surprised to see them during late afternoon of the
day they were passing directly south of Stockton, only a cou-
ple of leagues from the fort.

The medicine twins had sky-lined themselves on an emi-
nent rise and had done so not so much to see as to be seen
and become a rallying point, Kor-Káy decided, so he rode toward them. Others had seen them too. The scouting Kiowa
outriders were making their way in toward the rise from a va-
riety of directions.

When Kor-Káy reached them, the twins were, as usual,
mysterious about why they had taken such bold action and
would explain nothing to him. They dropped below the crest
of the hill to make themselves less visible, and waited silently.
When the six they had seen approaching, t'Hou-t'h, Intue-
k'ece, Tā, Kou-t, Tsei, and Tadl-doc, had reached them, Gui-
pah spoke importantly:

"We have found the horses. More than you have already!"

"How many more?" t'Hou-t'h inquired, emery-voiced, his
foxy face sharp with greed.

"More than a hundred," Gui-pah reported.

Addo-mah, unable to refrain from the conversation any

longer, declared, "They are not like those you have. These are the long-eared horses, the ones that cannot reproduce themselves. They shriek 'e-uah-anh-anh-anh-anh' in the early mornings, and evenings, and sometimes during the day."

Mules, thought Kor-Káy. The big beasts that carry the white-eyes soldiers' burdens, and pull their heavy guns and wagons. Undoubtedly, these hard-working beasts would be valuable for trade at Cibolero. "Where are they?" he asked.

"Not far from here, but still a long way from the fort," Addo-mah replied eagerly.

Perhaps the pastures near the fort had been grazed too closely, Kor-Káy thought, and these mules had been moved to thick grass, some distance from the fort.

"They are grazing in a loose bunch over just the other side of that tall hill," Addo-mah pointed to the uplift, a high rock-studded rise not much short of being a mountain—one of the foothills of the Chisos Mountains rising to their south.

"Are they well guarded?" Kor-Káy asked.

"Only two soldiers," Gui-pah interrupted before his brother could get credit for any more of the story. "It is so hot over there that the two soldiers are resting under a big shade tree a long way from the beasts. Too, they are not like the other soldiers."

This puzzled Kor-Káy, and he asked, "How are they different?"

"They sweat profusely, even under the trees," Addo-mah explained. "They are playing some game with little white blocks and pieces of paper and they laugh a great deal."

Drinking and gambling, Kor-Káy thought. He nodded, "I will ride back to tell Asa-tebo of this."

"We should take them now," Gui-pah argued. "We do not know how long they will stay here."

Kor-Káy confronted him, hard-eyed and firm of mouth. "The rest of the war party must know what we are going to do. If this is not done right, it could make much trouble." He turned Pintí and galloped off.

He rode to the south, calculating where he would intersect the traveling herd with those who drove it, and found them easily. Though short-handed, with most of the warriors off scouting for more booty, Asa-tebo, Koum-soc, a-A-dei, Touha-syhn and 'An-tsh' were keeping the cattle and horses moving. The dogs from Piedras Negras, as Asa-tebo had said they would, were helping, nipping at the heels and hurrying along any animal that fell into the drags. Juan Diego and the *carreta* raised a low plume of dust some seventy-five *varas* behind the working dogs.

Riding directly to Asa-tebo, Kor-Káy related the medicine twins' accomplishment, giving them full credit for finding the mules. Asa-tebo considered the information thoughtfully. With the air of a man whose mind is quickly made up, he said, "Go ahead and get the mules. There is a river that comes down out of the mountains about one sleep ahead of where we now are. Touha-syhn knows where it is. He will go with you." And to Touha-syhn he added, "Look for that place where the *álamos* and the salt cedar is so thick. We will be hiding there waiting for you. Be as quick as you can."

Kor-Káy and Touha-syhn rode back, as fast as their ponies could run, to where he had left the twins and the scouts. They were already gone. Apparently there had been some disagreement among them. From the confusion of tracks at that place, Kor-Káy and Touha-syhn concluded that, though separating widely, all were moving in the direction of the big hill Addo-mah had pointed out. Its broad base spread widely across the horizon before them. They hurried toward it.

What had happened here was distinctly visible. The scouts had formed a long skirmish line, probably following the twins' suggestion, and approached the big hill beyond which the mules were grazing. A belt of scrub oak timber skirted the foot of the hill. The skirmish line had ridden into it, but where it emerged from the timber the tracks of Gui-pah's and Addo-mah's war horses were missing. Kor-Káy felt a flush of resentful anger.

What were the twins up to? He hoped they had not done something foolish that would spoil everyone's chances of stealing the mules. It seemed certain they had devised some plan to use their witchery and try to appropriate all the honor of the exploit for themselves. But if they bungled it, and the mules escaped, there would be no honor to claim.

Touha-syhn was riding on up the hill a hundred *varas* to Kor-Káy's right. Kor-Káy lifted Pintí's reins and swept up the hill parallel to Touha-syhn. Approching the crest, they slowed, then dismounted. At Touha-syhn's signal, Kor-Káy left his pony ground-tied and, together, they bellied up to look out over the crest.

The mules were scattered widely over the broad plain on the far side of the hill, some of them still grazing peacefully on the prairie's cured, late summer grasses. The medicine twins had not exaggerated. There were surely more than a hundred of the mules, Kor-Káy decided. It was hard to tell how many, for those mules around the perimeter were in motion, being driven toward the center of the plain by the waving blankets of the advance scouts.

But someone, besides Gui-pah and Addo-mah, is missing, Kor-Káy thought. He thought through the list of the scouts, checking their names off on his fingers as he counted those out there riding in ever-tightening concentric circles, gathering the mule herd together: t'Hou-t'h, Intue-k'ece, Tā, Kou-t, Tadl-doc, Tsei—Tsei was the one that was missing.

This seemed unusually strange, for Tsei was one of the warriors most inclined to follow orders, one Kor-Káy had thought would surely wait while he had gone to talk with Asa-tebo. Tsei had more reason than most to be grateful to Asa-tebo, for Asa-tebo had healed him of the terrible wound in his body. Then Kor-Káy remembered that Tsei had been the only warrior who had been willing to greet Gui-pah and Addo-mah when they had come splashing across the Rio Bravo to rejoin the war party. *It is,* Kor-Káy thought, *that Tsei has so little will of his own that he is willing to follow the witches rather than remain loyal to Asa-tebo, who has the better judgment.*

The hovering shade tree at the foot of the hill must be the one beneath which Gui-pah and Addo-mah had seen the two soldiers who were supposed to be guarding the mules. Being high, and directly above it, Kor-Káy could see nothing through its dense leaves, but Touha-syhn, from his prone position off to the side must have been able to, for, with hand signs, Touha-syhn specifically called Kor-Káy's attention to the tree. Touha-syhn got up, and walking as if there were no further need for caution, went back to retrieve his horse. He mounted and rode down toward the tree.

Kor-Káy detected movement then in the edge of late afternoon shade beside the tree. It was Addo-mah. Kor-Káy whistled softly for Pintí and followed Touha-syhn down the hill. As they approached the tree, Kor-Káy saw Gui-pah and Tsei squatting beside the bodies of the two soldiers, searching their clothing. Both of the soldiers had been killed, shot with the arrows now protruding from their backs. Their throats had been cut.

Their bodies had been stripped, and Kor-Káy understood what Addo-mah had meant when he had said, "They are different." These were buffalo soldiers. Dark of skin, their black hair curled against their scalps like the black hair of the buffalo.

Their uniform jackets, which in the heat of the afternoon they had probably not been wearing, were stacked in the fork of the tree. When Kor-Káy stepped toward the tree, Addo-mah said, "Those coats belong to Gui-pah and to me."

The soldiers' shirts had been torn in removing them. Shoes, undergarments, stockings, and the trousers Gui-pah and Tsei were searching were piled beside the bodies. The loot in the tree fork included the soldiers' guns and knives, showing that Gui-pah and Addo-mah had claimed the things of most value. Tsei was having to satisfy himself by scavenging odds and ends from the soldiers' pants pockets.

The bloody dead men gave Kor-Káy a feeling of odd unreality, shock and sadness.

"It is a bad thing that you have done here," he said.

Gui-pah looked up from what he was doing. He held a belt with a polished and shiny buckle, and a handful of cartridges. His face wore a smirk of contempt. "We thought that, since they were different, you might be afraid," he said. "As you were afraid of the dwarf. We thought you might run away without even taking the mules."

"It was you and your brother who feared the dwarf's magic, not I," Kor-Káy said bitterly.

He saw only two "bottles"—both water canteens. The soldiers had not been drunk with firewater. They had been playing a game, for *dados*, dice, lay on the ground and money was scattered about. The laughter the twins had heard must have been amusement over some turn of their game.

Kor-Káy looked out across the plain at the mules, now gathered into a milling herd by the blanket-waving Kiowas. "We could have used our blankets to scare off the mules before the soldiers could have done anything. You have killed these men without any need, and the soldiers' friends will hate us far worse than if we had only stolen their mules. They will be out after us. It was different when we were in Mexico. We did not kill anyone there and those people did not even follow us to the big river. We had better get away from here quickly."

The Fort Stockton mules in cohesive *remuda* were being driven hard toward them now, a stampede pursued by their blanket-waving Kiowa captors. Touha-syhn and Kor-Káy leaped to horse and rode to turn the oncoming column. Gui-pah, Addo-mah, and Tsei were left behind, scrambling to gather up their loot.

As Kor-Káy and Touha-syhn swung the column of mules around the perimeter of the hill, they bent them south in a feint toward Mexico. If the Fort Stockton soldiers could be convinced that they were returning to Mexico it might provide a little more time for them to devise a deceptive withdrawal from the area.

❧ IX ❧

Slowing the tough, resilient army mules only at infrequent intervals through the night, walking them for a while to give them a blow, it was not quite daylight when Touha-syhn guided them in to the river rendezvous.

Asa-tebo was jubilant with the addition to their trading booty. "Eighty-four *wohaws*, one hundred and ninety horses and mules and one captive," he gloated, totaling them up. He was unmoved by Kor-Káy's account of the murdered soldiers. Seeming to forget his own past admonitions about unnecessary killings along the trail, he rebuked Kor-Káy in declaring, "This is a war journey. Dead men left behind are a part of war."

But Kor-Káy's somber attitude did turn Asa-tebo's thoughts toward a serious problem that confronted them.

"The river is dry," Asa-tebo pointed out.

The dry river gave him visible worry and concern. Wide, waterless, and powder-dry, the riverbed wandered northward into the infinity of desert distance. In past times it had sustained flood tides of rushing water, but now it looked as if no water had flowed over its crusty bed for months.

"We have no way to conceal our tracks," Asa-tebo fretted as he fell in the lead to point the direction of the trailing herd, "but we will stay in the riverbed anyway. There is no way of knowing when a storm up in the mountains may send down a torrent that will wash out our sign."

When Gui-pah, Addo-mah, and Tsei caught up with them later in the morning, Asa-tebo grinningly congratulated them on their loot, which further deepened Kor-Káy's sense of injury and anger. He rode up to Asa-tebo and, without asking permission, announced sullenly, "I am going to ride out with the scouts. The smell of the stinking carrion birds with us here is making me sick."

He urged Pintí up the cutbank, out of the dry riverbed, and rode off. Every warrior has the right to make up his own mind, and the act of Tsei and the twins was more than he could tolerate. *Everyone,* Kor-Káy thought, *has the right to decide what he is going to do. Now I am going to decide what I ought to do. Everyone has the obligation to listen to the most experienced man on a war journey. But perhaps I have listened to this one too long.* Red, sandy dust hung in the air like a long banner behind the column of Kiowas and their stolen stock as Kor-Káy rode out ahead, finally leaving them completely out of sight behind him.

Kor-Káy forged ahead at a steady pace, seeing no one, and, by late afternoon, knew he was several leagues ahead of the column, even far out ahead of its most advanced scouts. He followed the northwesterly trend of the narrowing riverbed until it thinned out and disappeared completely, sinking into the sandy earth of the rough, *arroyo*-marked country.

As the contour of the country changed, the drainage changed, sloping briefly easterly, then northeasterly as it began its gradual rise toward the high plains of the *llano estacado*. Though his mind was on other matters, Kor-Káy did not ride carelessly. He approached each ascending ridge with caution, never precipitously skylighting himself.

In this manner, he observed the far-distant, approaching puffy cloud of dust, and chose his passage over the thinly grassed plain so that he did not raise an answering dust. It might be only the track of a desert wind devil that moved toward him, lifted swirling in the warm air, then settling into its puffy appearance, but he would wait patiently, and prudently, and be certain, before he gave the phenomenon any hint of his presence.

Another hour's ride and he was sure that what he was seeing was man-made. Kor-Káy rode down into the swale of an old buffalo wallow and, from it, observed the coming dust until he knew what raised it. It was a detail, out from the fort. A white officer and three black, buffalo-soldier enlisted men. Behind them followed a pack train of four mules, brothers and sisters doubtless of the mules Kor-Káy had helped to steal. It was a meat detail, a hunting expedition, for the pack train was heavily laden with the meat killed on the hunt. Kor-Káy could see buffalo-hide- and deerskin-wrapped packets of meat, and panniers that certainly contained dressed quail, plover, wild turkey, pheasant, the plentiful game birds of these *llanos*.

The point that pricked Kor-Káy's thoughts most sharply was that, on the course they were now traveling, the soldiers of this detail would inevitably intersect the route of the fleeing Kiowas and their unwieldy trail herd. A glance at the sun, and a reflective calculation as to how long he had come this way, caused Kor-Káy to estimate that the encounter would come just at sundown and at about the time the Kiowas would be emerging from the dry riverbed.

A culpable and dangerous situation. For the soldiers would be coming at the Indians directly out of the setting sun. It would be nearly impossible for the warriors to see the soldiers coming at them out of the fiery, burning orb *al ras del horizonte*. That the soldiers were hunters implied that they were sharpshooters, and fast. Their own images right now were as elusive as ghosts in the desert's rising heat waves. Against the blinding setting sun, they would make poor targets. Some of the Kiowa warriors would be killed. The painstakingly gathered herd would surely be scattered, and probably driven back down the dry riverbed to entrapment and capture at Fort Stockton.

Kor-Káy picked out a spot yonder, beside the sprawling *nopales* of a prickly pear cactus, and decided that was as near as he could let them come. When they reached that spot, he dared himself to let them come a little closer. Then he burst from the buffalo wallow like a quail exploding from cover and ran for a distant fringe of bushy liveoak bordering the low range of hills.

It took the soldiers' captain a moment to recover his composure. He shouted, "Hold your fire, men. Follow him! That redskin will lead us straight to a war party."

Kor-Káy wished for Pein-hH and his bugle, though he had no real idea how Pein-hH could have helped him, and by then it made no difference anyway, for confusion had taken over. Kor-Káy could hear the buffalo soldiers shouting at their mules, at their officer, and at each other, in a patois he could not understand. The young second lieutenant in command of the hunters saw the foul-up that had been precipitated, and vacillated. He himself rode after Kor-Káy, then reined up, shouting more orders, meant to clarify the situation, back toward his men. Kor-Káy slowed Pintí. He would have to flee very slowly or he would lose his pursuers altogether.

The soldiers, trying to decide whether to abandon the meat-laden mules, apparently concluded too much work had gone into acquiring these comestibles, so they brought them ahead, running clumsily. The lieutenant was not eager to isolate himself too far from the support of his hunting detail. So Kor-Káy set a measured pace, outdistancing them, but slowly, so as not to withdraw the bait and make the chase seem hopeless.

Kor-Káy kept showing them his back, just out of gunshot range. Pintí was weary from last night's run with the mules. Kor-Káy had dozed in the saddle during the day. He knew his own tiredness was partly emotional but that Pintí's was entirely physical. Had the lieutenant and his soldiers been able to pursue them full out, it would have been a short race.

As soon after sundown as the silhouetting dusk turned to darkness, Kor-Káy went to ground. He found a creek branch running down out of the hills, its surface sand totally dry to the touch of his hand, and he began digging. After a while the sand became moist, and he continued his digging until enough water had risen in the bottom of the hole for him to scoop out double handfuls for Pintí to drink. Then he cupped water to his own lips.

Kor-Káy walked, leading Pintí, until they encountered a miniature meadow no more than twenty steps across, lush with summer-cured wild barley. Kor-Káy used his short grass rope to secure Pintí to his bare ankle, and lay down. The sky was clear, filled with stars, and Kor-Káy lay watching them and considering his decision. A door had opened for him here. He had already stepped out through it. It would be foolish to walk back in it now. Instead, he would continue northeast to the old Comanche Trail Asa-tebo had spoken of so often. Following it, he would return to his own village of the Washita band of the Kiowas.

He would steal T'sal-túa away and take her to the Chihuahua of his childhood. Perhaps he, like Juan Diego, could become an *arriero*, a freighter of merchandise. He doubted that T'ou-teinei would kill Diego now. Perhaps, after they reached Cibolero, Juan Diego would return to Chihuahua. Perhaps they could become freighters together.

Kor-Káy wondered if the soldiers were still following him. He had heard that the white-eyes officers and their black troopers were not very good trackers. *If they find us here, they will just have to find us,* he decided, and went to sleep hoping his pursuers would pick up his trail tomorrow.

When daylight came, he began leaving tracks. Not many, and widely interspread. A hoof-bruised leaf, his own moccasin print in a single crushed grass image at the edge of a clearing, Pintí's *quítaque*, a hoof-scuffed rock. The soldiers, in following him, would that much longer postpone a full alert of the Fort Stockton troops. He continued in this manner all day, saw no evidence that he was being followed, and with the coming of night, slept again.

Toward morning he awoke, dreaming of Asa-tebo. On starting out, he found that he had been sleeping less than a league from the traces of the old Comanche Trail. Soon, he discovered the tracks of a party proceeding up the trail ahead of him. He put the nightmare about Asa-tebo out of his mind and began at once to decipher the signs he followed.

In so doing, he left a plain trail that anyone could follow, intermingling his tracks with those of the Indians ahead of him. He was soon certain that the tracks he was following had been made by a northbound band of half-tame Kickapoos, returning to their reservation in the Indian Territory, after a visit with the wild, still renegade half of their tribe that had taken refuge in Sonora.

There were tracks of men, women, and children along the trail. They had few horses. Most of the men walking had quit wearing moccasins and were wearing the clumsy brogans issued to the reservation tribes, the kind of shoes that white men wore. Kor-Káy followed them until he sighted the straggling band. The nightmare of the early morning hours was again trying to dominate his thinking.

He pushed it aside to reason this through. If the men of the Fort Stockton hunting detail kept on following him, they would sooner or later catch up with the straggling Kickapoos. As soon as they discovered that they were following reservation Kickapoos, they would question them awhile, until convinced they had been up to no mischief, then probably return to Fort Stockton.

The choice that confronted Kor-Káy now was whether to pass around the Kickapoos and continue north, or give in to the dream that troubled him, and turn once more west. The evil dream was still growing in power. It seemed to fill him as poison fills a festering wound. It was beginning to cause real physical pain for him now, a subcutaneous pain that spread out under his skin and made his whole body hurt. His joints started to ache and his blood swelled in his head and throbbed in his eardrums. Kor-Káy put his hands over his ears and held them, for they felt as if they might burst.

He yearned to see T'sal-túa, to be with her, to take her away with him. But this dream that had possessed him and the pain that it brought pushed everything else out. Kor-Káy wondered if this could be the way Asa-tebo had felt on the night he had used the eagle shield to summon the medicine man to T'sal-túa's side. Whatever it was, it was beyond anything Asa-tebo had taught him, and Kor-Káy could clearly understand it. It seemed to interpret itself for him.

Instead of continuing north on the Comanche road and leaving plain tracks for the soldiers to follow as he willed himself to do, he turned west, into nowhere, and left no tracks at all.

With no plan whatever Kor-Káy traveled toward the westering sun. He strongly felt that if he could cut the trail of his own people, he could catch up with them before they reached Cibolero. He struck the course of what he knew, by the size of it, to be an important river. Knowing Asa-tebo's penchant for following rivers, Kor-Káy felt impelled to follow this one. It flowed shallowly. The Kiowas might have trailed the herd right up the middle of it, washing out their own tracks. But he followed its course for days, carefully observing the places where the river had risen and fallen, but never finding a human footprint nor a trace of the emergence of any sizable mixed bunch of cattle and horses.

At one crossing, marked with the bleached skull of a horse head tied high on a pole, he searched for one whole day among a myriad of horse and cattle tracks on both sides of the river, never finding a one he recognized. He continued upstream, with no reason for doing so other than that he had to travel some direction, and following the water course made more sense than striking out across barren prairie.

The country became mountainous. An immense range began building up to his left, with a skiff of snow visible on its peaks and crest. It reminded him that he was traveling northward. Here the thunder moon had already passed sufficiently for the first early snow of the falling leaf moon to touch the highest peaks.

He still found no recognizable signs of the passing of the war party, but this was cattle country, and Kor-Káy realized that Asa-tebo was clever enough to hide tracks when he wanted to hide them. The strong sense, the instinct that kept Kor-Káy traveling up the river valley never flagged. He became accustomed to it. At times when he was traveling he would briefly cease to be aware of its presence, but when he stopped to rest or sleep the feeling would begin to grow in him.

It seemed then even to strengthen, for each day he found himself going a league and part of another league farther. Though he had no idea where he was, the urge to continue motivated him somewhere far beneath his consciousness. Perhaps, he thought, with a persuasion similar to that which motivates a migrating bird.

He had passed the snow-covered peaks when he found the first trace of the passage of those he sought. And, at almost the same time, Touha-syhn found him. The trace he found was that of the wheel tracks of Juan Diego's *carreta,* coming up off a sandbar. The *playa,* washed down out of the mountains on the crest of some flash flood, lay like a sandy island on the valley floor, spreading out from the *arroyo* it had overflown. Kor-Káy wondered why Asa-tebo, so scrupulous at hiding their trail in all the leagues passed, had permitted those wheel tracks to be made here.

They were as plain as the rifle shot that then startled Kor-Káy, sending its ricocheting bullet whe-e-e-ing off a black lava boulder to Kor-Káy's right. The instinct that had been motivating him compelled Kor-Káy not to seek shelter, but to stand his ground. He caught sight of Touha-syhn, riding down out of the rising *mal país* to his right.

Waving his rifle, and shouting words lost across the distance, the short, stocky, Touha-syhn rode on down the slope. He muscled his horse to a halt, sliding off, and came running toward Kor-Káy with a bearlike fluidity of motion. "Asa-tebo is sick," he called out.

"Where is he?" Kor-Káy shouted back in reply.

Touha-syhn was excited and had to disgorge the information in his own order. "He has fallen down before the bitter cold. We found two old buffalo bulls which we killed, and took the robes. But even beneath those robes and lying beside a hot fire, still his bones shake and his teeth rattle."

Kor-Káy stood listening.

Touha-syhn went on, "Then he throws off the robes and his skin is as hot as a dry rock in the sun. The heat goes away with a sweat that leaves him so weak he can travel only by *travois*, and even then not very far."

"Where is he," Kor-Káy asked again, "and the others?"

"Some of them are beyond those hills, grazing our herd. Others are out hunting. Yonder comes Tsei and Koup-ei-tseidl, riding toward us."

Kor-Káy rode to the camp with Tsei and Koup-ei-tseidl while Touha-syhn returned to his watch post. He found Asa-tebo sitting up and cheerful.

"It is true," he said. "I have never doctored or seen a sickness like this. Sometimes, when the heat is upon me, I have power dreams. But none of them has shown me how to stop the sickness, or how to strengthen myself."

Kor-Káy had never seen anyone who seemed as pale and drawn as Asa-tebo. Hesitantly, he suggested, "Perhaps the medicine twins—"

"That pair!" Asa-tebo snorted and gestured obscenely. "I sent them away. They know nothing. They boiled water when I was cold, but I turned hot before they could even bring it to me. Then they offered to go up into the mountains for snow. I told them to go away. They got angry, and did."

Asa-tebo's thoughts seemed to wander. "We have been spending most of the time in the stream beds," he said. "You were right about that."

Kor-Káy had not told Asa-tebo he had been thinking that way. But it did not surprise him that the medicine man knew.

Asa-tebo said, "The rains of the falling leaf season had been coming high in the mountains. I let everyone come out only on sandbars the turtle told me would be under the water of a raise soon."

He sat for a time, resting. "Now those rains in the mountains are turning to snow. Winter is coming. And I am getting very cold."

"But also very hot," Kor-Káy reminded him.

Asa-tebo nodded, "I do not understand it." He sat, quiescent, and Kor-Káy sat beside him. They did not talk any more. Kor-Káy did not tell him about his decision to leave the war journey and return to the Washita. Nor did he tell about the soldiers he had deceptively led off, nor any of it. And Asa-tebo did not ask where he had been. Perhaps he knew anyway.

Asa-tebo dozed. After midday he aroused, and tried to mount his horse. He could not. Sa-p'oudl suggested that they once more make a *travois* in which Asa-tebo could ride.

They rigged the *travois*, to be drawn by Asa-tebo's horse. Soun-goucdl offered to lead it. Kor-Káy rode alongside the old medicine man, who seemed too weakened by the chills, fever, and sweating to even react to his plight. Kor-Káy was amazed at the debilitating effect of this disease during its relatively short duration. The age wrinkles in Asa-tebo's face had deepened perceptibly.

Flesh had fallen away from him. He looked thin, his muscles flabby, even stringy, in comparison to their bulging knottiness when they had started this long war journey, when Asa-tebo had demonstrated his agility in leaping on and off his horse only a little more than three moons ago.

As Asa-tebo rested and rode in the *travois*, however, he seemed to begin to recover some of his old demeanor. Presently he was looking out over the valley landscape, with his eyes flashing beadily.

The mountains behind them slowly receded. The mountains to the west continued along beside them, but the valley through which they rode became a flat plain that stretched out to the east for more leagues than Kor-Káy could see. Asa-tebo rode tensely, his clawlike old hands gripping the side poles of the *travois*, his black eyes darting feverishly, here and there, like a swift lizard poised for flight. Suddenly he looked as if he were angry.

"I should not be dragged along here like an old woman," Asa-tebo declared. "I am a warrior and should ride like one."

"But you are sick," Kor-Káy soothed. "I believe that you must have thought you were going to die. Otherwise you would not have called to me so strongly when I was away over there on that trail going north."

Asa-tebo speared Kor-Káy with an angry, reptilian glare. "You did not keep on running back to your mother and your sweetheart-sister as you intended to do."

Kor-Káy's own humor turned resentful, making him forget momentarily that he had set out to soothe and encourage this querulous old man.

"How can you know everything that happens to me when I am far off?" Kor-Káy demanded. "How could you summon me to you so strongly that I had no will of my own, and could do nothing but what your thoughts were telling me to do?"

"I am like the predator hawk," Asa-tebo gloated. "Have you never watched such a hawk, soaring high in the sky, seeing everything that moves on the earth below?" His eyes darted about sharply. "Those hawks and eagles know how to use that eagle shield medicine. I am going to use it to cure myself!"

Asa-tebo leaped out of the *travois*. "Take your knife and cut those thongs binding the poles to the sides of my horse," he demanded impatiently.

Kor-Káy stared at him in amazement.

Asa-tebo snatched his own knife from its sheath. Two swift slashes and the *travois* fell away. Instantly Asa-tebo leaped astride. "You are too slow, Grandson," he spat out.

His horse squatted on its haunches as he hit it with his hand. It made two long jumps then and settled into a hard run toward the head of the procession where Asa-tebo usually rode, far out in advance of everyone.

Bending his course steadily, Asa-tebo led them into a mountain pass. Well into it, they turned south. Here in the mountains they rode along ridges of middle height, with towering mountains in the background to the west of them. The foothills to the east were an infinite series lowering down into the flat, then blending off into the high plains that ran hazily to the far horizon.

Asa-tebo came riding back to tell them, "One more sleep and we will arrive at Cibolero."

Kor-Káy was glad to stop if for no reason other than to halt the creaking shriek of Juan Diego's *carreta* wheels. The wheels' protesting wails had begun to rend the quiet canyons as the moisture they had absorbed during the river travel was sucked out of them by the high, dry mountain air.

They made a dry camp for the night, rising as always well before dawn to be prodded and hurried by an impatient Asa-tebo. By full morning light they were coming up alongside the Comanchero settlement. It lay across the canyon from the ridgecrest trail that they rode, its *casas de adobes* and log cabins strung out along the parallel ridge *opuesto*. Most of Cibolero's structures were built of logs, both vertical stockades, and cabins of horizontal notch and groove construction. Both were chinked with adobe.

The cabins and adobe houses blended with the forest above and the valley below, in an almost idyllic setting. Early morning sounds coming from the settlement were sharply fresh and clear. Small boys, driving their goats off into the mountains for the day's grazing, went with the tinkling of their herd's bells, musical in the misty air. The long baa-a-a-ing of their charges, gentled by the distance, was the eager commentary of hungry young *cabritos*.

Smoke curled from chimneys, and the solid thunk of axe on wood resonated across the canyon. Kor-Káy could see each chopper pause as the Kiowa procession passed, staring momentarily across the canyon at the Indians and their considerable herd, then returning to the necessary business of chopping the morning firewood. Clearly they were accustomed to the approach of processions of wild Indians, coming in to palaver and trade.

Nor did it occur to Kor-Káy that their approach should strike terror into anyone's heart. These were the playmates of his childhood, his present friends and companions. He had never thought of them as threatening or frightening. They rode the full length of the ridge, to the trail crossing down through the canyon, at the far end of the village.

A good tactical arrangement, Kor-Káy thought, for the *ciboleños* could carefully scrutinize every approaching party as they came along the ridge. The bottom of the canyon was naturally fortified, by slabs of rock upended by ancient earthquakes and interlaced by impenetrable timber. There was no way to get into the village except down through the canyon at the trail crossing cleared across its far end.

The Kiowas rode down into the canyon, and climbed up toward the settlement, keeping the heterogeneous herd of tired livestock closely bunched. No *ciboleño* hailed them, or made any gesture toward them. The Comanchero village settlers kept their attention on the tasks to which they attended; chopping wood, one man driving a laden burro toward the small plaza in the center of the settlement, a woman hanging out clothes. Only the children stared.

A tall man in beaded buckskin boots, wearing a long leather coat against the chilly morning air, awaited them in the center of the plaza. He was not armed. But Kor-Káy noticed that, indistinctly visible, within the doorway of each of the log buildings around the plaza, stood one or two men. Each of them was armed.

The Kiowas were armed, as always. They sat their war ponies, silently stoic, no horseplay or idle talk here. Black hair in long braids twined with red wool and beaver fur, fringed shirts and leggings, blankets casually slung about shoulders or waists, upthrust rifle barrels in arms held akimbo, downturned mouths, faces held in dignified frowning.

"*Buenos días*," the tall Comanchero greeted them. "*Me llamo* José Tafoya—" he spoke Spanish, but his graceful, long-fingered hands repeated each statement in sign language as he welcomed them to Cibolero. He told them he had gifts for everybody. The man driving the burro had arrived in the plaza and as he began to remove the gifts from the burro's panniers, Kor-Káy said pleasantly, "Your sign talk is excellent, but you will not need it with us. We speak Spanish well enough."

The tall Spaniard looked at Kor-Káy, his attentiveness turning curious. "*Your* Spanish is excellent," he said. "How did you learn it?"

"In the same way you did," Kor-Káy smiled.

The burro driver was handing each warrior a heavy, well-made knife.

"Let us see what you have brought to trade," Tafoya suggested and walked toward the herd.

"Be careful," Kor-Káy advised. "There are fighting bulls in there."

"Fighting bulls?"

"Six of them," said Kor-Káy, "of the *divisa* Piedras Negras. They are tired and walked down, but a chance to get their horns into a man on foot might revive them quickly."

Tafoya stood, eying Kor-Káy quizzically.

"We have also to trade seventy-eight other cattle, one hundred and twenty-two mules, sixty-eight horses, and one prisoner," Kor-Káy winked at Juan Diego.

José Tafoya looked at Diego, who stood by his *carreta* load of *rurale* saddles and riding gear. In the milling herd, a cow brute now bawled impatiently, and one of the mules initiated a brassy, braying salute to the morning.

"*Amigo*," Tafoya nodded to Diego. "Do you have any rich relatives in Mexico who will be eager to buy your return with a high ransom?"

Diego shrugged, "I have many relatives in Mexico, each equally as rich as I."

Tafoya grinned. "Drive your livestock over into those holding pens beyond the plaza, friends. Our buyers will begin looking at them. While they are doing so, all of our stores around the plaza here are open. You may examine our stocks of merchandise. Then when we are all ready, we will trade."

The gathering broke apart. Tafoya moved up beside Kor-Káy's rawhide stirrup. "If you will detain yourself a moment here, *amigo*," he invited Kor-Káy, "we have a guest among us that you may find *gusto* in encountering." He turned to the burro driver who had passed out the gifts, "Parra, would you be disposed to make a *paseo por la iglesia* and see if our visiting priest would be disposed to join us here?"

Kor-Káy watched the plaza clear as the man called Parra departed with his donkey, moving down a narrow *sendero* toward a small church of logs, its adobe front painted with white *cal* and glistening in the bright morning sunshine. It stood perhaps two hundred *varas* distant along the ridge.

The stock herd had almost cleared the plaza and was being sorted into the adjoining pens by the warriors, under the guidance of shouting Comanchero traders who scrutinized each animal as it was hazed by. When all except the Kiowas' own spare horses were corralled behind shut gates, the traders climbed the corral poles to peer and point, calling terse, critical comments across the pens to each other. Koum-soc and a-A-dei, with the help of the Piedras Negras dogs, moved the Kiowas' spare horses to the far side of the corrals and held them there, waiting to be told where to move them.

Kor-Káy listened to the Comanchero traders shouting back and forth to each other. *"Tan vieja,"* called one. *"Tan flaca,"* shouted another. All this, Kor-Káy knew, was for the benefit of the warriors. There was not one old cow in the herd, though all were too thin from the distance and the hard trail they had traveled.

The Kiowas began to drift off, scattering themselves among the *puestos* surrounding the plaza and examining the merchandise the Comancheros had to offer. Kor-Káy hoped they would be prepared to drive hard bargains when the trading began. Yonder, down the *sendero*, Señor Parra had left his burro at the front doors of the glistening little church and entered it. He was inside only briefly, coming back out with a priest who hurriedly knotted the cord of his robe and pulled his cowl up over his head.

Even at this distance, and across the long years, Kor-Káy felt the subconscious tug of deep memory. The brown robe, the *cuerda Franciscana*. Some sense still remote spoke to Kor-Káy a matter of information so removed from this place and time that it did not summon up instant comprehension.

Kor-Káy dismounted. Tafoya took Pintí's halter rein, asking, "You are the chief of these people?"

Kor-Káy shook his head, "We have no chief." Inquisitiveness was not a custom among the Kiowas, and Kor-Káy looked directly at his inquisitor. "Our elder, Asa-tebo, advises us," he said.

"Then why does he not speak for you?" asked the tall Comanchero.

Kor-Káy hesitated, now realizing for the first time that he had relieved Asa-tebo of the burden of speaking for them. He noted that Asa-tebo was not among those around the corrals, nor was he examining the storehouse goods. Asa-tebo was sitting on the ground, alone, in the warmest sunshine of the center of the plaza. His war pony stood ground-tied beside him, towering over him. Asa-tebo sat hunched in his blanket, and shivering.

"He has been very sick," Kor-Káy said thoughtfully, almost to himself.

Tafoya, following Kor-Káy's gaze, said, "He does not look very well now."

Kor-Káy heard a sudden belligerence come into his own voice, "He healed himself, with the eagle shield medicine."

Tafoya nodded, his face a mask of unspoken doubt. "What was his sickness?" he asked mildly.

Kor-Káy described the chills and fevers that had wracked Asa-tebo, the sweatings that had weakened him.

"Have you been far south in Mexico?" Tafoya asked.

"In the hot country," Kor-Káy nodded.

"He has the malaria," Tafoya diagnosed. "It will be back."

Someone shouted at Tafoya from the corrals.

The Spaniard called back, "Vengo, Álvarez," and said to Kor-Káy, "Si me permite, amigo. If you will permit me. The trading has started."

He left, leading Pintí, whose rein he gave to a subordinate as he reached the corral where Pou-doc stood, holding a new rifle and pointing it among the stolen Piedras Negras horses at a *grullo* stallion he was offering to trade for it.

Leading his burro, Parra reached Kor-Káy and passed him, apparently to return on down the trail to his own domicile. But the priest who accompanied Parra stopped. He stood looking closely at Kor-Káy, from a distance of only a few *varas.*

The priest said then, hesitantly, in near incredulity, "*Tú eres* Jorge."

Kor-Káy, his eyes fixed, feeling frozen, did not reply. Then he said, "I'm Kor-Káy, of the Kiowas."

The priest stepped forward to seize his shoulders. "You are Jorge de la Vega," he was a lithe man, as tall as Kor-Káy, "You are my nephew."

"Padre Ignacio?" Though Kor-Káy's voice rose, it was not a question. His acceptance of a past that seemed irretrievably lost, was tentative. Kor-Káy stood unmoving, then he awkwardly lifted his hands as if to try to return his uncle's embrace. But his emotion remained turgid, as chill as the morning air.

The priest insisted, "I am the only brother of your mother, Lisa Calderón de la Vega." He hesitated, then explained, "José Tafoya, on his trading *viajes* to Chihuahua City spoke of a legendary young Spaniard, reputed to be living among the Kiowas. I could not credit it at first. But then—the tale he told would have you about the right age. I decided to travel to Cibolero with him. He had promised that he would then guide me on to the Kiowa country, where I might encounter you. To determine—" his voice choked. He reached again to embrace Kor-Káy roughly, "Jorge! Jorge!"

"I am Kor-Káy. ¡*Por favor!* That is my name."

"All that is over! You will now return with me to your homeland. You are all that is left of my family—your mother, long dead of the weakness which followed your birth—your father—his sister—both killed by these savages on that bloody day—and now you ask me to call you by the un-Christian name they have given you?"

"My name is as close as my family could come to saying Jorge," Kor-Káy stopped short, half angry with the feeling he was being forced to admit what he did not want, or was not ready, to admit.

"Your family?" the priest was thunderstruck. "Do you not remember—"

"Yes," Kor-Káy nodded grudgingly, "I remember. But this is now my life."

"You were nearly nine years old when they took you—a big boy. The years that have intervened seem long," the priest weakened, "and yet—so short—"

One of the Comancheros, the man Kor-Káy had heard Tafoya call Álvarez, approached them. "If the trading is not completed this afternoon," he told Kor-Káy, pompously brisk, "the *indios* must move back across the gorge. You may camp there wherever it suits you."

"Across the gorge?" asked Kor-Káy.

"Yes," said Álvarez. He was bustling, pharisaic, his sweat an odious stink in Kor-Káy's nose. "Our people are not accustomed to *indios*, even though we do business with many of you. Our women and children fear you. We cannot permit you to remain within the village overnight."

"I am not Indian," Kor-Káy declared, then contradicted himself, "We are all Indian."

The man Álvarez glanced at Father Ignacio, then directed his callous stare at Kor-Káy. "You look like an Indian," he said. "I mean no offense, but the padre here will also advise you; if your companions attempt to remain in the village overnight, there will be trouble. We will give you plenty of *aguardiente*." He smiled offensively, "You see there, one of your friends is drinking some now," he pointed at Tsei who was holding a *taza de barro*, being filled by one of the Comancheros. "There'll be enough to keep everyone warm and happy all night. Tell those small boys who are herding your spare horses to move them back out of the village." Álvarez smirked as he walked away, returning toward the stock pens.

➢ X ➣

Kor-Káy felt the frustration of a man caught with no one on whom to vent his fury.

He turned impotently on Father Ignacio. "That man just told me that we cannot camp overnight in this village. Because we are Indians!"

Ignacio shrugged. "There is much prejudice against Indians everywhere," he acceded. "In our own Chihuahua City, government officials will not even recognize that *indios* are human. They insist that the *indio* is an animal, and has no soul."

"But these people—" Kor-Káy protested, "—trading with us is the way they live. It is their business—what they do all the time."

"You are going to have to return to your own people," insisted the priest. "If you do not, you will become a pariah."

"The people with whom I journey are my people," Kor-Káy said obstinately. "I am among them now." He thought of T'sal-túa. "We intend to return to our home on the Washita, and I shall remain there." He called across the plaza to Asa-tebo, "Grandfather, are you ready to begin your trading?"

The medicine man sat cowering and shivering in his tightly clutched blanket. "You know the things I need, my grandson," he called back, shuddering. "Go ahead and do my trading for me."

At an impasse, Kor-Káy walked toward the shaking old man. "This is my first time at Comanchero trading," he reminded Asa-tebo. "I do not know how to go ahead."

The priest, crossing the plaza beside Kor-Káy, asked, "What do you have to trade?"

Trying to speak with composure despite his chattering teeth, Asa-tebo replied, "My grandson owns a calf, a heifer, two horses, five mules, one ox, and half of a fighting bull. I have two calves, a heifer, three horses, four mules, and the other half of the fighting bull." A pitiable and shaking Asa-tebo sat huddled, explaining to Kor-Káy, "We divided the spoils of our journey while you were away from us. There has since been much gambling and trading among the warriors. Some have more and some have less, but I held fast to ours. If I had been feeling better I would have done some trading, too, and would now own the finest animals in the herd. But I did not feel like gambling or trading." The old man pulled his blanket about him weakly. The long speech had exhausted him completely.

Kor-Káy stood, uncertainly, as the priest eyed Asa-tebo for a long moment, then turned his attention to Kor-Káy. "The man Álvarez, who told you not to stay in the village tonight, is the company disburser. We must talk with him."

Father Ignacio moved off toward the corrals. Tentatively, Kor-Káy followed. At the corral disbursing wicket the priest related Asa-tebo's inventory of trading livestock. The disburser Álvarez listened, meeting no one's gaze, and carefully wrote down a list of the animals Asa-tebo had enumerated. From a shelf below the counter, he counted out a sheaf of paper trading scrip and placed it in Kor-Káy's hand. Padre Ignacio, compressing his lips as his eyes made estimate of the thickness of the sheaf, suggested to Kor-Káy:

"Accept it for now. We will continue with your trading. If the amount does not cover your needs we will return here for further bargaining."

Álvarez said with restrained belligerance, "We trade fairly in Cibolero, Padre. I will always be here—to talk."

As they walked back across the plaza, Ignacio said, "Each

of these buildings is a small warehouse of trade goods. Each of the entrepreneurs is an independent merchant, banded together in this co-operative for mutual help and protection. Their caravans into our northern states—Sonora, Chihuahua, Coahuila, Tamaulipas, Nueva León—carry the results of the Indian trade. Your furs and peltries, livestock, even an occasional Anglo or Spanish captive are thus taken to Mexico. The returning caravans carry coffee, tea, sugar and other condiments, firearms, powder and lead, kettles and utensils, bolt goods, knives, beads, vermilion and face paint, glass gewgaws—and ransom money."

They had reached the first store. "This one belongs to Fidencio Sandoval," said Ignacio. "He deals in woolens."

Kor-Káy followed the priest inside, to see rough-hewn tables and shelves laden with bright woolen blankets. The north sidewall of the log cabin framed a fireplace and stone hearth, from which a blazing fire radiated heat to warm the room. Kor-Káy walked about, running his fingers over the soft, warm nap of the thick Saltillo blankets. A feeling of awe at seeing so many, all brightly new, of so many colors and textures, the fragrant pine aroma of the shelving and tables, the whole richness of the storehouse and the cheerful warmth of its fireplace, kept Kor-Káy silent, admiring, and forgetful. The priest reminded him.

"I am going to go outside and get your—grandfather," Father Ignacio stumbled over the word, hesitantly, overcame the hesitance, and struck out again bravely. "This high mountain sunlight contains little warmth, and he appeared to me to be very cold."

The padre brought Asa-tebo in and seated him before the blazing heat of the fireplace. Kor-Káy selected a blanket, draped it about the old medicine man's quivering shoulders, and held out his handful of scrip for the blanket trader, Sandoval, to take the blanket's value for the crudely hand-printed money.

Ignacio reached out to grasp Kor-Káy's hand and the money. "No, no," he shook his head urgently. "Make all your selections first. Then we will pay for them."

Asa-tebo interrupted, his teeth chattering even as he sat on the puncheon floor before the fire. "Our Indian way is always to pay for each thing as we get it," he said. "That way we never get more things than we can pay for."

The priest said firmly, "This time we will do it as I suggest," and to Kor-Káy he added, "Select as many blankets as you need and pile them up here beside your grandfather." The word did not seem to stick in his throat this time.

The medicine man still shivered violently despite the heat from the roaring fire before which he sat wrapped in his own blanket and in Kor-Káy's new one. The priest took Kor-Káy's next selection and added it to those about Asa-tebo's shaking body.

"Your grandfather is not well," Father Ignacio told Kor-Káy.

Kor-Káy's worried nod betrayed his anxiety. "José Tafoya says he has a sickness called malaria."

The Comanchero storekeeper nodded, in strong agreement, "Sí, la tiene—yes he has it. I have been watching him. ¡Yo tengo la misma!"

"He needs medicine badly." Ignacio frowned. "You say you also have malaria?" he questioned the storekeeper. "Do you have quinine?"

"Sí," Fidencio Sandoval still nodded, then quickly tempered his admission, "poquito."

"Bring me a dose of it," the priest instructed.

Sandoval continued to temporize, grimacing, "But I have only enough to last until I return to Chihuahua."

Ignacio's voice deepened. "I recall christening your little daughter soon after arriving here, Fidencio. I let you persuade me that Marisol is a Christian name because it contains Mari. You can spare a dose of quinine."

Sandoval's eyes rolled upward as his hands and shoulders lifted in resignation. He retired to the lean-to living quarters attached to his store, and returned with a folded tissue of white quinine powder and a pottery cup filled with water.

Kor-Káy passed these to Asa-tebo, telling him to swallow the powder, and concluded that his grandfather was even too sick to protest his authority to make medicine, for Asa-tebo poured the quinine in his mouth and gagged it down with a draft of water.

"*Soc-gyh*," Asa-tebo gutturaled harshly, using the Kiowa word for excrement.

Ignacio, of course, could not have understood the word, but Asa-tebo's wry grimace was expressive. "The nastier the medicine, the better it is for what ails you," the padre declared. "We will leave the old gentleman here before your fire, Fidencio my son. When his chills and fever break, give him cool water with which to bathe his face."

Kor-Káy and Ignacio walked from one small warehouse store to another, heaping up goods for Asa-tebo as well as Kor-Káy, two new rifles and a pair of dragoon pistols, powder and lead, a black iron kettle for cooking meat, needles, strouding and calico yard goods, skinning and butcher knives to complement the fine hunting knives they had received as gifts on arriving in Cibolero, beads, paint . . . in one of the stores Kor-Káy caught P'-ou admiring his face in a hand mirror set in a frame which sparkled with colored cut-glass jewels.

Kor-Káy immediately recalled a similar one his mother had used during his childhood, and quickly bought one for T'sal-túa. When all the piles were totaled up, there was not enough scrip to pay for it all. Ignacio led him back to Álvarez' office beside the corrals. The disburser was discernibly angry; he was also not disposed to argue intemperately with a priest.

Álvarez held his tongue lest his words affect his fate in eternity. The matter was settled. As they returned across the plaza to distribute the scrip among the storekeepers, Father Ignacio said, "I hope you do not find my scheming to get more money for your animals offensive. When you live under the vow of poverty as I do, it becomes a way of life. Unless you bargain, there is never enough to purchase even urgent needs."

A flurry of excitement was springing up in the plaza. A new procession was approaching along the ridge paralleling Cibolero. Tafoya and his lieutenants came sauntering out of the corrals to view the arriving newcomers.

Kor-Káy glanced curiously across the canyon toward them. He turned away, then what he had seen fully penetrated his consciousness. He turned to stare. The make-up of the procession fully arrested his attention. He had at first assumed it to be simply another procession of traders coming to do business with the Comancheros.

The lead riders in the procession, by their saddles, hats, garb and horse rigging were *tejanos*. There were eleven of them. Following were four Mexicans. Two wore the uniforms of the *rurales*. The third, clearly, was an *hacendado*. The wealthy rancher rode a high-forked Spanish saddle with ornate *tapaderos*. With him was one of his *vaqueros*. The rear guard of the procession consisted of a white army officer and two canvas-covered wagons.

Fully alerted, Kor-Káy observed that the drivers of both of the wagons were black buffalo soldiers, and a clear alarm sounded inside him. Kor-Káy beckoned across the plaza at Touha-syhn, who was coming out of the yard goods warehouse, his arms laden with bolts of material. Animated now by what seemed suddenly clear to him, Kor-Káy hurried to meet Touha-syhn.

"Get everybody together," Kor-Káy suggested to Touha-syhn. "Have them load everything they have traded for in Juan Diego's cart. See if you can work the cart over the ridge below the village, where the Ciboleros have denuded it of trees."

He returned to stand with Father Ignacio for a moment, watching the approaching procession. Kor-Káy said, "I must go to Asa-tebo."

As he hurried inside the blanket store, Ignacio, following, asked, "Is there reason for haste? I seem to sense excitement—"

"If they do not want us to camp in the village," Kor-Káy interrupted bruskly, "we will go right now."

He felt Asa-tebo's forehead. It was cool and sweaty. The medicine had worked and Asa-tebo was dozing. Kor-Káy told the storekeeper, "We will need some more of that medicine to take with us."

The storekeeper made no move to secure the quinine he had requested, and Kor-Káy pressed him urgently, "I will pay you for your medicine powder."

The storekeeper Sandoval stood stubbornly, glowering.

"But why in such haste?" asked the priest. "And why do you want to attempt going over the ridge?" Then an enlightenment began to appear in his face. Father Ignacio stepped back to the door to look outside at the approaching procession.

Kor-Káy could hear the squeaking wheels of Diego's *carreta* as it made its way through the plaza.

Ignacio said calmly, "Christian baptism, my son Fidencio, is ineffective for those who commit the sin of selfishness. Bring my nephew all the quinine you can, and plan a journey soon to Chihuahua to replenish your supply."

"I will pay for it," Kor-Káy reiterated, as the storekeeper departed, and returned, grudgingly, with seven tissue-paper packets. "No more than one daily," he warned.

Kor-Káy and Ignacio, helping a shaky-legged Asa-tebo to walk between them, went out into the plaza. The approaching procession had reached the canyon crossing at the far end of the village and was swinging down into the wash. In the center of the plaza, Juan Diego was replacing the end-stakes in his heavily loaded *carreta*. Beyond, Kor-Káy could see Touha-syhn, Tsoy, Intue-k'ece, Tā, and Soun-goucdl, their rawhide *riatas* already tied to the frame of the *carreta*, ready to help Juan's oxen in the attempt to heave their awkward burden over the ridge.

Kor-Káy turned to the priest. "*Tío*," he suggested hurriedly, "would you help my grandfather to find a place among the goods loaded in the cart. Perhaps he should ride there. I do not think his legs are yet strong enough to grip the barrel of his war pony."

Ignacio and Asa-tebo moved slowly on toward the *carreta*. Kor-Káy backed into the shadows between the warehouses. A nooning sun had flooded the small plaza with the glare of bright sunlight. It contrasted sharply with the patches of deep shade beneath the eaves of the scattered log structures surrounding it. Kor-Káy melted into one of the patches of darkest shade, and stood listening to the sotto voce conversation of Tafoya and his lieutenants. Their talking held a touch of apprehension as they speculated about the men who were crossing the canyon now, and their purpose in coming to Cibolero.

Kor-Káy surveyed the rock-strewn rise of the ridge above the village. In securing the logs necessary to construct the houses and stores of Cibolero, and in cutting firewood for the cold mountain winters, the villagers had stripped the ridge of timber. It had become a forest of stumps. Diego's high-wheeled cart might be able to make its way among them. If it did not break a wheel. Or become a runaway to crash into the trees on the other side of the crest. Kor-Káy put such disturbing thoughts out of his mind to concentrate on the matter at hand. The *tejanos*, the *rurales*, the *hacendado* and his *segundo*, had crossed the canyon and were curving up into the village.

Kor-Káy turned to watch the Kiowas on horseback ride over the crest. Minutes later, Diego's *carreta* went crawling up among the stumps, its oxen and outriders pulling and tugging, guiding it with taut ropes. It looked like some awkward, many-legged varmint.

The white officer and the covered wagons he commanded had crossed the canyon below and everyone in the coming *desfile* was riding up through the Comanchero settlement. As the Texas Rangers leading the procession rode into the plaza, Diego's *carreta* with its overload of trade goods disappeared over the crest.

On Tafoya's quiet order, his lieutenants were sauntering about the plaza, speaking softly into each door and window they passed. Around the plaza, every opening Kor-Káy could see was manned by an armed Comanchero. The tips of rifle barrels were visible in every small opening. Kor-Káy had noticed these openings before. Now he knew that every hole and slit had been put there as a place through which to fire a rifle.

Father Ignacio came hurrying up to Kor-Káy in the shadows. The priest's brown robe and *cuerda Franciscana* were flapping around his legs in his haste. "After making your grandfather comfortable in the *carreta* I lost you," he said. "I thought perhaps you had already gone with your friends."

Kor-Káy admonished, "Padre, you had better hurry to your church to protect the sacred objects there. There is going to be trouble here."

One of Tafoya's lieutenants paused, speaking into the doorway beside which they stood. "Stand fast, *compañeros*," he told the riflemen inside. "Don José will interrogate them to learn what they want."

"Yes, it is true I must go," said Ignacio. "The altar lamp burns and the chalice and sacred hosts are in the tabernacle. But what of you, my nephew?"

"As soon as I know of the plans of these men who have followed us, I must go to tell my Kiowa people."

"But I have just found you. After all this long time—"

"Go, Padre," Kor-Káy gently urged the priest. "The war talk is about to start here!"

Hesitantly, sadly, even walking backward for the first few steps, Kor-Káy's *tío* priest uncle went, turning then to run across the plaza among the arriving horses. He hurried on down the slope toward the little church.

The Rangers rode directly to the center of the plaza, halting before Tafoya. To Kor-Káy, the tall Comanchero leader seemed intrepid but somewhat forlorn as he stood there alone in the semisurround of tall *tejano* horses. The *rurale capitán* and his *teniente* dismounted. They waited at the edge of the plaza, a little diffidently, Kor-Káy thought, as if they felt uneasy so far from the soil of Mexico.

The army wagons were still pulling to a halt beside the plaza as, impatiently, the *tejano* captain opened the palaver.

"Howdy, neighbor," he spoke down to Tafoya, taking advantage of the superior height of his posture in the saddle. "You got some Kiowa Indians hid out around here?"

Tafoya replied, in Spanish, that he spoke little English. The *hacendado* stepped forward, holding his horse's reins, "If I am able to be of service here, *capitán*," he offered, and repeated the Ranger's question in Spanish.

"*No dejamos a indios quedarse en nuestro pueblecito durante la noche*," replied Tafoya.

The *hacendado* translated, "He says they do not permit Indians to remain in the village overnight."

"Then he's a damned liar," one of the Texans said abruptly. "There's one of 'em right now!" He pointed to Kor-Káy, standing in the shadow of the warehouse.

Kor-Káy stepped forward without hesitation. "*No soy indio*," he said, moving calmly into the center of the gathering. "*Estas cosas las hemos conseguido en comercio. Yo me las puse en broma, para ver como parecía en ellas.*"

The *hacendado* translated, "He says he is not Indian. They

took the things he is wearing in trade and he just put them on to see how he would look in them."

The Texan who had first pointed at Kor-Káy muttered, "He sure looks like an Indian to me."

"*¿Como se llama, joven?*" asked the *hacendado*.

"*Me llamo Don Jorge de la Vega, de una familia distinguida de la ciudad de Chihuahua,*" Kor-Káy replied haughtily.

"I am inclined to believe him," said the *hacendado*. "He could only have learned to speak such perfect Spanish at his mother's knee. He is the scion of a distinguished Chihuahua family. Doubtless he has come to these northern wilds in search of adventure, as do many of our young men."

The Ranger captain slung a leg over his saddle horn. He pulled a sack of tobacco from his pocket and began building a quirly, drawling ironically at Tafoya, "We'll all tell the truth —or take the consequences here." He leaned on his saddle horn, indicating the other Rangers with a sweep of his quirly, "We rode into Fort Stockton a little more than three weeks ago. A bunch of Kiowas had run off with the fort's mule herd and killed the two soldiers who were mounting guard over the mules. They had done a good job of making few tracks, but you can't run a herd as big as they were and not leave some sign.

"From the tracks, we figured it was the Indians we'd run afoul of once earlier in the summer. None of our boys was hurt that time, though we sure left some marks on them. Then we caught up with these four aliens—"

"*¡Vecinos dando caza a ladrones!*" the *hacendado* contradicted, meaning to file his own complaint. "I am Señor Don Ayón Heriberto Tuñón, *patrón de la hacienda Piedras Negras*. Here is my *segundo*, Lazo Chacón. The Indians stole from me an *encierro* of six bulls on a dark night of the month past. They stole also my yearling calves, and the cows for breeding we had selected during the *tientas* of that day. *El* *acto mas malo,* they stole the horses of the *caballeros* who were my guests.

"With our best *vaqueros* we were soon in pursuit, but rain and bad weather hampered us. *Por suerte,* we came upon *capitán* Ruido Torres and his *rurales* who had been unhorsed by the savages. We realized the United States might attack so large a force of us in crossing the border, even though we were in hot pursuit of thieves. *Capitán* Torres and his *teniente* Gan, with myself and my *segundo,* continued in pursuit of the *indígenas,* leaving the *vaqueros* and *rurales* to greet us when we return to the border."

Tafoya shrugged, his face bland. His voice honeyed with innocence, "It weighs on me," he said, "to hear of all these difficulties. We are reputable traders who deal honorably with all who pass. Never would we knowingly deal in stolen property."

The army officer, escorted by two black soldiers, came shouldering his way into the conference. "Knowingly or unknowingly, sir," he charged, "you are certainly dealing in stolen property. I can recognize the ears of an army mule from any distance. Those corrals yonder are full of them!"

Siding his commanding officer, one of the black enlisted men jogged the shoulder of *segundo* Chacón. Chacón, a man of craggy face adorned with a full handlebar mustache, received the Negro's carom off his shoulder with poor grace. The tips of his mustache quivering in indignation at being so rudely jostled, he turned to accost the black soldier angrily.

"¿A dónde vas? ¡Cuidado, cabrón negro!"

The Ranger captain had enough Spanish to comprehend the gravity of the insult. He spurred his horse between the pair.

"None of that! We've got enough of an international incident on our hands without fighting amongst ourselves!"

The situation edged toward eruption. As angry babel in two languages and many dialects arose around him, Kor-Káy eased around the group toward the corral where Pintí was confined.

When the war pony nuzzled him at the corral gate, Kor-Káy let him out, mounted swiftly, and rode up the rise to leave the disputing voices behind. One of the Texans shouted, "Captain! Suh! That Injun is escapin'."

Kor-Káy broke for the crest.

The captain replied, "The rest of them have *already* escaped. Those Indians are long gone."

The white army officer was shouting at Tafoya. Loudly, Kor-Káy assumed, because Tafoya did not speak English and the officer thought that if he yelled loud enough Tafoya would be forced to understand, whether he understood English or not.

"I intend to have my mules out of those corrals," the officer was yelling at Tafoya as if he were a deaf man. "I intend to have them now!"

Kor-Káy, glancing over his shoulder from the back of a running Pintí, saw the officer turn to face the covered wagons and shout, "Men, fall out and advance on those corrals as a line of skirmishers!"

The canvas-wagon covers were thrown off and black soldiers, at least thirty of them, came swarming down out of the wagons. The soldiers, their rifles at ready, were running toward the corrals as Kor-Káy ran over the ridge and the melee of Texans and Mexicans was lost to his sight.

The cracking of rifle fire and the full-throated roar of .45 caliber six-shooters set up a steady din that faded only slowly as Kor-Káy rode off among the low stumps of the cut trees.

He easily followed the ruts of Juan Diego's high-wheeled *carreta*, surrounded by the pony tracks of the war party. The tree-stripped brow of the crest ran on for a league beyond the end of the village of Cibolero. Here pony hoofs had sliced through the layers of leaves and browned pine needles to the

moist black earth below. Now the trees of the forest closed in
again, becoming an impenetrable wall of timber.

At the timber's edge they had had to abandon Diego's cart.
It stood empty, the long shaft of its tongue pointing into the
timber, the yokes of the oxen that had drawn it abandoned
beside the trees. The forest floor around the cart's rough-
hewn stakebed had been thoroughly gouged and scored, torn
up during the work of unloading the cart. Pony tracks then
led off into the forest.

Kor-Káy followed them down into the glade of a scissors-
shaped canyon, emerged at the hilt of the *tijeras*, and continued on through a long pass, beside mountains that turned wa-
termelon red with the late afternoon fall of the setting sun.
Half a night of riding, in darkness until moonrise, ultimately
brought him to the Kiowa camp.

Knowing that their trail of retreat had been plain, they had
chosen to make camp in the most defensible place possible.
They had climbed to the top of a steep-sided mesa that
stood alone, a monster mushroom of rocky earth thrusting up
from the barren plain surrounding it. Atop it, at its edge, Kor-
Káy found Sa-p'oudl.

The Kiowas had spread themselves around the circular perimeter of the mesa, to take turns at staying awake, each to
make sure his adjoining neighbor was awake before letting
himself fall asleep.

"We saw it in the distance about sundown," the beefy Sa-
p'oudl whispered to Kor-Káy. "'H-'ei-p'eip and 'An-tsh' hurried on ahead to climb it. They found water standing in the
rock basins from a former rain. It is so steep our ponies could
hardly scramble up through the same shallow wash you
found."

Kor-Káy nodded in the moonlight. "It is a good place to
wait."

"If they are going to come after us," Sa-p'oudl said, "we
can see them from a long way off and decide whether to hurry

on and run some more, or try to fight them here. I have been watching you come toward us ever since moonrise."

"What if it had not been me?"

Sa-p'oudl scoffed, "Not know the way Pintí reaches for the sand with his forefeet with every long jump? If it had not been you on his back I would have killed you as you came scrambling up the wash."

"We should roll a big rock into that wash and close it up," Kor-Káy said.

"One is beside it and ready," Sa-p'oudl replied.

Kor-Káy nodded approvingly, "Then go to sleep. I will watch for you."

"You just got here and you are tired," Sa-p'oudl countered. "You go to sleep."

"I am too awake now. We will both watch. How is Asa-tebo?"

"The medicine the brown robe priest gave him has driven away his sickness. He is tired, but well. Diego sleeps near him back there on the mesa."

Is it possible that my uncle, Padre Ignacio, makes stronger medicine than Asa-tebo? Kor-Káy wondered. "Did my grandfather ride up here?"

"On his own horse," Sa-p'oudl nodded. "After we had to unload the cart because it would not go through the thick timber, Asa-tebo would not let us make another *travois* for him. While we were unloading, Intue-k'ece, Pou-doc, and Tsoy sneaked back into Cibolero to get Asa-tebo's horse. They stole another for Diego to ride, and a *cabe* of the *burros mejicanos*. We tied on them the things we had traded for. We have Diego's oxen to kill and eat if we cannot find anything else." Sa-p'oudl chuckled. "Intue-k'ece told me that our enemies in the plaza were all frowning. Can they not get along with each other?"

XI

Through the remaining hours of the night Kor-Káy and Sa-p'oudl took turns, dozing, then staring off into an infinity of shapeless dark and dim shadows. As the hours passed, one thought grew in Kor-Káy's mind. He was returning to T'sal-túa. He was determined that however many leagues remained, he would let nothing deter him from a steady march. He intended to persist toward the rising sun until he reached familiar country and could find the camp of the Washita band. Then he could determine for himself whether she had fallen to 'N'da's persuasion and become 'N'da's bride.

He took up his flute and played a soft prayer song toward the sinking moon, then awakened Sa-p'oudl. Kor-Káy dozed, and slept soundly. Sa-p'oudl's touch awakened him soon after the false dawn had given way to the real coming of morning. The big warrior was pointing toward the distant, haze-shrouded horizon. Kor-Káy ran his gaze along the long line of that pointing. He saw nothing.

Carefully, he retraced the route, and repeated his scanning, until the slow sweep of his eyes at last separated from the myriad of tiny, round *piñones* one minuscule dot that did not seem to stay fixed in relation to the objects around it. There, at the limit of his vision, one object was moving infinitesimally, not with the erratic purpose of a grazing or hunting animal, but steadily, implacably, it was coming toward them.

By the time the other warriors were up and about, the faraway speck had become a shape slightly more physical, proceeding forward among the dark oblongs of *piñón* through which it traveled. Sa-p'oudl, to break his fast, was chewing on a jaw full of the jerked beef. He offered the tough, stringy morsel to Kor-Káy.

Kor-Káy nodded his thanks and bit off a chunk. As he chewed it, the first light of the rising sun caused the approaching object, slowly, gradually, to take on color. It became a richer brown than the sandy wastes over which it crept. Sa-p'oudl spread the word of this among the rest of the war party. They suspended their preparations to travel to come and stand around Kor-Káy and Sa-p'oudl on the brink of the mesa, watching.

It continued to take shape, and Kor-Káy felt pique, for he was able to identify what he was seeing. It was an annoyance to be followed like this. He had left the matter an unresolved irritation simply by putting it out of his mind. No one commented. The brown-robed figure, head hidden in peaked cowl, came on astride a burro. Presently Asa-tebo's dimming eyesight made out its identity and he put into words what everyone else already knew.

"It is the brown-robed medicine priest from Cibolero," he said, "the wearer of wooden beads who spent all his time in haranguing my grandson." Asa-tebo turned to hurry toward his pony, saying urgently over his shoulder, "Let us be gone before that enemy catches up with us."

The warriors did not seem to consider Father Ignacio of any great danger. No one followed Asa-tebo off toward the scattered war ponies and burros grazing idly around the top of the mesa. Two full grown jacks and a jenny grazed with the burros, Kor-Káy noted. Intue-k'ece, Pou-doc, and Tsei must have been a little careless in their gathering up of pack animals during their covert return to Cibolero. Perhaps they had not wanted to delay too long in those environs should the contending forces in the plaza be distracted from their preoccupation with glaring at each other, and note that three Indians had returned to the village to be shot at.

Tsoy lost interest in Father Ignacio's coming. He moved off to catch his pony and pack burro, making ready to depart. Kor-Káy heard Pein-hH call out teasingly to him, "You are hurrying because you fear the brown-robed bead wearer?"

Soun-goucdl, standing nearby, grinned impishly. "No, he is anxious to get home!" He thrust his left hand past his right, making the sign for "baby."

Tadl-doc made an even more suggestive hand sign. "We are all anxious to get home," his laugh was libidinous.

The impulse seemed to ripen for all of them. They began drifting off toward the mounts and pack animals.

Soun-goucdl pressed his salacious jest. "That is so," he teased, "but Tsoy had already made his baby."

Kor-Káy recalled that Lupe had been visibly with child when they had departed on this war journey. Tā ran to catch up with Tsoy, poking him good-humoredly, "Our brother is anxious to get home and find out if he is the father of a son, or of just another daughter!"

Sa-p'oudl came leading a husky black burro up to Kor-Káy. He slapped the burro's dusty, long-haired hip. "The priest tied the plunder for which you traded in Cibolero on the back of this burro. We brought it with us. It is piled up over here."

"I thank you," Kor-Káy said, and moved off through the sage brush and shinnery to do his own packing.

The warriors were efficiently making ready to depart. Asa-tebo packed his own burro, waited grimly, and finally struggled aboard his own pony. As they proceeded single file down the narrow wash from the mesa to the plain below, Kor-Káy heard Yih-gyh challenge the others, betting that Tsoy's expected child would be a boy.

P'-ou said haughtily, "I will take that bet. Already he has two girls, and is almost certain to have a third."

"That is why I am betting he will have a boy," declared Yih-gyh. "Everyone's luck is bound to change sometime."

They reached the foot of the mesa and turned off toward the rising sun. Looking back toward the mountains, across the *piñón*-dotted plain, Kor-Káy could see that his uncle was drawing very close. So, ignoring the hostile glances of Asa-tebo, Kor-Káy turned away from the war party and rode in the opposite direction to meet his priest uncle.

They greeted each other cautiously, Ignacio drawing up on the frayed rope reins of his burro as Kor-Káy halted Pintí. Then they sat looking at each other, Kor-Káy from his perch on Pintí, Padre Ignacio looking upward from his somewhat lower seat, riding bareback on the burro.

Kor-Káy cleared his throat. "You did a good thing in getting the medicine for Asa-tebo," he said. "He is much better."

The slender, middle-aged priest smiled with dignity. "I am pleased to hear it."

Kor-Káy cleared his throat again.

"I told you that I would not return with you to Chihuahua City," he said stubbornly.

Ignacio smiled agreeably.

Kor-Káy felt a little admiration at how well his uncle maintained his aspect of dignity despite his awkward seat on the burro.

Father Ignacio explained frankly, "I felt that we had not had adequate time to consider the matter. José Tafoya told me how to follow out through Tijeras canyon and swing east at the Sandía uplift. He said that if I then followed the old trail east through the *llano estacado* I might likely, at some point, overtake you. I decided to ride through the night, as long as my strength would last. I am glad it took only one night." He shifted his weight uncomfortably on the hard hide and bony spine of the husky burro.

"Why did you not steal a horse?" Kor-Káy demanded rudely.

Ignacio's face became shocked and serious, "Steal? I could

not steal anything! I bought this burro from Rafael Parra. It was all I could afford."

"It is an honorable thing to steal horses from your enemies," Kor-Káy declared proudly. "The Kiowas are the best at it of any Indians. You could easily have stolen one of those *tejano* horses after the shooting started."

They turned to follow the war party. As they rode, they fell steadily behind. Kor-Káy was too stiff-necked to make conversation. Padre Ignacio appeared willing to let the fates work out their will in quietude rather than in noisy contention. So they rode in silence.

When they came into camp late that evening, the warriors had already roasted and eaten the day's kill of cottontails, young jackrabbit, plover, and prairie chicken. While Kor-Káy and his uncle chewed on cold jerky, the warriors wanted to hear about the fight at Cibolero. They asked in Kiowa, Kor-Káy relayed their request in Spanish.

"It was more sound and fury than blood and death," Ignacio said, speaking slowly, then glancing at Kor-Káy as if expecting him to translate his Spanish into Kiowa.

"I have taught them, Uncle, Father," Kor-Káy said impatiently. "They understand Spanish well enough." It seemed an anachronism, trying to reaccustom himself to use the title "Father" after all these years. Kor-Káy felt ill at ease and was glad when his uncle took up the narrative, making the embarrassment of further questions unnecessary.

"There was much shooting in the air at first," Ignacio said. "As the groups attempted to intimidate each other, they were firing over each other's heads. But as the struggle kept up it grew more serious. Tempers began flaring and in their anger several were wounded. Some seriously. I heard some last confessions. A few may die."

"Are the *tejanos* following us?" asked Koup-ei-tseidl.

"No. Two of them are wounded, and they have the stolen animals, which they seemed to consider of first importance. I

heard their captain tell Tafoya they would return to Austin
for reinforcements, then 'with blood in their eyes' come
back to Cibolero to 'wipe out that nest of illegal aliens,' if
they did not abandon their illicit trading. The Cibolero settlers were packing up to take refuge in our northern outpost
of New Spain at Santa Fe. Tafoya said they may later return
to Cibolero, or they will start a new trading rendezvous for
you and your Indian friends in a canyon called Palo Duro,
which is closer to your country."

"What of the buffalo soldiers?" Touha-syhn asked in
Spanish.

"The army officer and his black men will be very busy returning the mules to their fort. I understand they have no orders to attempt to pursue now, though they feel you should
all be punished, for thievery and for murder. That, they vow,
will come later."

Asa-tebo chuckled grimly, "We will soon be where they
cannot find us. I will regain my strength and make strong
medicine to blind their eyes."

"There were the two from Piedras Negras, and the two
rurales," Kor-Káy mused.

Padre Ignacio accounted for them together. "The four
from Mexico realized the good luck of their passing alliance
with the Texans and the force of black soldiers," he said. "It
made them strong enough to regain possession of their stock.
With it, they intend to return to Mexico immediately." He
looked directly at Kor-Káy, "Which I had hoped we would be
doing."

Kor-Káy got up and walked to his heap of trade goods
acquired in Cibolero. From it he took a heavy woolen blanket
that he gave to Father Ignacio. With the taciturn comment,
"I am going to sleep now," he left the group, found a place of
solitude, and wrapped himself up in his blanket.

Instead of going to sleep, he lay awake. He did not resent
the priest's presence, only his repeated insistence that Kor-

Káy should return to Mexico. To be rid of it, Kor-Káy knew that he wished his uncle would depart, and knew equally well that Father Ignacio had no such intention. Kor-Káy tried to think as Ignacio thought, trying to plumb his own probable emotion on finding a member of his own family, Dagoomdl, T'sal-túa, or Asa-tebo, after they had long been lost. This disturbed him, forcing Kor-Káy to decide that he might as well try to find his uncle a more suitable mount, so that the priest would not fall so far behind tomorrow. Beyond that, everything seemed very uncertain. Kor-Káy gave up thinking about it, and turned over and went to sleep.

In the morning, Kor-Káy sought the owner of the grown jenny he had seen among the grazing burros the previous morning. She would doubtless be easier to ride than either of the two jacks he had seen at the same time.

Pou-doc admitted to quasi ownership of the jenny. "She is the *amiga* of the burro on which I pack my trade goods. They are so friendly I cannot keep them apart," he declared half angrily. "It is a nuisance!"

Kor-Káy promptly offered to trade his burro for Pou-doc's. In the trade, which Pou-doc welcomed, he acquired the jenny. Kor-Káy was adapting his own rawhide saddle to her back when Father Ignacio joined him.

Hesitantly, the padre protested.

"What will you ride?" he asked, instinctively denying the need for any thought given his personal convenience.

Kor-Káy threw the blanket Ignacio was carrying, the one on which the priest had slept, across Pintí's withers.

"I learned to ride without a saddle," Kor-Káy demurred, "and always strip Pintí's back when we are preparing to go into battle. Riding bareback has many advantages."

"Not for me," Ignacio admitted ruefully. "The back of that burro is as hard as iron. His bony corrugated spine has made my seat as sore as a paddled schoolboy's."

"You will not find a rawhide saddle soft, but it provides a

security for long riding. I will use this blanket as a saddle."
He swung astride.

Father Ignacio mounted the big jenny with somewhat
more difficulty. He followed as Kor-Káy rode out to assume
the place where Asa-tebo had always ridden before his
sickness. No one questioned, or challenged, his position.

Behind them the mountains foreshortened and fell behind
in the climbing of the sun. Before them the land lay rolling in
long swells, a varying sameness in its patterns of rocky tan
earth sprinkled with obelisks of *piñón* brush. Fading northward the distant illusory snow-capped peaks were sometimes
visible in clean clear air, though often seeming suspended in
that air, with no contact with earth; sometimes disappearing
altogether in vague dusty remoteness.

To the south curled a rimrock of mesas, without beginning
or visible end. The arid basin became a looping crescent of
dry riverbed that circled and recircled, an *arroyo redondo* as
limitless as space itself.

Padre Ignacio rode in silence until it seemed to become cer-
tain that Kor-Káy would never speak at all; then he said,
"Can you put into words what it is that draws you to these
Kiowas? Why have you become so attached to them?"

Kor-Káy rode thoughtfully. "First," he said finally, "it is
Asa-tebo."

"Why is he so significant? He is sick, withdrawn, an
ineffective old man. What is especially important about Asa-
tebo?"

"He is my adopted grandfather," Kor-Káy asserted defensively. "He is a buffalo doctor, an owl prophet, and he has the
eagle shield medicine. What is more, he is giving me his
power—"

The troubled padre interrupted, distressed, "You mean
that he is a medicine man. I suspected that! And he is making
of you a heathen priest," his shock was palpable.

Kor-Káy rode in a mix of mildly defensive anger at the aggressiveness of his uncle's accusation, but strongly tempered by his own recent experiences, his own uncertainty and doubt regarding the efficacy of Asa-tebo's medicine. "On the night of my capture," Kor-Káy said with some belligerence, "I first saw him make magic. I was tired and frightened," he paused, thinking how inadequately those words expressed the exhaustion and terror that had possessed him then. "Asa-tebo made a small heap of earth, changed it into a rattlesnake, then chased the snake away. My fear ran away with it, and I went to sleep."

Father Ignacio said without hesitation, "Hypnosis." Then he paused, musing argumentatively with himself, "Of course you did not understand the Kiowa language then. But hypnosis can be induced by using nonsense words, so why not with a language you do not understand?" To Kor-Káy, he explained, with a confident and infallible certainty, "Hypnosis induces sleep."

"Does it make rattlesnakes?" Kor-Káy asked.

"It could make you *think* you saw a rattlesnake."

"But Lupe saw a puppy dog."

"Who is Lupe?"

"Lupe was captured with me."

Father Ignacio turned concentrative, probing the past, then came a glow of recollection. "I had forgotten," he burst out. Becoming more excited as he talked, he recalled her full name, "Guadalupe de la Fuente Mares. She came from a poor family. Her father was a *peón* of the Avellano *finca*, on the *camino* Cuahtemoc. And another girl was captured at that same time. Pilar Bonilla! Pilar's people, I know well. Is it possible that both of those girls are still living?"

"Both of them are the wives of men on this journey." Kor-Káy was surprised. That the priest might think otherwise than that the girls were alive and well was astonishing. Surely by now, Kor-Káy thought, this priest should know that the Kiowas are kind, that they capture small children only to replace their own children lost in death, and pretty girls only to become wives. That Lupe and Pilar should be alive and well struck Kor-Káy as a commonplace; like the fact that with the years men grow old, and women garrulous. "Lupe is a true Kiowa," he told his uncle. "She has two," he recalled the camp gossip, "no, by now three children. Pilar is barren, and is a shrew who makes everything difficult for her husband, Intue-k'ece."

Father Ignacio listened to this, but with his attention clearly wandering. He returned abruptly to the previous subject.

"When Asa-tebo did this magic, of which you spoke, you say that Lupe saw something other than your rattlesnake?"

"She saw a puppy dog."

Father Ignacio nodded, "The hypnotist had suggested that you would see something, but he could not control what you would see. So you happened to imagine a snake, and Lupe a dog. What did Pilar see?"

"Nothing."

"She probably is not subject to hypnosis. Some people cannot be hypnotized."

"I do not understand what you are saying," Kor-Káy protested.

"That your *brujo*, your witchdoctor's magic is false."

Kor-Káy remembered well the self-untying neckerchief, the objects he had helped appear and disappear in the dark cave on the big bend of the Rio Bravo, and the "owl's prophecy" before that, but he found himself still feeling defensive.

"I have seen Asa-tebo cure a wounded man by feeding him a road-runner cock that he caught at the risk of his own life, and cooked in a special way. Using his own eagle shield, I brought him back from a long way to cure T'sal-túa. I saw him suck out the thorns that Gui-pah and Addo-mah had shot into Sa-p'oudl's body. He cured me once when I was little. He has taught me all that I know about how to use the plants and medicine the earth and animals provide for healing people." Kor-Káy's feeling surged strongly. He finished with defiance. "He is still teaching me all the time!"

A sage hen flew up from the *piñón* brush near Pintí's hoofs. In smooth movement Kor-Káy's short bow was in his hand strung with an arrow from his quiver, and the bird swerved groundward with the arrow thrusting from its breast. Kor-Káy suggested, "Let us stop and eat."

The priest watched this act of unexpected swiftness in dumfounded awe. "At least he has taught you to kill quickly," he pondered.

"We live in a world filled with enemies," Kor-Káy said blandly.

Father Ignacio countered, "We live in a world filled with God."

Kor-Káy built a small fire. He dressed the bird and showed his uncle how to slice its meatier parts into thin portions that could be roasted and eaten unhurriedly, yet in a minimum of time. When they departed, the brown-robed Franciscan held the jenny sidling under tight rein while he surveyed the ground behind them. There remained no trace of where the fire had been, no visible indication that they had stopped and eaten here. Kor-Káy's rapid ministrations had repaired and replaced; the sandy semidesert earth appeared to have been undisturbed. There was no perceptible evidence that they had been there.

Father Ignacio reiterated his assurance of the night before, "I now not only feel positive that you will not be followed. I do not see how anyone could follow if you did not want them to."

"It is all part of Asa-tebo's teaching," Kor-Káy said simply, "that of leaving whatever you find just as you found it."

Passing midday, Father Ignacio asked with sudden sharpness, "What is that ahead of us?" He stared at a mirage-like apparition that seemed to be proceeding ahead of them, indistinct in the rising, wavering heat waves of the afternoon. With mild surprise that the priest would not know, Kor-Káy replied, "It is our friends."

"The Kiowa warriors?"

"The ones who are on this journey," Kor-Káy affirmed.

"But they were behind us!"

"Now they have passed us."

"But how—"

"When I shot the bird they scattered to hunt."

Understanding dawned on the priest's face. "When the grouse went down they accepted it as a signal to forage. I suppose if I had thought to look behind us they would simply have disappeared in the desert. That I am with you slowed your eating, and permitted them to pass us."

"Now that they have regathered, they are ahead of us," Kor-Káy confirmed patiently, "but we will camp together tonight."

In ensuing days a *desarollo* of the continual acquiring of pieces of new knowledge for Father Ignacio Calderón became for him an entry into a new world. Sporadic driblets of information fell on him like the spattering of raindrops over thirsty earth. He steadily pressed Kor-Káy with questions, explicitly eager to know more. His fascination with what he was seeing and learning turned childlike in its evidence, and he would grow restive during the long, intervening drouths of silence when the Indian reticence so deeply ingrained in Kor-Káy took command.

Ignacio pried from Kor-Káy a detailed account of his nephew's physical training, and did not withhold his admiration of the robust and muscular physique it had given him. The priest probed deep after Kor-Káy let slip a hint of his vision quest. Then, hearing the account of it, disparaged that meaningful experience to the point of ridicule.

Kor-Káy's drouths of silence became even longer after that but, as Asa-tebo had done for him, Kor-Káy occasionally pointed out a wild herb or other growing plant and explained its use in healing.

"I have noticed that the Kiowas eat only meat," Ignacio commented one day, "though you use plants for medicine. Are there no green plants in your diet? If you eat no fresh vegetables you must suffer from scurvy."

"Is that the sickness that causes your teeth to fall out? I have heard that the men at the soldier house get such a disease," Kor-Káy acknowledged. "It is because they eat only a part of the animal and reject the rest, as you do. We eat the whole animal, especially the buffalo, intestines, the liver raw and seasoned with gall, the animal's eyes, brains, everything, and we have no such sickness."

Wry-faced and turning palpably green, the priest fell silent.

They traveled in a mode of suspended time, ignoring the distance reaching out before them, measuring their way patiently, persisting in the certainty that after an adequate number of nights of sleep, and long days of steadily gnawing at that distance, the familiar landmarks of home country would begin to appear.

Emerging from the *mesas secas* they set forth across the great flattening plain of the *llano estacado*. "It is a colossal saucer. With the horizon for a rim," Father Ignacio marveled. "One always seems to ride in the saucer's center. When we camp at night I can see that horizon beneath the bellies of the horses, however far away they graze."

He expressed amazement that the Kiowas could find water here, where there should be none. His increasing enjoyment of the company of the Kiowas was apparent, and he commented often on how they could ride silently for hours, with no bodily motion other than that caused by the movement of their horses, then, suddenly, they would become animated.

A practical joke by one played on another, a rousted jackrabbit, a meadow lark flying by with its bright twisting song, anything, nothing, could cause a comment which became a conversation, and they were chattering at one another, with much laughter, their language of gutturals and glottals musical and incomprehensible.

This laughing, and not infrequently shouting, crescendo of effervescent animal spirits and rough play would accelerate in tempo to a climax, then taper again into the long silence. They seemed always congenial, living together in easy camaraderie, fitting the patterns of their lives together with a sure and frictionless discipline.

After so many days that Ignacio lost count, and he noted to Kor-Káy that the Kiowas did not seem to keep count, the priest said argumentatively, "These Indians are not savages!" To which comment Kor-Káy did not respond at all.

Attaining the cap rock, that summit of the plains where the wind seems eternally to blow with ripping, tearing force, its endless chaffing of stone has exposed the craggy face of the land. The crags focusing toward the morning sun become draws, up which the Kiowas found *ojos*, running springs, that rarely dried up. The sparse rainfall following these draws makes of them creeks and streams that eventually form the river Washita.

Within distant sight of where it passes into the Kiowa country of the Indian Territory are three hill-like mesas, known to Kor-Káy for the fact that when hunting, antelope could always be found there. Directly south of these antelope hills they began following the main course of the Washita, and Asa-tebo rode forward to join Kor-Káy and Father Ignacio. Kor-Káy sensed that his aged mentor had recovered his physical well being enough to respond to the urge to resume his place in setting the pace for the journey.

Asa-tebo looked well. Ignacio greeted him cordially, receiving in response a noncommittal grunt. Kor-Káy said nothing, for Kiowa courtesy does not provide greetings for such circumstances. They would have then ridden in silence had it not been for Ignacio's need to make conversation.

"The daily dose of quinine seems to be doing its work well for you," he commented in genial Spanish.

"I have taken all of it," Asa-tebo replied, accompanying his words with the proper hand signs. "But that is all right. In another sleep we should reach our village and there my medicine is too strong for any evil spirits to get inside of me."

Father Ignacio replied conversationally, "Splendid," and said to Kor-Káy, "if we are so near our destination we should pause in the morning to say a mass of thanks to God for bringing your people safely home."

"*Misa?* Mass?" It was a word Asa-tebo had not heard. "What is that?"

Kor-Káy replied, hesitantly, "It is a ceremony of my uncle's medicine." He told his uncle, "We will ride on while you are doing that. You can catch up easily." Kor-Káy was eager to avoid any clash between Ignacio and Asa-tebo over matters of power and religion, but Asa-tebo was curious.

"No, no," he chided Kor-Káy. "We will stop and watch, unless your brown-robed relative is afraid I will steal his medicine."

The priest smiled, "I would be glad to have you present and watching."

Kor-Káy noted that Asa-tebo observed Father Ignacio diligently from that point on. When the priest did not break his fast with the warriors the next morning, Asa-tebo nodded approvingly. "Fasting before any power ceremony is always good," he told Kor-Káy.

Father Ignacio set up an improvised altar on a ledge of stone on the bank of the Washita in the bright autumn sun and the warriors ranged themselves around to observe this strange medicine. It was, for Kor-Káy, a journey into the past. As soon as Father Ignacio chanted, "*In nomine Patris, et Filii et Spiritu Sancti—*" Kor-Káy was back inside the great cathedral of Chihuahua and a child again. The huge, drafty, echoing interior of wooden pews and marble columns seemed as real as if he had attended yesterday. He heard the reading of the epistle and the gospel through a mist of memories, of his father, his acerbic aunt, and recurrent flashes of the spacious house of his childhood. These memories came and passed with no emotion of homesickness or longing.

His only sense of yearning was to see T'sal-túa, and his heart raced at the thought that he might be with her before another nightfall. Father Ignacio consecrated the wine and the wafer. Now he was reciting the Pater Noster and presently raised his voice in the Agnus Dei: *qui tollis peccata mundi, miserere nobis. Agnus Dei, qui tollis peccata,* striking his breast with his hand, and Kor-Káy knew the mass was near an end.

The Kiowa warriors listened respectfully through the last "*Ite missa est. Deo gratias.*" When sufficient silence had elapsed and the priest's gathering up all the increments of the mass convinced them it was finished, they arose and began catching their horses.

They resumed the trail, Asa-tebo continuing to ride with Kor-Káy and Ignacio, and they had traveled almost a league before Asa-tebo remarked courteously, "It is a good power ceremony."

Father Ignacio said, "I yearn to explain its meaning to you. Will you permit me to do so?"

Asa-tebo's negative hand sign, gracefully but emphatically given, warned the priest, "Explaining your power only weakens it. I have never explained any of my ceremonies, even to my grandson when I give them to him. The old men, who gave them to me, never explained them either."

Father Ignacio tried to clarify, "I could not 'give' it to you in the sense that you could then do it. I meant to interpret or explain it to you. But you would not be able to perform the mass, even though I told you all that it means."

This visibly angered Asa-tebo. He declared impatiently, "If you are going to give me your power, you should give it all to me and not try to hold on to part of it. No, I think you had better not explain anything. I might decide to steal it."

The warriors were so eager to get home they could not stop even to make the proper preparations. As they rode they were beginning to paint themselves for arrival at the village. They had been gone so long that their eagerness to return overcame their desire to do so with full and proper ceremony. They need not have hurried. There would have been plenty of time. For when they reached the site the village had occupied when they had departed more than three moons ago, it was deserted.

The village was gone. Everyone scattered out to look for signs of what had happened. There were no scraps of anything that had been destroyed, not even any ashes, or circles where tepees had stood.

Touha-syhn suggested, "I do not think there has been any fighting here. Nothing has been torn down or burned up. Maybe they have only moved downstream."

"That would have been a good thing to do," Asa-tebo confirmed. "The rains of the beaver moon will soon be coming. It is better to get where the banks are higher so that the river cannot come out into the camp."

They rode on. Pein-hH unslung his bugle and began playing all the lively bugle calls he knew. He blew a spirited retreat, saying he had wanted to play that one to confuse the fighting at Cibolero, but thought it might anger the soldiers who had heard him play it before. Pein-hH speculated, "It might have caused them to chase us this time."

"Those Texas Rangers would not have paid any attention to the bugle calls anyway," Asa-tebo said. "They do not play any horns as the soldiers do, or even sing. All they know how to do is fight!"

"Strangely," said Father Ignacio, "I believe that at Cibolero I observed an illustration of what you are saying. The *tejanos* were the most anxious to injure others. Everyone was doing a great deal of shooting in the air, over each others' heads, but the Texans grew vindictive and the shooting became more serious. The two Rangers who were shot were grievously wounded—"

Koup-ei-tseidl and Tsoy came charging past them. 'H-'ei-p'eip rode up to shout, "They have heard the bugle!"

"They remembered it from before," Asa-tebo nodded, "and were not frightened by it."

A procession was riding to meet them.

Intue-k'ece heeled his horse forward happily. "It is our own people," he declared. "I see my wife."

XII

Intue-k'ece's cause for joy was short, for Pilar had not ridden
out to welcome him. She had come to berate him for being
gone so long. As she flayed him with her sharp tongue, he interrupted to accuse her acidly, "I had hoped that you were
with child when we left and would at least be showing a fat
belly by now! I even purchased a charm from the medicine
twins to assure it!"

Asa-tebo urged his horse in between them. "Stop this and
be glad of our home coming," he chided. "You should have
known better than to waste anything on those twins," he
reproved Intue-k'ece. "It is a good thing I drove them off and
I hope they will never come back."

In the confusion of families reuniting, Kor-Káy saw Tsoy
and Lupe. He was holding his new baby. Kor-Káy hurried to
ride alongside the slender, usually sober Tsoy.

Tsoy proudly displayed his new daughter. "Is she not beautiful?" he asked Kor-Káy.

Kor-Káy recalled Tsoy's frequently expressed wish for a son,
and Yih-gyh's and P'-ou's bet. "One day," Tsoy bragged, perhaps apprehending Kor-Káy's thought, "my daughter will
catch a fine husband who will be like a son to me."

In the milling crowd, Kor-Káy found Da-goomdl. He was
astonished and saddened at how much she seemed to have
aged during the time of their absence. He embraced her tenderly, but could not keep from asking, "Where is T'sal-túa?"

"She could not get up her courage to come and meet you,"
Da-goomdl admitted.

With his heart pounding, Kor-Káy asked, "Has she become the wife of 'N'da?"

"No, my son, but the worry that she would do so has shortened my steps and lined my face while you have been gone!"

"Where is she now?"

"She ran away as soon as we heard Pein-hH's bugle. Perhaps she is hiding at the same spring—"

Already Kor-Káy had Pintí extending himself in a hard run. The moving of the camp would have brought it very close to the spring where the mountain lion had wounded T'sal-túa. That *ojo* would likely be where the camp was now securing its drinking water.

As Pintí ran through the deserted camp, Kor-Káy unslung the sacred flute from where he had so long carried it beneath his buckskin shirt. Nearing the edge of the timber he flung himself down, leaving a panting Pintí ground-tied, and began his silent approach through the timber surrounding the spring.

As he neared it, he saw movement on the ledge above the water. Kor-Káy halted abruptly, brought the flute to his mouth and searched his mind for the exotic melody he had rehearsed so often during the lonely marches south, through the hot tropical *matorral*, and in the returning.

The melody he had created came to him, and he began playing it, wildly, beautifully, putting all of his yearning into its lyrical pentatonic mode as he slowly walked the last short distance to the spring and stepped into the clearing. The movement he had seen was T'sal-túa, as he had been certain it had been.

She sat sadly on the limestone ledge above the spring, her arms clasped about her, hugging her knees to her breast. Her face, her whole body was poised in an attitude of defense, tinged with the anticipation of defeat.

On the sand below her and beyond the spring, where the panther had been playing with her body while she lay bleeding, sat 'N'da. His scornful face was ugly with triumph, his knotty, muscular legs stretched out naked and relaxed toward the pool of water that had once been stained with T'sal-túa's blood.

'N'da glared up at Kor-Káy. "You play prettily," he said derisively.

Kor-Káy snatched the silenced flute from his lips. He stood staring at 'N'da, who glared back contemptuously. 'N'da snarled, "I have just been telling your *sister*," he emphasized the word strongly, "that Asa-tebo's medicine cannot help her this time. Nor can you, nor anyone. She is going to become my wife."

"Why?" Kor-Káy demanded belligerently.

'N'da replied cynically, "I am sure that you know by now."

T'sal-túa arose and came to stand before Kor-Káy. He longed to take her in his arms, and intuitively felt from her a warmly responsive desire to be taken in his arms.

But T'sal-túa folded her hands pristinely before her and said, "'N'da says that Asa-tebo's medicine is not true. That it is all false . . . tricks he makes by cleverly using his hands and the help of others to make things appear, and to hide things. 'N'da says that Asa-tebo was giving him this power. He helped Asa-tebo, in a long ago sun dance, to make white things appear out of the dark. Then you, his grandson, went to Asa-tebo and asked to learn his medicine. Asa-tebo was so pleased that his own grandson wanted to learn his medicine that he refused to show 'N'da anything anymore."

"It is shameful," Kor-Káy said coldly, "that someone could not have shown 'N'da how to be brave. Then he would have had the courage to free your father Toné-bone when he was staked out before the Utes. Toné-bone himself told me before they went into battle that he had given that privilege to 'N'da. But when the Utes charged in fury, 'N'da lost his courage and fell off his horse. Instead of pulling the stake out of your father's sash and freeing him, 'N'da ran, and left your father to die."

T'sal-túa's hand covered her mouth and tears came to her eyes.

"If 'N'da feels that he must accuse Asa-tebo," Kor-Káy said boldly, "I feel that I must accuse 'N'da."

'N'da was standing now, his eyes aflame with fury. "If you make such an accusation of me before the people," he threatened, "I will kill you."

As 'N'da stormed off into the timber, T'sal-túa came into Kor-Káy's arms. He held her for a moment, guiltily, then said, "We must go and see Asa-tebo."

She nodded, wiping the tears from her eyes. They walked toward Pintí, their hands touching but not clasped. He swung her up, onto the waiting pony, but this time, instead of leading Pintí as he had when T'sal-túa had been so gravely wounded, Kor-Káy swung astride also. She rode with her arms clasped about his waist to keep from falling off.

The beaver moon clouds were scudding across the sky as they rode toward camp. They were dark, and many, reminding Kor-Káy that Asa-tebo had complimented the camp's wisdom in moving downstream where the Washita banks were high before the coming of the late autumn storms. These heavy clouds blowing in, and the sticky wetness of the atmosphere, were convincing indicators that the camp move had been timely.

They found Asa-tebo in his tepee, sitting among the emblems of his power, his aged wife Darcie hovering in the shadows of the tepee's dark side. Asa-tebo had another guest.

Father Ignacio sat with crossed legs on the far side of the fire, beyond the tepee entrance. When Kor-Káy and T'sal-túa entered, the priest arose politely, greeting them warmly. There was no need to introduce T'sal-túa for the priest guessed at once who she was and told her that he was Kor-Káy's uncle and only living relative.

"I have come to tell Asa-tebo the meaning of the mass," Father Ignacio explained, "as well as its message of salvation for him."

In contrast to the priest's dark brown robe, Asa-tebo had dressed himself in bleached buckskins of sparkling white. He sat calmly, smoking his long, carved and ermine-decorated red pipestone calumet.

"Sit down, all of you," Asa-tebo invited. "You have showed me your medicine ceremony," he told Father Ignacio, "and before you tell me about it I would like to show you some of mine."

Casually, Asa-tebo tapped the tobacco from his pipe bowl out into his hand and tossed it into the fire. A great burst of flame, seeming to fill the whole tepee, bloomed out of the fire. Kor-Káy looked around to be sure that no one had been burned by it. The great ball of fire rolled upward and out the tepee's smoke hole.

Asa-tebo reached to the ground beside where he sat and picked up the fur hat he wore in winter. Carefully, he turned it upside down to show that it was empty. Then he extended it toward Father Ignacio. It was full of dried plums.

Father Ignacio looked at them strangely. "May I eat one?" he asked.

Asa-tebo nodded.

The priest put one in his mouth and chewed it thoughtfully. Swallowing it with difficulty, Father Ignacio said, "I prefer fresh ones."

Asa-tebo turned the fur hat over, emptying it of the dried plums. He righted the hat, and extended it once more toward the priest. Now it contained fresh, newly ripened plums.

Kor-Káy knew there had been no ripe fruit in any of the small plum trees along the Washita for nearly three full moons. The plums ripened early in the heat moon, when they were gathered and dried by the Kiowa women for later beating into the winter's pemmican.

Father Ignacio scowled at the ripe plums and said, "I did not come here for this sort of thing."

A low roll of thunder penetrated the tepee walls. Glancing up through the tepee's smoke flaps at the approaching storm, Kor-Káy could see that the sky had darkened perceptibly. The air seemed unseasonably warm, and there was not much of it. It was getting hard to breathe.

Father Ignacio, even having expressed his displeasure, took one of the plums and tasted it. He handed the plum to Kor-Káy. It was very sweet and juicy. Kor-Káy passed it on to T'sal-túa, who ate the last bite of it.

Old Darcie's voice creaked out of the shadowed side of the tepee. Addressing her husband, she said, "You are so good at making things, let us see you make some meat. There has been very little in this tepee all the time you were gone." Her voice, in castigating Asa-tebo, was filled with resentment.

Asa-tebo picked up a scrap of buckskin from the tepee floor, a piece of the hide old Darcie had been working in making him the new bleached buckskin outfit he now wore. He laid the scrap of hide in his hands and spat across it into the fire. Again smoke and flames bloomed from the fire and rolled skyward. When it cleared, a fat forequarter of deer meat lay weighing down Asa-tebo's forearms. He passed it to his wife. Expressionless, she carried it out of the tepee to hang it up.

The sky above the open smoke flaps flashed sullenly as lightning streaked across it, followed by thunder's reverberations. Kor-Káy could hear the coming of voices outside and Darcie came running back. Within moments the big tepee was rapidly filling with people as the storm swept in on the rising wind.

A few big drops of rain splatted noisily down on the tepee and Kor-Káy rushed outside to close the smoke flaps before the coming downpour could start. The horizon was black. While Kor-Káy knew tornados did not often sweep this country late in the beaver moon, he was sure the coming storm would be intense. By the time he had lifted one of the smoke pole flaps, and then the other, swinging them into place, the rain was pouring down and he was drenched.

Kor-Káy met Father Ignacio as he tried to re-enter the tepee. "Where are you going?" he asked his uncle.

"I don't know," said the priest, "but neither I, nor my message, is welcome here."

Kor-Káy seized his arm, pulling him back into the tepee. People were still coming, crowding inside. Kor-Káy called to Asa-tebo, "Grandfather, my uncle feels unwelcome. Please invite him to stay until the rain has passed."

The deluge was pouring down. Asa-tebo crowded across the tepee to stand between them. He said nothing to either, but looked slightly upward, full into Father Ignacio's face. Asa-tebo leaned over and walked out into the rain. Kor-Káy knelt to see him as he stepped farther out into the downpour.

Asa-tebo stopped, standing still in the drenching water. A few hailstones began to strike the taut buffalo-hide sidewalls of the tepee, bouncing off. The wind still rose. In the span of time that Asa-tebo stood out alone in it, the hail splashed in deepening rain, water puddled about the old medicine man's moccasins, running off along the ground in swirling wind-swept currents.

Asa-tebo turned then, lowered his head and came back inside the tepee. His buckskin garments, his hair, even his moccasins, were still as dry as if he had been standing outside on a sunny summer's day.

Asa-tebo triumphantly fixed Ignacio in his most penetrating glare. The old medicine man asked, "Could you do the power ceremony of your medicine while standing out in the rain and not get wet?"

A violent crash of thunder and the wind rose to near tornadic violence as the tepee rocked with its force. The noise of the storm grew to preclude conversation and a few of the restive crowd filling the tepee cried out in fear. Kor-Káy could hear one of the women start singing a prayer song.

Asa-tebo shouldered his way back to his seat of honor. Through the mingle of moving people Kor-Káy saw the medicine man seat himself calmly and start refilling his pipe. The thunder storm began to abate. The crowd of people inside the tepee quieted as the wind and rain tapered, and the tornadic squall passed on over.

When only splatters of large drops again fell against the hide walls, Father Ignacio left the tepee. Kor-Káy and T'saltúa followed him. The camp lay in shambles, its colorfully painted tepees blown-down and mud-spattered, among broken tepee poles. But Asa-tebo's tepee, its earth red walls rising to the black cone of its crown, stood erect and undamaged.

Touha-syhn emerged from the tepee to stand beside Kor-Káy. Looking out across the wreckage, he said, "We might as well go ahead with having the victory dance. Nobody is going to get any sleep tonight anyway."

The sun appeared boldly, stretching long rays earthward among the remaining dark cloud patches of the storm. As the sky became increasingly visible, it seemed washed and infinitely blue. Kor-Káy watched the brown-robed back of his uncle grow smaller as he walked, in retreat, down toward the solitary river.

As darkness fell, the keeper of the drum turned it before the great fire where he had it drying in the center of the village. He began to tune its dry side. Singers, carrying their especially made, woven and weighted drum sticks, drifted slowly into the arena.

They sat, encircling the big drum, talking but little and watching, as the drum keeper concluded his tuning. With the drum in place, the slow, time-marking beat of the singers—tump, tump-tump, tump-tump—replaced the erratic strokes of the drum keeper. Sa-p'oudl, serving as camp cryer, came to the center of the dance ground to call out his inviting, "*Bé-ha. Bah-kó-bah.*"

This he repeated frequently, urging the villagers to gather. They came, spreading their new blankets to sit on the drier earth within the covered circle of the dance ground, protected by its wide-spreading brush arbor. Humming conversation, punctuated by the summons of the camp cryer, passed the time until the warriors in their gorgeous feathered finery, and the younger women, in fringed buckskin dresses, began to respond. Some of the older women were still re-erecting tepees, and Kor-Káy saw that the stack of spare tepee poles that had lain at the camp's edge was almost depleted.

As the round dance songs began, his eyes followed T'sal-túa's graceful circling step, step-step, step-step, in the firelight, among the backs of the dancers, mostly women, their buckskin fringes swaying enticingly. He moved out there, his dance bells jingling, to dance beside her. Kor-Káy's own sunburst bustle and decorative feathers were fancy and bright, as were his colorfully beaded moccasins, shining copper arm bracelets, and dignified headdress of coup feathers.

Custom dictated that women and war dancers remain virtually oblivious to each other's presence during these social dance songs of the early evening, and when Kor-Káy saw his uncle and the *arriero* Juan Diego appear in the circle of observers at the edge of the firelight he left the round dancers and went to stand beside them.

"Juan Diego and I will begin our return to Chihuahua tomorrow," said Father Ignacio. "I still hope that you will return with us."

Kor-Káy asked carefully, "After what you saw today, are you still so sure that Asa-tebo has no power?"

"I am no magician," said the priest. "I do not know how he performs his tricks. But I am certain they are no more than *magia de la sala*, parlor magic."

"I know how he does some of them," Kor-Káy admitted.

"He has given me much of his eagle shield power, but when his tepee stands while others fall," Kor-Káy hesitated. "Father Ignacio, why is it that when I learn of the trickery in Asa-tebo's eagle shield medicine I know I would feel guilty in using it? Asa-tebo feels no guilt—he has told me that all these things are a part of his medicine, as it was given to him by his elders before him."

"*Sobrino*—nephew," the priest said sympathetically, "during your early years you were thoroughly taught the Christian ethic. Asa-tebo was raised from birth with primitive ethics. You were taught to feel guilt at deception and trickery. Asa-tebo was taught that it is 'medicine.' "

"But how can he sit underwater for such a long time?"

"I am told that pearl divers along our seacoast learn to hold their breath and stay underwater for as much as five minutes," said Ignacio. "Five minutes can seem an interminable time when you are watching someone stay underwater."

"He is teaching me the uses of herbs and plants."

"Our medicines, too, are derived from herbs and plants. That is true medicine."

"How can he stand out in the rain without getting wet? Is that not true medicine, too?"

Father Ignacio paused, observing his nephew with sympathy and with measuring eyes. "That is something you will have to decide for yourself," he said quietly.

A social dance done together by men and women holding hands interlocked was about to begin. Kor-Káy went away thoughtfully, to seek out T'sal-túa, when, unexpectedly, another woman barred his way. It was Pilar, and astonishingly, she threw her blanket about Kor-Káy, pulling him to her.

He was stunned. Such an imperative invitation to dance was customarily issued only by girls who had been long courted by the young man they were entrapping in their blanket. Kor-Káy did not want to dance with another man's wife.

He wanted to dance with T'sal-túa. Impatiently, he threw Pilar's blanket aside and walked to meet T'sal-túa.

Pilar began screaming behind him, "Así! You prefer your sister. Admit the way it is between you two. It has long been a lot more than just brother-sister love. It is a wonder she is not carrying your child."

In Kor-Káy's shock he could think only that this must be another scheme contrived by 'N'da. Kor-Káy shouted, "It is not true! Where is he who dares to scheme with you to make such a charge?" He reached to seize Pilar's arm, looking for 'N'da to confront them together, but Pilar spun and ran away from him. Boldly, Kor-Káy walked to stand defensively beside T'sal-túa. He took her hands, intending to dance with her, but Pilar's noisy scene had brought everything to a halt. The singers were silent.

Da-goomdl came forward. "What my son says is true. Pilar is lying," she told the crowd. "Go on with your dancing. I will go and get Pilar and make her come back and admit it before all of you."

Tentatively, the drummers began their tump, tump-tump, tump-tump again, and the lead singer commenced the high wailing of the dancing song. As his voice descended, other singers joined in. Kor-Káy and T'sal-túa locked hands and arms together and began the skipping steps of the dance.

"I do not know," she said, "why you hold back from going where your uncle lives."

Kor-Káy continued to two-step glumly around the dance circle. He could not quite bring himself to say, "*You are the reason.*" Instead, he said irresolutely, "I am Kiowa!"

"You are Spanish," she replied.

"Asa-tebo is giving me his power," Kor-Káy countered insistently.

"I think that old age is stealing away his power," T'sal-túa said regretfully. The singing grew more powerful and they stepped with renewed vigor to its wild euphony.

Frankly, sadly, T'sal-túa said, "You know our people will never let us marry."

"Da-goomdl will make Pilar tell the truth," Kor-Káy declared stubbornly.

"It makes no difference whether Pilar tells the truth or more lies," T'sal-túa demurred regretfully. "It would be better if you lived far away from here, so that we would never even have to see each other."

Kor-Káy could see Da-goomdl searching among the tepees for Pilar.

Timid and hesitant, T'sal-túa asked, "Could we make a marriage in that place where your uncle lives, if I were to go there?"

It was a stunning new thought, and Kor-Káy tried to probe it, vacillating, "There are other ways of doing things there, customs made different."

"What are these customs?"

He could not even remember much about the ingrained traditions of courtship in his native Chihuahua. Kor-Káy replied lamely, "For one thing, making a marriage is not quick and easy as it is among us. They have a long ceremony in a big building called a church and there are a lot of social affairs called *fiestas* with many kinds of dancing—"

T'sal-túa giggled. "It sounds exciting."

Da-goomdl was returning now, alone. Hurrying up to them, she announced in a voice loud enough for all to hear, "I cannot find her. She has run away."

Intue-k'ece, who stood nearby in all his dance finery said resolutely, "I will find her."

Kor-Káy watched his warrior companion of the long journey trot quickly to the war pony tied outside his tepee, kept there to be prepared for the always present danger of surprise attack by Utes or perhaps some of the enemies the Kiowas had so callously made during their long journey. Intue-k'ece slid smoothly onto his pony's back and rode to circle the camp.

He was not gone long. Returning, bringing the animal that she had stolen to escape with Pilar still astride its bare back, Intue-k'ece reported bitterly, "It was easy to find her. She had stolen this great worthless jackass that followed us from Cibolero. They made a trail as plain as a hungry dog running away from the meat rack. I could see it in the dark. The jackass would go only a little ways then balk and she would have to wait until it was ready to go again." He dragged her down from her perch high astride the stallion jack. "Speak! And tell the truth!" he ordered her, "or I will cut off your nose the way the Sioux do."

Sulky, with malevolent downcast gaze, Pilar seemed to give a moment of thought to whether her angry husband might carry out his threat. Tangibly afraid, she muttered grimly between clenched teeth, "I know of no scandal between Kor-Káy and T'sal-túa. I thought perhaps I could make myself inviting to Kor-Káy and he would take me with him when he returns to my home country. I am sick and tired of living in the dirt with this Indian who calls himself my husband!"

"You are free to go if Kor-Káy will have you," Intue-k'ece declared. "I will not keep for a wife a woman who lies—and is barren besides."

Father Ignacio reached out a restraining arm. "*Hacer mal es humano—perdonar, divino,*" he quoted.

Tears filled Pilar's smoldering eyes. She sobbed out angrily, "I do beg forgiveness, Padre, but I am sick with loathing of this terrible place and will die if I must stay here."

Father Ignacio told the assemblage, "I am well acquainted with this woman's family. They have mourned her loss greatly." Father Ignacio touched the crown of her bowed head with a gentle hand. "Diego and I will take you with us when we depart tomorrow," he said. "There will be sufficient

time on the way for you to complete your confession, make
your penance and receive absolution."

Kor-Káy felt clawlike hands seize his arm and turned to
face old Darcie. She had been running, and stood muttering
and trembling, on ancient legs that hardly seemed able to sustain her. She leaned weakly against Kor-Káy.

He heard Yih-gyh shout laughingly, "Asa-tebo's ancient
wife has come to dance with Kor-Káy, too."

But Kor-Káy knew that was not so. As soon as she could get
her breath Darcie began wailing. Unable to speak, her fingers
moved toward her forehead in the hand sign for *come*, then
both hands agitated themselves across her chest, signing *sick*.

"It is Asa-tebo!" T'sal-túa burst out, and she was running
toward his tepee.

Kor-Káy and Father Ignacio followed, but Kor-Káy passed
them all to enter the medicine man's tepee first. He found
Asa-tebo cowering, crouched over the fire with buffalo robes
heaped about his shoulders.

With Ignacio's help, Kor-Káy persuaded the old man to lie
down on the tepee's ground cloth.

"You see," Ignacio said sternly, "his walk in the rain was
only another illusion. He did get wet, and it has given him a
chill."

Asa-tebo shook his head in determined denial. Through
chattering teeth, he said, "The little men in the trees who
would not talk to us in that far away place threw this curse
down on me."

"Getting wet has caused a reoccurrence of your malaria,"
Father Ignacio insisted.

"We must have more quinine," Kor-Káy said urgently to
Father Ignacio.

"The priest's medicine?" said Asa-tebo. "It will not help
now. It only worked for a little while anyway. Just the same
as when I cured myself with the eagle shield medicine. But
this is not the *mal* you call malaria. I tremble now because I

am going to meet D'ah-kih. When I have gained enough courage to stop trembling, I will go."

The old man lay miserably, shaking and drawn with pain. "There is this thing I must tell you, my grandson," he reached out from beneath the robe to seize Kor-Káy's hand, holding it while he then reached to farther grasp T'sal-túa's forearm. "You are not brother and sister," he said. "Now I want you to get married. It will not offend tribal customs."

"Then why?—" Kor-Káy's face became a mask of puzzlement.

Asa-tebo rested for a while. "I did not want you to marry until I had given you all my power. Now you have it."

"No, no," Kor-Káy protested, "there are many things you have not told me—"

Asa-tebo interrupted firmly, "You have all the power I can give you."

"I cannot stand in the rain and remain dry. I do not have that power."

"You have it now," Asa-tebo nodded emphatically. "I have just given it to you. Perhaps at first you will not know how to use it just right. But if you keep trying, it will come. As you get older, all your power will get stronger, if you use it right."

He paused again, resting. His trembling had unmistakably diminished. His eyes remained only partially open, eyelids hanging unevenly, over blurred, half-focused pupils.

" 'N'da came to me," he said. "A long time ago I was giving him power. Then I saw that he was not meant to have it. He told me that unless I took you on a long journey, leaving him to persuade T'sal-túa to marry him while you were gone, he would tell the people evil things about me that would weaken my power."

The old medicine man closed his eyes, his lips moving, but no words came. The trembling had stopped. Asa-tebo lay quiescent. He released Kor-Káy and T'sal-túa, composing himself.

"I must leave you now," he said softly, and began to sing his death song.

Father Ignacio shepherded Kor-Káy and T'sal-túa out of the tepee. Facing them, his hand searching inside the breast of his brown robe, he asked incredulously, "You thought you were brother and sister?"

Both nodded. The priest shook his head. "Surely you understood there is no blood relationship between you."

Kor-Káy shrugged. "We were raised as brother and sister—"

T'sal-túa cocked her head quizzically. "Then would you be willing to marry us?"

"After you have been baptized," Father Ignacio assured her.

"Does baptizing hurt?" T'sal-túa inquired curiously.

Kor-Káy gasped, "Of course not!"

"Then I will do it," T'sal-túa agreed willingly.

Father Ignacio had taken his breviary from inside his robe. "I must return to read the prayers for the dying," he said, and lowered his head to re-enter the tepee.

Kor-Káy and T'sal-túa remained outside, listening to the strange but peculiarly euphonious harmony of the priest's low-voiced reading, his chanting of prayers, and the high, wind-wild falsetto of the death song Asa-tebo sang. Both were resonant with timelessness; the ancient prayers of man disciplined, subdued, submissive before implacable death, speaking of its inevitability though still faithful to things everlasting; and the wild-wind yearning of an aged man near death for a beyond dimly perceived and unknown.

T'sal-túa said, "I shall return with you, to your country."

Kor-Káy replied, "We must first be certain that Asa-tebo is prepared for the spirit world and laid to rest in the old way."

"If we are to stay here and do that, we will have to be married in two ways," T'sal-túa reasoned practically. "In the Indian way for while we are here, and in Father Ignacio's way for later."

"Asa-tebo will live in a new world we cannot see," Kor-Káy pondered, "but we must remain on this earth, and live in two worlds."

Asa-tebo's song was finished. Father Ignacio's prayers ended. As the priest came out of the tepee the sky had begun to glow with odd curtains of wavering, ethereal light. The abnormal light increased in intensity, becoming colossal hanging cycloramas of frost-white beams alternately tinted with umber, red, and green.

Father Ignacio looked skyward at the display. "Ah," he said. "The aurora borealis. The northern lights. They are seen almost nightly, I have read, in the far northern provinces, but are rarely visible this far south. My father told me that once, as a boy, he saw them even in Chihuahua."

The Kiowas, leaving the dancing ground, were moving slowly, in awe at the lights in the sky, to stand encircling Asa-tebo's tepee. All stared at the bewildering lights, and at Kor-Káy. Touha-syhn separated himself from the murmuring people and came to place his hands on Kor-Káy's arms.

"It is Asa-tebo's power," he said, "coming to settle like a robe about your shoulders."

Raising his voice, in erudite Spanish, the priest explained to the encircled Kiowas what they were seeing.

"Not all of these people," Kor-Káy said, "understand Spanish."

"Then you must explain the light in the sky to them in Kiowa," Father Ignacio insisted.

Kor-Káy hesitated, asking T'sal-túa, "Are there Kiowa words for aurora borealis? I have never heard of it."

"It makes no difference what either of you tell them," T'sal-túa answered. "They will believe what they want to believe."